DALVARON STATION

SINGULARITIES BOOK 3

ANTHONY JAMES

Illustration © Tom Edwards
TomEdwardsDesign.com

Sign up to my mailing list here to be the first to find out about new releases.

ONE

Having recently captured the huge alien warship *Ragnar-3* and escaped from the underground facility on Ilvaron, Captain William Lanson had set a course for a location, the coordinates of which he'd discovered within the vessel's databanks. That location was a place called Dalvaron, though he wasn't sure if the name referred to a planet or a facility.

In ten days, the *Ragnar-3* would exit lightspeed, and then Lanson would find the answer.

For the first two days after escaping the massive enemy vessel known as *Tyrantor*, Lanson and his crew had devoted themselves entirely to the task of familiarising themselves with the *Ragnar-3*'s operation. Luckily, the controls, the monitoring tools, the sensors and almost everything else had been designed with similar underlying principles to the equivalents on a Human Confederation warship. This ensured that by the end of the two days, Lanson was confident that he and his crew were ready to take the *Ragnar-3* into battle.

Unfortunately, the Singularity option on the weapons panel remained locked down, as did the related data files.

Given that Lanson and his crew had been given command access to the *Ragnar-3* on Ilvaron, and the Singularity menu was still greyed out, it seemed likely that vital weapons and defensive functions were contained within.

This was the reason for the mission to Dalvaron – a place which Lanson believed was the central control station for the Infinity Lens. Once there, he hoped to find a way to elevate himself and his crew to a higher security tier – a tier with access to the Singularity menu.

Whether his plan would work, Lanson had no idea. All he knew was the alien hardware recognized that he and his crew, along with the squad of soldiers accompanying the mission, had been physically modified by the Galos device located on Cornerstone and this, for some reason, permitted them high level access to primary assets like the *Ragnar-3*.

Equally, he could only hope those same Galos modifications would be sufficient for the hardware at the Infinity Lens central control station to grant him access to the Singularity menu.

Two days after deciding to set a course for Dalvaron, Lanson was still coming to terms with the fragility of the threads holding everything together.

On the plus side – albeit a minor plus – Lieutenant Fay Perry, one of the warship's two sensor officers, had discovered that the species responsible for the construction of the *Ragnar-3* had called themselves Aral. While knowing the name brought no tangible benefits, Lanson was nonetheless pleased at the discovery.

At the same time, Perry had learned that the aliens which had arrived at Scalos on the warship *Tyrantor*, were known as Ixtar. Other than the names, facts were few on the ground.

Once the *Ragnar-3*'s controls were no longer a challenge,

Lanson decided it was time to explore the vessel's interior, and he excused himself from the bridge.

Despite the vastness of the warship, its personnel areas were relatively compact. Tight passages led to claustrophobic rooms, where consoles and wall panels had been only sparsely installed. The lighting was low to the point of gloominess and the temperatures bordered on freezing. A tangy scent of metal pervaded the air, and the drone of the propulsion was soothing.

During his circuit of the interior, Lanson discovered several maintenance hatches in the floors and the walls. Opening each as he found them, he discovered either long passages which vanished into the distance, or steep, dark steps, some of which seemed to continue forever.

These were likely the maintenance access tunnels, and Lanson was sure that if he followed them, he would find his way to the *Ragnar-3*'s missile clusters, or its Gradar magazines, or perhaps to the main control hardware which governed the warship's engine modules. Maybe he'd even end up in the turret housing the two massive topside guns.

Given the overwhelming size of the *Ragnar-3* – at more than five thousand metres in length and approaching two thousand metres where its flanks were the highest – Lanson didn't want to commit himself to explorations which might potentially last for the better part of a day, with no real benefit except to assuage his own sense of curiosity.

Lanson's sleeping quarters were located not far from the bridge, along a passage only just wide enough for two to pass. His room was one of twelve designated for use by the *Ragnar-3*'s original bridge officers, and contained a bed, a metal-frame chair, and a wall-mounted screen. Showering and toilet facilities were accessed through a powered door.

The bed itself was about the right length and width for Lanson, suggesting the alien species which had constructed the *Ragnar-3* were approximately the same size as a human. Aside from that, the Aral were a mystery, though he was keen to learn more about them.

With the warship's controls mastered, and its interior explored, Lanson spent his off-duty hours in his quarters, either asleep or in thought, or in the *Ragnar-3*'s main mess area, which was no more than five minutes' journey from the bridge.

During his years in the military, Lanson had visited numerous mess areas, and this one hardly varied from the standard template. Two rows of rectangular metal tables were bolted to the floor, each with two benches for seating. Lanson estimated the mess area was designed to accommodate in the region of forty personnel, depending on the ass space required by the original aliens who built the warship.

On one occasion, four days into the voyage, Lanson was standing at one of the two replicators in the mess area, deciding whether his breakfast for the day should be purple solids, green mush, dark blue liquid, or a combination of all three.

Settling for a green mush, which he knew would taste vaguely like fried potato, and a cup of water, Lanson sat at the nearest table. He was currently the only occupant of the mess room, and he spent a quiet few minutes thinking about events since his ill-timed arrival on Cornerstone.

Movement made him turn his head, just as Sergeant Evander Gabriel arrived, accompanied by several members of his squad.

"Captain Lanson," said Gabriel in greeting.

"Sergeant," said Lanson with a nod.

Soon, Gabriel had made his selection at the replicator. He waited for an invitation and then sat opposite Lanson, having placed his suit helmet and gauss rifle carefully at his feet. On his tray, the soldier's meal consisted of a variety of colours and textures, none of which looked particularly appetising.

Private Mitch Davison parked himself next to Gabriel, looking somewhat pleased for himself.

"Can I tempt you with an insect, Captain?" he asked, indicating the metal bowl on his tray, which contained many of what did indeed resemble locusts, albeit with a light red colour.

"Thanks for the offer, Private," said Lanson. "I've just eaten a big pile of mush, and I'm not sure I'm ready for anything more."

"Your loss, sir," said Davison, crunching down on a couple of maybe-insects and chewing with a look of enormous pleasure that was probably faked.

Lanson turned his attention to Sergeant Gabriel. "Have you finished testing the weapons you found in the *Ragnar-3*'s armouries yet?" he asked.

"Pretty much, Captain," said Gabriel. "Like we already discussed, there's a bunch of different armaments, and crates of ammunition. The light gauss rifles seem to possess a similar punch to our own, and the high-calibre ones could likely put a hole through a squad of Sagh'eld if they were stupid enough to be standing in a line."

"But you're happy to stick with what you know," said Lanson.

"For the moment, Captain," said Gabriel. "Of course we have no way to replace the ammunition for our current load-outs, so it may be that we have to start using these Aral guns sooner rather than later."

"I can't promise you a return to base anytime soon, Sergeant, so maybe you should get in some practice with these new weapons."

"Yes, sir, that's already underway." Gabriel gave a half smile. "Except for the explosives. There's not enough room to test those on the *Ragnar-3*."

"How many rockets is Private Castle carrying?"

"Six in the tube and six spare. And the pack of explosives Private Galvan found on the New Beginning is half empty - he used a bunch of charges in the Scalos facility," said Gabriel.

"You might have to do some field testing, Sergeant. I can't tell you whether there'll be a need for a deployment once we reach our destination, but I wouldn't lay bets either way."

"If you're hoping to obtain higher level access to the Aral hardware, I have a feeling we'll need to attend a security station in person, Captain."

"That may well be the case, Sergeant," said Lanson.

"Have you learned anything more about the *Tyrantor*, or the Ixtar, Captain?" asked Private Ashley Teague from the adjacent table.

"Nothing beyond what I told you all yesterday, but there is some good news, though it's not one hundred percent confirmed," said Lanson. "Lieutenants Turner and Perry are nine-tenths sure the area encompassed within Sector 3 does not include Human Confederation territory."

"That's great!" said Teague. "What about the Sagh'eld? Is their territory within Sector 3?"

"We're not so sure about that, Private," said Lanson. "It's likely they're outside the current range of the Infinity Lens, but we can't be sure."

"Do we know what happened to the Aral, Captain?" asked Private Miguel Damico. "It seems to me like the Aral were fighting the Ixtar, and now they're extinct."

"That's one possibility," said Lanson. "But it wouldn't explain why the Aral facility on Scalos, and the Ilvaron base were undamaged. If the two species were at war, I wouldn't have expected those places to be abandoned – the Ixtar would have had to take them by force."

"Does it matter one way or the other?" asked Private

Stanton Castle. "Aral or Ixtar, we're just going to shoot them anyway."

"Humanity already has enough enemies, soldier," said Lanson patiently. "I'd rather not kill anyone or anything that might end up as our friends."

"I'd like to think those friendly aliens exist, Captain," said Castle. "Somewhere out there in the universe." He shrugged.

"What if the Aral knew about the Ixtar because they have the Infinity Lens up and running in a different sector?" asked Corporal Catina Hennessey. "Maybe they were watching from afar, without the two species ever meeting."

"I reckon there's elements of truth in that, Corporal," said Lanson. Hennessey was good at coming up with ideas. "But there's plenty still unanswered."

"What would be the fun in life if we knew everything?" said Hennessey.

Lanson smiled. "I'd settle for knowing more than I do right now."

"Do we have any idea how long the *Tyrantor* will take to find us once we arrive at this control station, sir?" asked Gabriel, obviously keen to ask a few of the questions he'd been thinking up.

"The short answer is *no*," said Lanson. "It's possible the enemy warship won't have a way to reliably track us because of the false trails the *Ragnar-3* is leaving, but this is all new to us Sergeant. The Ixtar might have other tech we don't know about."

"Maybe the *Tyrantor* has bigger fish to fry," said Corporal Brad Ziegler. "The enemy warship could have gone after a different target."

"You almost said that with a straight face, Corporal," said Private Rocky Chan.

"Yeah, I nearly believed you were serious," said Castle.

Lanson looked down at his tray and wondered if he was ready for another helping of mush. Deciding against it, he drained his water and rose from the bench. "It'll be a few days before we arrive, Sergeant Gabriel. I'm sure we'll speak again beforehand."

"Yes, sir."

With the conversation over, Lanson returned to the bridge, his stomach gurgling either from an excess of mush or because he hadn't eaten enough of it. His mind was turning once more, fruitlessly, as was so often the case. Answers to Lanson's many questions awaited, almost a week away and, until then, all his restless thinking was no more than a waste of time and energy. Or so he told himself.

Settling into his seat at the command console, Lanson spoke briefly to the other members of his crew. They weren't exactly on edge, but they were clearly feeling the same frustrations. Sometimes, the only option was to put up with the stresses of the mission and Lanson's crew were experienced enough to ride through times like these.

The remainder of the journey was more of the same. Lanson slept well and his mind gradually settled. When he craved solitude, he occupied himself by wandering through the *Ragnar-3*'s interior. The warship hadn't been built by human hands, but he felt comfortable here anyway. After all, metal was metal, and tech was something Lanson had always loved, regardless of the form it took.

When he desired company, Lanson killed time in the mess area. The soldiers were accepting of the future, whatever it might be. Lanson supposed they had little choice – when death was always a likelihood, they had to find a way to cope. The alternative was madness, or a fear so debilitating it would render them useless on the battlefield.

Aside from this, Lanson found himself grudgingly developing a taste for the alien food – even the insects, which he'd felt obliged to try in case the soldiers began thinking he was lacking in bravery. The textures were completely different to anything he was accustomed to, but the flavours were good in a peculiar way, and he was mostly left with a feeling of contentment after finishing a meal.

This was in stark contrast to his experiences of the low-grade replication facilities found on a Carbine class, where a requested cheeseburger might look like a cheeseburger, it might smell reminiscent of a cheeseburger, but when the food was eaten, Lanson would always feel as if he'd consumed a quantity of nutritionally balanced cardboard.

And so, the journey, which could have been one of ill-temper and agitation, ended up as something different, though not in a way that could be entirely classed as a positive experience.

When Lieutenant Gus Abrams – the *Ragnar-3*'s senior propulsion officer – called out his one-hour warning of the warship's return to local space, it seemed to Lanson as if the journey had passed in a shorter time than ten days.

The *Ragnar-3*'s arrival at its unknown destination – known only as Dalvaron - was imminent. Sitting at his station, Lanson clenched and unclenched his fists in anticipation of what he might find.

TWO

"Ten minutes!" yelled Abrams.

"Is everyone ready?" asked Lanson. He continued, without waiting for an answer. "Remember, this is no different to any other mission. Once we exit lightspeed, we'll go through the same routine as always and proceed according to whatever we find. Lieutenant Abrams entered a ten-million-klick offset for the Dalvaron coordinates in the *Ragnar-3*'s databanks, so we should be out of immediate detection range."

"We're heading to a place that was originally friendly to the *Ragnar-3*, but we can't afford to assume the facility we're hoping to find hasn't been captured by hostile forces," said Commander Ellie Matlock.

"That's right," said Lanson. "But I'm really hoping we'll be the first to arrive."

"Are you putting a time limit on how long we're staying, Captain?" asked Matlock. "Just in case the *Tyrantor* shows up?"

"I'm not setting a time limit, Commander, since it would be based entirely on guesswork," said Lanson. "Whatever we find at Dalvaron, we'll have to deal with it quickly and be on our way."

"To hunt for another of the Singularity class warships like the *Ragnar-3*," said Lieutenant Becky Turner.

"Maybe," said Lanson. "Or maybe the outcome at Dalvaron will be different to what we hope. In which case, the best course of action might be something else."

"You're still thinking about using the *Ragnar-3* to draw the *Tyrantor* into Sagh'eld space?" asked Matlock.

"I'm tempted," Lanson admitted. "However, we don't know the location of any Sagh'eld populated worlds, nor the movements of the enemy fleet, so there's no way to guarantee the effectiveness of such a move." He sighed. "Plus, I'm not sure how comfortable I'd be leading the *Tyrantor* to a Sagh'eld planet anyway. That would be a lot of deaths to carry."

"Good job it's not an option, then," said Lieutenant Abrams.

Lanson smiled. "Yes. For now, we're keeping our full focus on Dalvaron. If we're lucky, we'll find a way to unlock the Singularity menu and also recover a few extra Galos cubes at the same time."

The conversation died off, since this had already been discussed at length during the previous ten days, and with the lightspeed exit coming soon, it wasn't a time for further deliberation.

"Two minutes!" called Abrams shortly after.

As the seconds counted down, Lanson felt the chill of adrenaline pumping through his body. The stakes were high – and there was far more than the lives of the mission personnel at stake. Lanson believed he'd been granted an opportunity to lay his hands on some exceptionally potent alien hardware. Should the beleaguered Human Confederation manage to detonate a couple of Galos cubes within the midst of an attacking Sagh'eld fleet, it would surely give the enemy something to think about. Perhaps even drive them to the negotiating table.

At the same time, Lanson knew that if he succeeded here at Dalvaron, his future would become even less clear. The Ixtar clearly intended to fire up the Infinity Lens and use it for hostile purposes. They couldn't be allowed to succeed, though Lanson wasn't sure how he could defeat an entire species.

The destruction of the Infinity Lens is the only logical solution.

It was a galling thought. Although a few Galos detonations might inflict notable damage to the Sagh'eld fleet, the Human Confederation really needed the extreme tactical advantage offered by the Infinity Lens in order to defeat the enemy.

Cursing sourly beneath his breath, and wishing he had fewer plates to spin, Lanson watched the digits of the lightspeed timer as they approached zero.

With a faintly perceptible shudder, the *Ragnar-3* entered local space. Lanson immediately requested power from the propulsion and he sensed the suppressed acceleration as the warship tore away from its arrival point.

"Sensors coming up," said Lieutenant Turner.

On an HC warship, the sensors were usually offline for five or six seconds after lightspeed exit. The *Ragnar-3*'s arrays came online in less than three. Lanson stared at the feeds on the curved screen which was projected into the air directly above his console. So far, nothing was to be seen other than the usual panoply of stars and the void's darkness.

"Running local area scans," said Lieutenant Perry.

"I'm searching for Dalvaron," said Turner. "I have the coordinates, so it shouldn't take long."

Lanson held onto the controls and breathed the cold air through his nostrils. So far there'd been no opportunity to test the limits of the *Ragnar-3*, but the velocity gauge was already showing five hundred kilometres per second, which put the warship above the maximum of an HC battleship. The propulsion sound continued climbing, but without becoming deafening.

"Let's see how far this gauge will climb," said Lanson.

"Captain, the scan for Dalvaron will take much longer if we're travelling at high velocity," said Turner. "And we're already at a long range."

"I hear you," said Lanson, drawing back on the controls. He'd find time to test the *Ragnar-3*'s limits soon enough.

The velocity gauge tumbled and Lanson allowed the warship to coast at a sedate twenty kilometres per second.

"The local area scans are clear, Captain," said Perry. "The default scan volume is huge and the *Ragnar-3*'s processing cores chewed right through the data."

"I'm glad to hear it," said Lanson truthfully. "Keep scanning until I tell you otherwise."

"Yes, sir."

"Lieutenant Turner, what progress?" asked Lanson.

"I've found something, Captain," said Turner. "I was just waiting for the enhancement before I told you about it. Dalvaron isn't a planet – it's a space station."

"Show me when the enhancement is complete," said Lanson.

"It's finished now, Captain. Check your screen."

Lanson turned his gaze to the sensor feed which, despite the distance, was surprisingly clear. In the centre of his screen, a construction made from the darkest of alloys was astounding both in terms of its size and the complexity of its build.

"Three hundred klicks from one end to the other," said Lanson in disbelief, as he read the information overlay.

"Yes, Captain. The station is three hundred klicks by two

hundred by two hundred at its maximum along each axis," said Turner. "It's motionless and nowhere near anything else."

For a time, Lanson stared. The Aral central control station was almost beyond his comprehension. Overall, its shape was akin to a cylinder, but with a multitude of rectangular protrusions, some of which measured as much as thirty kilometres in length. In addition, hundreds of slender towers dotted the station's hull, and, though the distance made certainty difficult, Lanson thought he could see narrow horizontal beams jutting from each.

"Are those comms transmitter towers?" he asked.

"I wouldn't bet against it, sir," said Turner. "If this place is sending out real time updates from the Infinity Lens, it's going to need plenty of hardware."

"Are we going to approach at lightspeed, Captain?" asked Matlock. "Or attempt comms contact with the station?"

"I'd like to watch for a while longer from our current distance, Commander."

"I don't think I can obtain any significant additional feed enhancement, sir," said Turner.

"Do what you can," said Lanson, his gaze locked on his viewscreen.

"What's the matter, Captain?" asked Matlock, her eyes narrowed.

"I don't know, Commander. Just a feeling is all."

Five uneventful minutes went by. Lanson began to wonder if he was being overly cautious, and yet his internal alarm bells were ringing.

"You think the Ixtar got here first," said Matlock after a time.

"Maybe."

"If the enemy have access to the Infinity Lens, they'll know we're here, Captain. They'll have detected our lightspeed exit.

The fact we haven't yet been attacked suggests our presence here is not known."

"There's so much we don't understand, Commander," said Lanson. "What if the *Tyrantor* is the only Ixtar warship with access to the Infinity Lens? What if there are other vessels in the enemy fleet which need to authenticate to also obtain access?"

"In which case, we should either attempt comms contact with the station or execute a lightspeed jump that takes us to a position from which we can view anything currently outside our sensor arcs."

In circumstances like this, the usual procedure would be to run a sweep for comms receptors – like Matlock had suggested - and then initiate contact. However, Lanson was feeling some-what on edge, having been told by Sergeant Gabriel how easily the *Tyrantor* had cracked the security on the Scalos facility. Should the enemy already be at Dalvaron, they might have subverted the comms.

Damnit, we can't sit here watching all day.

"Lieutenant Turner, run a scan for receptors," said Lanson.

"Yes, sir, running the scan." Turner was quiet for a few moments. "Dalvaron receptor located. Should I request a comms link?"

"Do it," said Lanson.

"Comms link requested...comms link accepted!" said Turner.

"Is there going to be anyone alive on that space station?" asked Massey.

"Doubtful," said Lanson. "I'm hoping there'll be a backup comms AI designed to handle traffic in emergency situations."

He drummed his fingers while he waited for Turner to report. Less than a minute later, she spoke.

"Captain, Dalvaron station reports it is under attack from

an Ixtar vessel called *Ghiotor*. I've been given access to the station's sensor feeds, along with a 3D model showing the position of the enemy vessel."

"Let me see the model," said Lanson.

"I'm putting it on your screen, Captain."

The model was highly detailed and rendered in such a way that it appeared entirely real. Using one of the touch panels on his console to rotate the view, Lanson marvelled anew at this technological wonder. However, when he'd rotated the model 180-degrees around its vertical axis, he saw the enemy warship parked close beside one of the rectangular protrusions.

The *Ghiotor* was another monster, just like the *Tyrantor*, and similar in design, with a rectangular solidity that spoke of a vessel designed to soak punishment, while giving out twice as much in return.

"Almost nineteen thousand metres from nose to stern and with an estimated mass of one-point-one trillion tons," said Lanson, shaking his head at this new glimpse of just how far behind the Human Confederation was in the universe's technological arms race.

"I'm speaking with an AI on Dalvaron, Captain," Turner confirmed. "It tells me that the *Ghiotor* arrived less than two hours ahead of us."

"What's the nature of the Ixtar attack?" asked Lanson.

"The enemy are seeking to break the Dalvaron main security modules, sir," said Turner. "If they accomplish that, they'll have access to the space station's data arrays and control hardware."

"The control hardware?" said Lanson, twisting in his seat. "That would allow the Ixtar to block the Infinity Lens transmissions to anyone apart from their own warships."

"I don't know, sir. It's possible."

"Maybe it would be for the best if Dalvaron had self-destruct routines it could activate under circumstances like this," said Abrams.

"The AI confirms it has no self-destruct capability," said Turner. "The requirement to destroy the Dalvaron station was not foreseen."

"Does the AI have an estimate on how long it'll take for its security modules to be overcome?"

"Negative, Captain." Turner went quiet again, listening. "Apparently Dalvaron does not house the Infinity Lens, and it is not the only transmitter."

"Then where is the Infinity Lens?" asked Lanson in curiosity.

"Our security tier is too low," said Turner. "The AI will not provide that information."

"We came here to authenticate for a higher tier," said Lanson. "Can we do that remotely?"

"No, sir," said Turner, after listening to the AI for a few more seconds. "However, we are invited to attend in person. The authentication is required to take place within Dalvaron."

"Isn't that just great?" said Lanson. "There's a trillion-ton enemy warship in the way. Besides, we can't all leave the *Ragnar-3* at once."

"Apparently personnel on the highest security tier are able to elevate others to the same tier, sir," said Turner. "Only one of us needs to go."

"Where does the authentication take place?" asked Lanson.

Turner held up a hand to indicate she was listening. When she was done, she raised her head, and her face wore an expression of worry. "There's only one place on Dalvaron capable of handling elevation from Tier 1 to Tier 0, Captain," she said. "And it's on the far side of the structure where the *Ghiotor* is currently parked."

"Well, shit," said Lanson.

He cursed again for good measure and turned his attention once more to the 3D model of the space station. Lieutenant Turner had highlighted a new area, showing the closest docking bay to the authenticating station, along with the route to get from one to the other. The bay entrance was in the adjacent face of the rectangular protrusion to where the *Ghiotor* was positioned.

"That bay doesn't look as if it could accommodate the *Ragnar-3*," said Lanson. "And even if it could, we'd have to risk a lightspeed jump from here to there and hope we landed right where we intended."

"The angles don't work in our favour anyway, Captain," said Abrams. "I reckon the *Ragnar-3* would become visible to the *Ghiotor* if we attempted to dock on that adjacent face."

"There has to be another way," said Lanson.

He leaned back in his seat, thinking. Should Dalvaron succumb to the Ixtar, the enemy would have gained control over one of the Infinity Lens transmission stations, and doubtless they'd go for the rest as well. Maybe they'd already taken control of one or more of the other stations. Eventually, the Ixtar would gain full control of the Infinity Lens output, and that was not acceptable.

With their massive warships and their ability to turn up exactly in the places they weren't wanted, the Ixtar were already looking unstoppable.

Lanson, however, was a man who didn't like admitting defeat. While he couldn't see a way to accomplish everything he wanted, he had a plan – of sorts – that, should it be successful, might reveal a way forward.

Taking a breath, Lanson readied himself to tell the others.

THREE

"I'll lightspeed over to Dalvaron in one of the *Ragnar-3*'s shuttles," said Lanson. "A transport should be small enough to enter the docking bay while remaining outside of the *Ghiotor*'s visibility arc."

"I thought you might say something like that," said Matlock.

"And do you have a problem with the idea, Commander?"

"No, sir - I can't think of a better way. You might want to check with the Dalvaron AI to see if any Ixtar soldiers have broken into the station's interior."

"Good idea," said Lanson. "Lieutenant Turner, ask the question."

"Yes, sir."

"Lieutenant Perry – get on the comms and tell Sergeant Gabriel he's going on a trip to somewhere nice," said Lanson. "Shuttle Bay 1 is the closest – he should make his way there."

"Yes, sir."

"What are your orders for the *Ragnar-3* while you're absent, Captain?" asked Matlock.

"Travel outwards to two hundred million klicks. The extra distance won't make any difference to my return journey, since I'll be travelling at lightspeed, but it should reduce the chance you're spotted by the *Ghiotor* if it changes position."

"If the enemy warship cracks the Dalvaron security, the Ixtar will gain access to the space station's sensor data, Captain," said Lieutenant Perry. "When that happens, two hundred million klicks won't be enough."

"You'll have to play it by ear," said Lanson. "With any luck, the Dalvaron comms AI will continue to function for a time after any security breach. You should have enough advance warning to escape into lightspeed."

"That would make it tough for all of us," said Matlock. She smiled thinly. "But we'll handle it."

"I have faith in you, Commander."

"Captain, the comms AI reports a heavy presence of Ixtar troops within the Dalvaron interior," said Turner.

"How heavy?" asked Lanson.

"5250 Ixtar in total," said Turner. "They are not currently near the authenticating station, but groups of them are moving in that direction."

"Damnit," said Lanson. "Are their movements intentional or nothing more than exploratory?"

"That is unknown, sir."

"Assuming the Ixtar decide to head directly for the authenticating station at highest speed, how long will it take them to get there?"

"The lowest time is estimated at one hour," said Turner.

"I'd best get moving," said Lanson. "Has the AI confirmed it will open the shuttle bay door upon our arrival?"

"Yes, sir."

Lanson was quiet for a few seconds as he downloaded the

3D model of Dalvaron into his suit computer. Then, he turned to face Matlock. "The bridge is yours, Commander."

"I'll try not to break anything, sir."

Grabbing his gauss rifle from the floor adjacent to the main command console, Lanson rose from his seat. Exiting the bridge, he descended the narrow steps outside and then made haste towards Shuttle Bay 1. His mind wanted to think about the crap it had just got him into, but he didn't give it the opportunity. Focusing on his passage through the *Ragnar-3*, Lanson breathed deeply and steadily, and his head stayed clear.

Shuttle Bay 1 was the place where Lanson had first arrived onto the warship, during his escape from the Ilvaron facility. Like every other docking bay, it was a utilitarian space, low-lit and cold.

The single shuttle parked here was a little over thirty metres in length, and clad in angled plates of thick armour. From memory, Lanson remembered the vessel to be fast in comparison to most other transports, and it was equipped with port and starboard repeater turrets, which were installed midway along its length.

Light spilled from the shuttle's single open door. Waiting at the entrance was Corporal Hennessey, her gauss rifle held in one hand. Lanson knew her well enough to detect the signs of tension in how she was standing, though it didn't reflect in her expression.

"We've been waiting for you, Captain," Hennessey said with a hint of smile. "We thought you were never coming."

"I decided to make a stop at the replicator," said Lanson, who'd done no such thing. He stepped across the twelve-inch gap separating the shuttle from the adjacent platform. "I never start a mission on an empty stomach."

The soldiers waiting in the passenger bay watched as

Lanson hurried towards the steps leading to the cockpit. Something caught his eye, and he stopped mid-stride.

"What's that you're carrying, Private Castle?" asked Lanson.

"This, sir?" asked Castle, holding up a two-inch-diameter grey tube which was about the length of his forearm. At one end of the device was a round-edged cube the size of a fist.

"Yes. That."

"I found it in one of the *Ragnar-3*'s armouries, Captain." Castle looked suddenly shifty. "Behind a secondary inner door. The Sergeant knows about it."

"I see," said Lanson.

He left the passenger bay and climbed to the cockpit. Sergeant Gabriel was already in the right-hand seat, and Private Stacie Wolf was in the left. Sitting himself between them, Lanson cast his eyes upon the control hardware.

"Has Lieutenant Perry filled you in, Sergeant?" he asked, taking hold of the vessel's twin joysticks. A faint vibration ran through the metal.

"Yes, sir," said Gabriel. "We're attempting to sneak onboard a space station of unbelievable dimensions beneath the nose of an enemy warship, also of unbelievable dimensions."

"That about sums it up," said Lanson. "Have you received the 3D model of Dalvaron?"

"Lieutenant Perry planted it in our suit databanks, sir," Gabriel confirmed. "We've got a long run to the authenticating station."

"And not much time to do it in," said Lanson. He had an idea. "Private Wolf, contact the *Ragnar-3*'s bridge and ask if the Dalvaron control AI will provide us with real time updates on the Ixtar movements within the space station."

"Yes, sir, I'll ask." Wolf spoke for a short time into the comms and then turned to face Lanson. "The control AI has agreed to provide us with those updates. They should appear as model overlays anytime now."

Lanson checked his HUD. Given the size of Dalvaron and the smallness of the HUD screen, only a fraction of the 3D model could be legibly viewed, and he was required to scroll and zoom for a few seconds before he located the first of the Ixtar troops – these being represented as red dots. Overall, the result was imperfect, but in theory it should give the mission personnel a huge advantage in avoiding the enemy soldiers.

Drawing his attention once more to the pilot's console, Lanson gave the hardware one final check. The shuttle was good to go.

"Private Wolf, inform the *Ragnar-3*'s bridge that we are ready to depart," he said.

"Lieutenant Perry acknowledges, sir."

"Then let's get this mission underway," said Lanson.

As he fed power into the shuttle's engines, he realised how calm he was about the whole situation. Maybe that would change once the cold dark of space began pressing against the transport's hull, and the Dalvaron station loomed like a taunting monument to humanity's technological inferiority, but for the moment, Lanson felt like he was in absolute control of his emotions.

The shuttle had previously docked nose-first, obliging him to guide the vessel backwards along the tunnel. When the transport approached the first of the three interior blast doors, the huge slab rose upwards into its recess. Then came the second door and finally the third. Moments later, the shuttle emerged from the protection of the *Ragnar-3*, whereupon Lanson brought it to a halt.

Viewed from only five hundred metres, the alien warship appeared huge beyond measure, and even its Gradar repeater turrets dwarfed the transport. Lanson thought he'd become accustomed to the way technology could transcend its creators, but the sight of the *Ragnar-3* reminded him the universe still held many secrets.

"Hunting for a sensor lock on Dalvaron," said Private Wolf.

"Good luck at ten million klicks," said Lanson.

To his faint surprise, Wolf proved him wrong, though the distant station appeared as no more than an indistinct grey blob on the feed, showing no useful details whatsoever. Still, Lanson doubted the arrays on his old warship *Gallivant* would have done a better job.

"Readying us for lightspeed," said Lanson, tapping the coordinates into the navigation system.

The backend computer accepted the data and gave a predicted time of eight minutes to lightspeed entry. After a few moments, the shuttle's smoothly droning propulsion note deepened, and the vibration Lanson felt through the joysticks increased.

As lightspeed warmup commenced, he glanced to his right. The concentration on Gabriel's face suggested the soldier was watching the movement of the enemy troops. Meanwhile to the right, Private Wolf was digging around in the comms system settings, as if she needed the distraction.

"I see Private Castle has found himself a new weapon," said Lanson.

"Yes, sir," said Gabriel.

"I thought you hadn't been able to test any of the explosives, Sergeant," said Lanson. "And that sure looked like an explosive launcher to me."

"I—" Gabriel stopped himself and sighed. "My apologies, Captain, I should have spoken to you about it. We found the launcher a few days ago, but it was only about an hour ago that Private Castle figured out how to release the magazine so we could see what kind of ammunition it was holding."

"And?" said Lanson, with great interest.

"The launcher holds one projectile, sir," said Gabriel. He twisted to face Lanson and held up his right hand with the thumb and forefinger held about an inch apart. "It's about this big and shaped like a cube."

Lanson was momentarily lost for words. "A Galos launcher?"

"I don't know, sir," said Gabriel, his expression pained. "Maybe."

"You should have told me, Sergeant."

"It was my intention, Captain. Just with the *Ragnar-3* arriving at Dalvaron, I figured it would be best to speak with you later. And then, when we got the order to head to this shuttle, I thought maybe we'd find ourselves in a position where we'd need some extra firepower, so I ordered Private Castle to bring the launcher along with him."

Despite everything, Lanson couldn't help but laugh. "If it really is a Galos cube in that launcher—" He shook his head in a mixture of horror and wonder.

"Yes, sir," said Gabriel. "It'll do some real damage to whatever it hits."

"Of course we might be letting our imaginations run away with us," said Wolf. "The cube in that launcher might be no more destructive than one of our plasma grenades. Hell, it might not be an explosive at all."

"Spoken like a true cynic, Private," said Lanson.

"Someone has to keep their feet on the ground, sir."

The conversation died off. Wolf continued tinkering with the comms system, and Gabriel's gaze become remote once again, as he studied the enemy movements on his HUD.

"Two minutes," Lanson announced. "Private Wolf, advise Lieutenant Perry that the *Ragnar-3* can prepare for its own lightspeed jump to two hundred million klicks from Dalvaron."

"Yes, sir."

For the last sixty seconds of the warmup, Lanson's eyes darted between the sensor feeds and the lightspeed timer.

"Ten seconds," he muttered, looking once again at the smear of grey – Dalvaron – on the enhanced forward feed. If the *Ghiotor* made a late change of position, such that the arriving shuttle was visible to its sensors, then the mission would end in a fiery detonation of enemy missiles.

Three...two...one...

The transport's engines rumbled with a depth that belied their mass, and Lanson felt the kick in the back of lightspeed entry. No sooner had his brain registered the transition, than the re-entry followed.

"Waiting on the sensors, Captain," said Wolf.

Lanson held tightly to the control joysticks and muttered curses under his breath. After only a few seconds – which felt like an age – the feeds came up, and a few seconds later, Wolf had corrected their direction and focus.

"We are four klicks from the nearest wall of the space station, Captain," she said.

"Damn," said Lanson in awe at the sights.

He'd already known that Dalvaron was huge, but seeing it from such close range was something else. On and on it went, like a god created by its subjects, rather than the other way around. The cylindrical main section of the station was about thirty kilometres from the shuttle's underside, and now that he was so close, Lanson could see deep etchings in the metal surface. He was sure these etchings – which were a combination of straight lines and angles - weren't random, but his mind was unable to comprehend a pattern.

Drawing his eyes away, he checked a different feed, this one focused on the rectangular protrusion behind which the *Ghiotor* was currently parked. Lanson's chosen destination had brought the shuttle to the opposite side of the protrusion to the enemy warship, but the entrance to the docking bay was on the adjacent face.

So far, there was no visible sign of the *Ghiotor*.

"Private Wolf, confirm our comms link to the *Ragnar*-3 is active," said Lanson.

"Yes, sir, the link is active."

"In less than one minute, the warship will enter lightspeed. Before that happens, I want you to establish a connection to the Dalvaron AI."

"I'm on it, Captain."

Wolf was a fast worker, and, while her talents were wasted in a ground squad of ten, Lanson was glad she was here, rather than elsewhere on the bridge of another officer's warship.

"We now have a comms link to the Dalvaron station, Captain. The AI confirms the *Ghiotor* has not changed position," said Wolf.

"Can we have a positional marker placed on our tactical?" asked Lanson.

"One moment, sir, I'm making the request."

A moment later, a huge red dot appeared on the tactical screen. The *Ghiotor* was exactly where it had been before on the opposite side of the protrusion, and it was stationary.

"The AI has also provided route details for our approach to the docking bay, which should keep us out of the enemy vessel's sensor sight," said Wolf.

A green line appeared on Lanson's tactical. This line indicated a course leading directly to the corner edge of the rectangular protrusion, followed by a low skim across the next face, then an entry into the docking bay. It was straightforward enough.

"Lieutenant Perry advises the *Ragnar*-3 will enter lightspeed in ten seconds, Captain," said Wolf.

"Acknowledged," said Lanson.

It was time to begin the approach to the docking bay. Rotating the shuttle, Lanson requested a trickle of power from the engines, as if anything more than a whisper would bring the *Ghiotor* racing into sight from the far side of Dalvaron.

Slowly and steadily, the shuttle accelerated towards the corner of the protrusion edge, only a few thousand metres away.

FOUR

When the shuttle arrived at the edge, Lanson brought the vessel once more to a halt, in a position where its topside forward array had a view across the face adjacent to the *Ghiotor*, while the rest of the transport was out of sight.

"Looks clear," said Wolf.

Lanson nodded. Narrow towers and slender constructions of fine alloy blocked much of the view ahead, but not so much that a vessel like the *Ghiotor* would remain hidden should it have changed position.

"The docking bay entrance is twelve thousand metres from here," said Lanson. "Private Wolf, has the AI confirmed the entrance is open?"

"Negative, sir. The AI states that the bay will stay closed until we're ready to enter."

"I love taking things on trust," said Lanson sourly. "Especially when it's my life on the line."

Even so, he wasn't about to call a halt to the plan just because an alien AI was sticking to protocol. Requesting power from the engines, Lanson guided the shuttle over the corner edge and across the face of this huge structure. His calmness from earlier was no longer so absolute, and he felt a cold sweat prickle his scalp.

The first of the narrow towers obstructed the shuttle's journey and Lanson guided the vessel around it. Other towers and structures lay ahead, though he knew their cover was illusory. Should the *Ghiotor*'s crew decide they needed to see a different part of the space station, they'd easily spot the transport if they decided to come this way around the protrusion.

"Ten thousand metres to the bay entrance," said Wolf.

Keeping the shuttle low to the grey surface of Dalvaron, Lanson piloted it along the route line on his tactical. The bay entrance remained out of sight, and he guessed he might not see the way in until the doors opened.

"Oh crap, the station AI reports that the *Ghiotor* is in motion, Captain," said Wolf. A moment later, she breathed out in relief. "It's going around the other side of this protrusion - so it shouldn't spot us."

Lanson's eyes jumped to the tactical. Sure enough, the alien vessel was accelerating without apparent urgency and it would soon be on the opposite side of the protrusion.

"It won't spot us *now*, Private," Lanson growled. "But if the enemy warship comes around behind us, it certainly will."

"Maybe we should get our asses in gear, sir," said Gabriel.

"That's exactly what I was thinking myself, Sergeant."

Lanson increased the shuttle's velocity and guided it around another of the towers. The distance to the bay entrance fell to eight thousand metres and then to seven thousand.

Despite the obstacles in the shuttle's way, Lanson still had time to watch the *Ghiotor*. The alien warship was travelling much faster than the transport, and he began to worry that the enemy crew had caught wind of something.

"Six thousand metres to target," said Wolf.

"We aren't going to make it if the *Ghiotor* doesn't slow down," said Gabriel.

Lanson could see it too, but he didn't respond. The way ahead was now crowded with towers and elaborate structures made from metal beams – structures which rose high above the surface, occasionally freestanding and at other times connected to the towers.

Although large enough gaps to accommodate the shuttle existed between the beams, Lanson's skills would have been tested had he chosen to fly through these transmitters instead of around them – particularly at the transport's current velocity. So, he avoided them, figuring that in this case the safest route would also be the fastest.

"Five thousand metres to target," said Wolf.

"The *Ghiotor* is no longer in motion, Captain!" said Gabriel.

Lanson glanced at the tactical. The enemy vessel was indeed stationary, halfway along the adjacent face of the protrusion and only a few hundred metres from its surface. Despite knowing just how fast a warship could accelerate, Lanson was almost shocked at how rapidly the *Ghiotor* had completed its half-circuit.

"We have to get into that bay," he said.

"Four thousand metres to target," said Wolf.

Although Lanson knew he wasn't nearly out of the woods, he felt much better with the *Ghiotor* once again motionless. Then came the bad news.

"Captain!" yelled Wolf. "An enemy shuttle!"

Lanson cursed at the sight. The Ixtar transport was about two thousand metres ahead and partially concealed behind one of the towers. From here, he couldn't be sure of its size, nor its armaments, but it was unmistakeably an enemy vessel.

Banking hard, Lanson brought his own shuttle to a halt and out of sight behind a nearby structure.

"I don't think it detected us, Captain," said Wolf.

"But what the hell is it doing there?" snarled Lanson. "Why didn't the station AI add it to our tactical?"

"I'll find out, sir."

A short time later, Wolf had an answer, though it wasn't one which Lanson had wished to hear.

"The station AI states there are no vessels on this face of the structure except for our shuttle, Captain," said Wolf.

For a split-second, Lanson wondered if he'd and his crew had mistaken something entirely different for an enemy shuttle. He shook his head angrily – it wasn't a mistake.

"We all saw that transport," he said.

"Yes, sir," said Gabriel. "It wasn't anything else."

"Which makes me think the Dalvaron security systems are already partially compromised," said Lanson. "That means the space station might soon lose sight of the *Ghiotor* as well."

"What if the bay door won't open, Captain?" asked Gabriel.

"Let's hope it's controlled by a different security system to the external sensors," said Lanson.

Whatever the truth, time was running out. The bay entrance was only four thousand metres away, but the Ixtar shuttle was directly in the path. In other circumstances, Lanson might have taken a circuitous route to his destination, hoping to avoid detection by the enemy vessel. Here and now, he was considering the direct approach, but success would depend on knocking out the enemy transport in double-quick time.

What if the transport is fitted with an energy shield in the same way as the Ixtar soldiers? Lanson wondered.

Neither the attack nor the avoid options were especially palatable and he wavered between the two. The decision was taken out of Lanson's hands. Suddenly, the *Ghiotor* accelerated again, heading once more along the adjacent face of the structure. Despite the towers and the transmitters, there wasn't a place where Lanson could hide the shuttle well enough to avoid detection from the enemy warship.

"Think you can handle those side repeaters, Sergeant?" asked Lanson.

"Yes, sir."

"Private Wolf, order Private Castle to the starboard flank door. Tell him to open it up, and be ready to hit a target."

"Yes, sir," said Wolf. "I'll let him know he should hold on tight."

Now he was committed, Lanson felt his mind clear. He requested power from the engines and the transport accelerated hard along the edge of the tower. As soon as the vessel came to the corner, Lanson banked around it. More towers and thin-beamed structures lay ahead.

Although the enemy shuttle wasn't on the tactical, Lanson remembered its last position. His plan was to approach from the rear and unleash his vessel's flank repeaters to gain a quick kill. After that, he was relying on a short delay while the *Ghiotor*'s crew realised what had happened. That delay, Lanson hoped, would be enough for him to make it into the Dalvaron bay.

It was going to be tight.

When the *Ragnar-3*'s shuttle emerged from behind the tower, Lanson increased its velocity until it was racing low across the surface of Dalvaron. Ahead, he could see the structure behind which he'd spotted the enemy vessel.

"The Ixtar shuttle is out of sight, Captain," said Wolf.

"Let's hope it's right where we saw it last time," said Lanson grimly. An orange light appeared on his console, indicating that the starboard flank door was open. "It looks like Private Castle is ready."

"He'll know when to take the shot, Captain," said Gabriel.

Lanson nodded in response. He threw the shuttle around one of the spindly transmitters and then back onto course. The surface structures were coming up fast and Lanson didn't need to look at the velocity gauge to understand he was pushing to the limit. Fortunately, the Aral shuttle was agile enough to handle the rapid changes of heading and its hull barely groaned with the strain.

"Here we go," said Lanson.

With another heave on the joysticks, he brought the shuttle tightly around the tower behind which the Ixtar transport had first been sighted.

"There!" yelled Wolf.

The enemy vessel was stationary, and in exactly the same position as before. Lanson sized up his opponent – the Ixtar shuttle was the longer of the two vessels by about fifteen metres, though its flanks weren't so high, and, from his current viewing angle, he believed it was also fitted with twin repeaters.

All-in-all, it was just another shuttle and Lanson reckoned he was in with a good chance of taking it down, assuming it didn't have an immensely powerful energy shield.

"Sergeant Gabriel, give them hell," he said.

"With pleasure, sir."

The Aral shuttle's flank repeaters opened up with a clanking, metallic roar, which was loud even in the cockpit. Projectiles spewed out in their thousands, but the bullets were prevented from striking their target by the dull red energy shield which sprang into existence around the enemy vessel's stern and portside flank.

"Damnit!" said Gabriel.

"Don't let up, Sergeant," said Lanson.

"No, sir, I won't."

Repeater slugs drummed without cease into the enemy vessel's shield, and Lanson watched closely for signs it was weakening. Already the Ixtar shuttle was rotating, in preparation to fire its own guns in return.

Lanson was ready for the enemy response. Without reducing velocity, he piloted his own shuttle straight past his opponent, while rotating so that Sergeant Gabriel could maintain fire from both of the flank guns.

In a moment, Lanson's shuttle was past the enemy, with its guns still on target, and holding a course for the bay entrance.

As a consequence of his manoeuvre, Lanson found himself piloting his shuttle backwards at high velocity across the surface of Dalvaron. The previously straightforward journey was now tougher than before, and Lanson concentrated on avoiding the obstacles in his way.

Meanwhile, Sergeant Gabriel fired without cease at the Ixtar transport. The vessel's shield had taken a pounding and it was clearly weakening, such that the red patches of energy were both shrinking in size and dimming in intensity. However, the enemy would, in moments, have their own guns on target, and Lanson wasn't keen to duke it out with this opponent.

Unfortunately, he had no choice. With the element of surprise gone, and the enemy hull preserved intact by their energy shield, it looked as if it would soon come down to a bruising exchange of repeater fire.

"The *Ghiotor* hasn't increased velocity, but it won't be long before it's in sensor sight, Captain," said Wolf. "Two thousand metres to the bay entrance."

No sooner had Wolf finished speaking, than the enemy repeaters opened up. A hail of projectiles smashed into the Aral shuttle's nose section and the noise of it was tremendous, like the inside of a metal-roofed hut as the rain from a tropical storm crashed down. Lanson gritted his teeth and banked his vessel left and right, hoping to prevent any one section of the armour plating from suffering too much damage.

"The enemy shield has failed, Captain!" said Gabriel. "Let's see how that transport's armour holds up to some real impacts."

Projectiles poured in both directions, and the nose section of the pursuing Ixtar shuttle became visibly distorted from the fusillade of shots crashing into its protective plating. However, the sound hadn't diminished in the cockpit of the Aral transport and Lanson doubted his own vessel was looking any prettier.

"We have less than ten seconds before the *Ghiotor* has us in sensor sight, Captain," said Wolf, her voice rising with both the urgency and the need to be heard over the relentless drumming of the impacts. "One thousand metres to the bay entrance!"

Lanson's eye was drawn to movement on the forward feed. A streak of orange – the propulsion of a shoulder-launched rocket - raced towards the enemy shuttle, curving sharply as it homed in on its target. Too late the Ixtar pilot saw the danger and tried to avoid the incoming missile.

In a flash of expanding plasma, the missile detonated on the weakened nose section of the enemy transport. With its forward sensors momentarily blinded by the explosion, the Ixtar pilot was unable to avoid an oblique impact with one of the Dalvaron towers – an impact which knocked the shuttle off course. All the while, Sergeant Gabriel directed a torrent of repeater slugs into the target vessel's armour.

"The *Ghiotor* is accelerating, Captain!" said Wolf. Her voice climbed in volume again. "The bay door is opening – we're less than five hundred metres away."

Lanson could feel the tightness of the margins like hands around his neck. Although the stricken enemy shuttle was almost defeated, the *Ghiotor* was nearly upon him. The moment that monstrous vessel obtained a sensor lock, the Aral transport would be obliterated by gauss projectiles or missiles.

On the rear feeds, Lanson could see the bay door had now vanished completely into its recess. The bay opening – a five hundred metre square – was far larger than was necessary for the Aral transport to dock, but at least it gave him a big target to aim for.

At last, the Ixtar transport succumbed to the incoming fire. It didn't break apart, but with its engines in a state of failure, the burning vessel crashed into one of the spindly transmitters. The beams of the structure were stronger than they looked, and they didn't buckle beneath the impact.

Lanson couldn't afford to spend any time watching and he concentrated on the feeds. The bay opening was coming up fast and he hoped it would offer the sanctuary he and the mission personnel needed.

"Oh shit, there's the *Ghiotor*," said Wolf.

Of their own accord, Lanson's eyes darted to the forward feed, where they witnessed the sight of the immense enemy warship rise above the towers and the transmitters. With barely fifteen thousand metres separating his shuttle and the *Ghiotor*, Lanson knew his remaining life could be measured by the blinking of an eye.

This was not his moment to die.

With its engines thundering under maximum acceleration, Lanson piloted the Aral shuttle into the thick darkness of the bay and out of the *Ghiotor*'s sensor sight. A split second later, an immense projectile smashed into the edge of the bay opening, before ricocheting into space.

Guiding the shuttle deeper into the bay, Lanson willed the bay door to close before the enemy warship could appear once more. He got his wish – the protective slab emerged from its recess and the gap narrowed rapidly. Before the door could fully close, Lanson caught sight of an immense shape overhead.

Before the *Ghiotor* could fire its weapons into the bay, the door closed fully, blocking the warship's sensor sight. Lanson didn't even have a moment to feel relief. The Ixtar would not want intruders inside the Dalvaron station. They'd act to root out Lanson and the mission personnel, of that there was no doubt.

How brutal the Ixtar would be in their pursuit, Lanson could only guess. Right now, his guesses were erring strongly towards an enemy response of indescribable savagery.

FIVE

A few seconds after the bay door closed, the lights came on, illuminating the space in blue, though only dimly. The bay was huge, and could have certainly accommodated a Human Confederation destroyer - maybe even a Blade class cruiser at a push.

Guiding the shuttle deeper into the space station, Lanson's eyes jumped between the different feeds as he familiarised himself with the bay. Numerous platforms intruded into the space, some big and some small. Dozens of vessels were parked, either atop the platforms or adjacent. A few hundred metres away, Lanson spotted a five-hundred-metre spaceship against one of the walls, with a studding of turrets and missile clusters identifying it as an attack vessel.

Without warning, the warship accelerated sideways from its docking platform and then rotated about its vertical axis.

"What the hell?" said Gabriel.

Lanson wasn't sure what was going on either. When the Aral warship finished its rotation, he thought for a moment that its nose was aimed directly at the shuttle. Then, he realised it was in fact aimed at the bay doors. With another burst of acceleration, the warship raced past the shuttle and came to a halt a short distance closer to the bay exit.

"I know what's happening," said Lanson in understanding. "The *Ghiotor* is about to break through those bay doors and when it happens, that Aral warship is going to soak whatever the enemy vessel sends our way."

"It's not going to soak for long," said Wolf.

"We need to get out of this bay and quickly," said Lanson.

"I've assigned north to be that way on our maps, Captain," said Gabriel, indicating portside to one of the four longest walls of the bay. "The exit lies somewhere over there."

Lanson guided the shuttle that way. He looked hard for a place to dock, though it was difficult for him to study his HUD and use that data to identify the exit. Numerous docking platforms had been fitted to the northern bay wall, several of them clustered, and he couldn't be sure which of them would lead most directly to the authenticating station.

"That one, Captain!" said Wolf. "I've highlighted it on the feed!"

Immediately, Lanson altered course and increased velocity. The platform Wolf had indicated was only a few hundred metres away and higher up the bay wall. Another shuttle was parked there already, but Lanson was sure there'd be enough room for a second.

"How come the *Ghiotor* hasn't broken through that bay door yet?" said Wolf. "It's only metal."

"I'm sure Dalvaron has more to protect it than just the walls, Private," said Lanson, hoping he was right.

The shuttle quickly covered the short distance to the docking platform and Lanson decelerated at the last possible moment. In his quest for speed, he misjudged a fraction and the vessel thudded into the bay's solid metal wall, before he set it down with much less of an impact.

For a few seconds, Lanson didn't move from his seat while his eyes hunted for the platform's exit door. The platform itself was about eighty metres long and twenty deep. Here on its upper surface, he could see crates, doubtless once used to hold supplies when the Aral worked inside the station. Then, Lanson spotted the narrow seam of a door, about forty metres from where he'd parked the shuttle, and next to a stack of crates.

"That's the place," he said. "Let's get out of here."

Lanson, Wolf and Gabriel climbed quickly down into the shuttle's passenger bay, while the latter barked orders on the squad comms. By the time Lanson was out of the stairwell, Corporal Ziegler was already in the portside airlock. The soldier didn't hesitate, and he thumped his hand onto the access panel.

As Lanson hurried towards the airlock, he heard the drone of pressurised air being sucked out of the shuttle's interior, and he felt the movement of it as it went by. Soon it was his turn to exit the transport and he followed the others by dropping the short distance to the docking platform.

The moment he set foot on solid alloy, Lanson sprinted after the rest of the squad. Corporal Ziegler was nearly at the exit door.

Lanson felt a sudden urge to look behind. Twisting mid-stride, he saw the Aral warship only five hundred metres away. Beyond, the edges of the bay door were also visible and, in the moment Lanson was looking, he saw the grey of their metals turn from grey to dull red.

"Shit, here comes the *Ghiotor*," he said.

Ahead, Corporal Ziegler had arrived at the door and he

stood next to the access panel. "Want me to open this, Captain?"

"Do it!"

As Ziegler's hand descended onto the panel, Lanson tried to eke out some extra pace. In the space of only a couple of seconds, the blue light of the bay changed first to purple and then to a deep, intense orange, like the inside of a furnace. Lanson didn't dare another look over his shoulder and besides, he knew what he'd find.

"The door's open!" yelled Ziegler. "Inside!"

Those soldiers who were ahead of Lanson dashed out of sight into an opening that was partially concealed by the stack of one-metre crates against the bay's northern wall. Lanson was nearly there when he heard the strangest sound – it made him think of a wild animal groaning with the pain of spilled innards, only infinitely deeper and with a terrifying edge that was almost supernatural.

This time, Lanson couldn't help himself. As he approached the crates, he glanced once more over his shoulder, to see the bay door sagging inwards, its metals bright like a star. In the centre of the door was a dark hole, through which the thin atmosphere of the bay was exiting and creating the sound Lanson could hear as the air was superheated and drawn outwards into the vacuum of space.

A droning sound began, afflicted by a dullness caused by the near total lack of air. For a moment, Lanson didn't understand what he was hearing. Then, he spotted the Gradar turrets on the Aral warship adjusting onto target and he realised the vessel was shooting at incoming missiles.

Crap.

A couple of seconds later, Lanson was through the door and into a square space he took to be an airlock. Sergeant Gabriel was last man and, as soon as he was across the threshold, Corporal Ziegler touched the access panel to close the door.

Once the outer door was closed, a green light appeared on the inner door. Corporal Hennessey was already at the panel and she activated it at once. The second door opened and the soldiers dashed into the passage beyond.

When Lanson exited the airlock, he paused for a moment to listen. He could hear the booming sounds of detonation from back in the docking bay, distant and muffled by the airlock door.

Then, Hennessey closed the inner door and the sound faded away. The first thing which struck Lanson was the near silence of Dalvaron. If the space station was fitted with engines – which it almost certainly was – then they were completely offline. The moment he noticed the absence of sound, Lanson found himself craving the familiar drone or rumble of a light-speed drive.

By now, Gabriel had made his way to the front of the pack.

"We have to move!" he yelled. "The *Ghiotor* wants us dead, and that means there's a good chance it'll saturate this area with missiles. Or worse."

"If the Ixtar blow up these walls, they won't be able to land a shuttle nearby, Sergeant," said Ziegler.

"That's a good point, Corporal," said Gabriel, setting off north along the corridor beyond the airlock door. "However, I'm not going to bet my life on how a bunch of aliens might or might not behave. We need to put some distance between us and that bay."

"I reckon they're going to hit us with a death ray attack," said Hennessey. "That'll be clean and easy for them."

Hennessey had called it right back on Ilvaron and she repeated the trick here on the Dalvaron station. A wave of sickly energy struck Lanson and he grimaced with the feeling of sudden debilitation. As quickly as it came, the weakness faded and he felt as good as new. Having been struck several times by the weapon already, its effectiveness was heading towards zero as his Galos-modified body became rapidly better at shaking off the effects.

"Take your death weapon and fire it up your own asses!" said Hennessey, raising a middle finger towards the unseen alien warship. "Because we ain't dying from it. Assholes."

"Come on, we're getting out of here," said Gabriel, urging the mission personnel to keep pace.

Lanson stayed in the middle of the line as Gabriel rapidly accelerated to a sprint. The passage was almost four metres wide at floor level, but the walls sloped inwards, such that the four-metre-high ceiling wasn't much more than three metres from one side to the other.

Already, Lanson was feeling vulnerable in his TL-1 all-purpose spacesuit, what with the soldiers wearing full GK-3 Frontline armour. The lesser weight of the TL-1 would make him a little more agile, but it wasn't like he'd be dodging bullets in it.

As he ran, Lanson looked ahead to see what was coming up. He wanted to check his HUD map, but it was difficult to focus on it when he was running so hard. This corridor continued straight for about fifty metres, and then it opened into a larger space. A short distance before that, intersecting corridors went east and west, and Lanson glanced into them as he went by. He saw rooms and tech, but he was travelling so rapidly that his brain was unable to retain the details.

As soon as Gabriel entered the northern room, he barked an order to halt. Once every member of the squad was inside, Corporal Hennessey thumped her hand on the access panel to the left of the entrance and the door closed.

Lanson stared around him. This room was a storage area,

measuring about forty metres from east to west and twenty from south to north. Hundreds of grey crates were stacked against the walls, as well as across the middle of the floor. A couple of gravity vehicles with lifting forks hovered nearby, their drives humming quietly.

"Listen up," said Gabriel. "It strikes me that if the *Ghiotor's* crew were hoping to make absolutely sure we're dead by bombarding the docking bay, we'd already know about it. That makes me believe they'll be sending a shuttle filled with their soldiers to look for our bodies."

"Bodies they won't find," said Ziegler. "Then they'll come looking for us."

"The Ixtar are already to the north of us," said Private Teague. "Once they know we escaped the death weapon, they'll come this way."

"Our best hope is that the Ixtar don't have layout plans for Dalvaron," said Lanson. "So far, their movements indicate they're conducting a sweep through this area of the space station, without knowing exactly where they're going."

"Let's hope they get lost, huh?" said Teague.

"I estimate we're less than two thousand metres from the authenticating station as the crow flies, and the enemy currently to our north are almost fifteen hundred metres beyond that," said Gabriel. "We can't afford to take it easy."

"If the Ixtar head directly south, we might be able to avoid them by heading west and then north, Sergeant," said Lanson. "That'll take us off the route line given to us by the comms AI, but we'll have a better chance of making it to the authenticating station."

"Yes, sir," said Gabriel. "That's what I'm planning."

"If – when – the Ixtar land their shuttle in the docking bay behind us, will they appear on our HUD maps as well?" asked Private Chan.

"I haven't spoken to the Dalvaron AI since we docked," said Private Wolf.

"Do it now," said Gabriel. "And do it quickly."

"Yes, sir."

Gabriel didn't immediately order the squad to move out and it was evident he was studying the enemy troop movements on his HUD. Lanson did likewise, but at the same time, he approached the nearest crate. The surfaces of the container were dull and scuffed, and the lid was sealed with an electronic lock.

When Lanson placed his middle three fingers on what he took to be the crate's security scanner, the lock disengaged with a click. Taking hold of the lid, he lifted it to the vertical, where it stayed without falling closed again. Peering into the crate, Lanson saw hundreds of magazines for hand-held weapons.

"Will any of those fit this Galos launcher?" asked Private Castle, who was one of the soldiers taking an interest in what Lanson was doing.

"Doesn't look like it," said Lanson. "I'd guess these are magazines for rifles."

"So many bullets and nobody to fire them," said Corporal Hennessey. "I wonder what happened to the Aral."

"That's a question I've been asking myself," Lanson admitted. "So far, I haven't come up with an answer."

"Maybe we'll find something here on Dalvaron, Captain," said Hennessey.

"I'll be keeping my eye out, Corporal."

"Sergeant, I've contacted the comms AI," said Private Wolf. "It confirms that any new enemy arrivals will be added to our HUDs."

"That's good," said Gabriel.

"But there's something else, Sergeant," Wolf continued.

"The AI isn't responding quickly. I don't think we have long before it's either shut down or subverted by the Ixtar."

"A shutdown I can just about handle," said Gabriel. "However, if the enemy gain control of the internal monitors, we're well and truly screwed."

"It's worse than that, Sergeant," said Lanson. "If the AI is purged by the Ixtar, I might not be able to authenticate."

"Damn, is there a way to prevent that happening?" asked Gabriel.

"Maybe," said Lanson. "Private Wolf – request that the AI sends a command to the authenticating station, instructing the hardware to authenticate us even if there's a security breach elsewhere."

"I'll send that request now, sir," said Wolf. She paced for a few seconds. "The AI has sent the command," she said. "The authentication should begin even if there're failures elsewhere in the security network."

"Good," said Lanson. In truth he had no idea if his plan would work, since he didn't know how the Dalvaron security was set up. Still, he'd done as much as he could, and it would soon be time to move.

First, Lanson wanted to speak with his crew on the *Ragnar-3*. He ran a receptor sweep for the warship, which turned up no results. It was an outcome he'd been prepared for, since he'd expected the walls of Dalvaron to block any outbound transmissions.

"Private Wolf – I have another request for the station AI. We need access to the external comms arrays."

"I'm asking now, sir." Wolf went quiet as she waited for a response. "I'm only receiving a bunch of garbled crap from the AI, sir."

"Try again," said Lanson.

"Yes, sir." This time Wolf was quiet for only a moment. "Same result."

"So we have no comms to the *Ragnar-3*," said Lanson. He wasn't downhearted. "If we can find the right type of console, I should be able to manually give us external comms access."

"Something to add to the list," said Gabriel.

"We should get going, Sergeant," said Lanson, refusing to let himself worry about the comms situation.

Gabriel nodded. "We're heading out of the western exit," he said, pointing towards a closed door that way.

As the squad moved out, Lanson kept one eye on the HUD map. He'd already committed a couple of different routes to memory and he hoped the Ixtar wouldn't have enough knowledge of Dalvaron to block them off.

Suddenly, the red dots representing the Ixtar soldiers on his HUD winked out for about two seconds, before they reappeared.

"Did you see that, Sergeant?" asked Lanson.

"Yes, sir."

"We're running out of time."

"That's one thing there's never enough of, Captain."

With that, Gabriel planted his hand on the exit door access panel. The door opened and he broke into a sprint along the passage outside.

Lanson followed the others, trying to pretend the mission was still under a semblance of control. He was desperate to complete his elevation to Security Tier 0, and he was equally keen to find out more about the Aral. Accomplishing both goals was possible here on Dalvaron, as long as the Ixtar weren't quick enough and aggressive enough to prevent it happening.

Despite his limited experience with this new enemy, Lanson was sure they were going turn the mission into a damned tough one.

SIX

The new passage stretched away into the distance and, before the squad had travelled more than fifty metres, a new cluster of Ixtar appeared on the soldiers' HUD maps. Lanson estimated their numbers at more than two hundred.

"The enemy have docked in the bay behind us," said Gabriel. "They're going to search for our bodies and when they find thin air, they'll head north."

"We have to stay ahead of them," said Corporal Ziegler.

Soon, the passage entered another large space, measuring about a hundred metres by forty, and with a high ceiling which, bizarrely, was arched and intricately decorated with a colourful scene of a beautiful lake surrounded by purple, alien trees and green grass, with a three-moon sky of the deepest red.

Lanson wanted to stare, in the hope he might gain an understanding of the Aral through their art. Instead, he tore his eyes away and scanned the room for anything which might be of use.

Many consoles of a type Lanson remembered from Scalos

occupied the floorspace. The top panel of each was illuminated so dimly that the light was hard to distinguish.

"These are in sleep mode," said Lanson. "It won't take long to bring them online."

"Is there anything here you can use, Captain?" asked Gabriel.

Lanson thought about it and then shook his head. "Once we're done with the authenticating station, and assuming circumstances permit, I'll do some digging through the hardware then. For now, we should keep moving."

"Yes, sir," said Gabriel. He almost managed to hide his relief at Lanson's decision. "Let's go," he said. "We're heading west again."

Lanson got himself in gear, and part of him was glad to be leaving this room behind. Something about the artwork – which was both bewitching and desolate at the same time – made him feel sad for the species who'd constructed this space station. Lanson was sure the Aral were long since extinct and yet their technology remained operational. Whatever had befallen the aliens, their creations were left behind in memory.

The western passage led past intersections heading north and south. As he sprinted by, Lanson did his best to see what lay in those directions. The passage north was sealed by a door, while south, he caught a glimpse of what may have been a security monitoring station.

Fifty metres farther along, the passage opened into a room of similar dimensions to the one which preceded it. Here, the ceiling was flat, not arched, and upon its surface was another image of equal wonder. In the centre of a canvas of pure darkness, a trillion pinpoints of light spiralled inwards towards a centre. When Lanson's gaze lingered, he felt as if he were being drawn inwards, as if he were teetering on the event horizon of the black hole he knew was pulling those stars to their doom.

Blinking and shaking his head, Lanson hauled himself back, and yet his gaze wanted to return once more towards the centre of this unknown galaxy, as if losing himself in the forever would see his consciousness find eternal peace within the universe.

"Shit," he heard Corporal Hennessey whisper from nearby.

Reaching out, Lanson placed a hand on her shoulder and gave her a gentle shake. "Snap out of it, soldier," he said. "You don't want to stare too long."

"I do want to stare Captain," said Hennessey. "I—" She cut herself off and her faraway expression returned into the present. "It felt for a moment like everything I ever wanted."

Lanson attempted a smile. "We've got too many people relying on us, Corporal."

None of the other soldiers appeared to have noticed anything untoward about the ceiling, though Gabriel was looking directly towards Lanson.

"Is there a problem, Captain?"

"The ceiling—" said Lanson. This wasn't the time to explain. "There's no problem, Sergeant. We should be on our way."

Gabriel nodded slowly and then turned. "Two more rooms west and then we cut north," he said, jogging towards the exit.

Another passage led to another room, this one filled with grey tech and nothing else. By now, the docking bay was about three hundred metres away. However, the enemy were spreading out and moving rapidly. In addition, another five hundred of the alien scumbags had docked, and these were following the earlier arrivals in pursuit of the squad.

The final room before the intended change of direction to the north contained more of the same tech as elsewhere, though a huge screen on the southern wall was illuminated and displayed an enormous quantity of data. Lanson slowed briefly to look. The screen was evidently showing a portion of the output from the Infinity Lens. Colourful lines appeared in places, their overlay text too small to read from this distance, despite the size of the screen.

"Keep going, Sergeant," said Lanson, forestalling Gabriel's coming question.

"Yes, sir."

Gabriel headed for the farthest of the room's two northern exits. He paused at the access panel and then cursed. "A bunch of the Ixtar to our north are now moving west," he said.

"Coincidence or something else?" asked Private Damico.

"Damned if I know," said Gabriel. "The enemy are still being watched by the Dalvaron monitors, so it shouldn't be too difficult to avoid them." He swore again. "Unless they locate the authenticating station and recognize it for what it is."

With a force borne from anger, Gabriel struck the access panel and the door opened. A long corridor went north and the lights here were flickering on and off at random intervals.

Only a short distance into the passage, Lanson was already irritated as hell by the lighting, and that irritation climbed yet higher when the corridor went completely dark for a full three seconds. The moment he switched on his night vision enhancement, the lights came back.

Forced to slow down, Gabriel dropped his pace to a fast jog and ordered the squad members to turn on their helmet flashlights. Beams of yellow appeared, jumping with the movement of each soldier's head. When combined with the flickering lights, the effect was unpleasant, though Lanson found it more tolerable if he narrowed his eyes.

Sixty metres farther, Gabriel followed a short passage east. This passage then went north and brought the soldiers into a compact room which gave access to three airlifts.

"According to the HUD map, these all go to the same place," said Gabriel.

Choosing the middle lift, he stepped forward and pressed his hand onto the operation panel. The door didn't immediately open and several seconds went by.

"This car must be a thousand levels below us, Sergeant," said Ziegler.

"I'll try these other two," muttered Gabriel.

Before he could operate a second control panel, the centre lift opened. The car looked as if it could accommodate all eleven of the mission personnel, but it would be a tight squeeze.

"In," said Gabriel brusquely.

The soldiers entered the car and Lanson went in second-last after Gabriel. Space was indeed at a premium and he found himself pushed up against the side wall of the car.

"Sorry, Captain," said Damico, trying to make some extra room.

"Don't worry about it, soldier."

"Down we go," said Gabriel. "We're about five hundred metres above our destination level."

The lift door slid quietly shut and Lanson sensed the acceleration as it descended the shaft. He used the opportunity to check the positions of the enemy troops on his HUD map. Just like before, the dots vanished and then reappeared a couple of seconds later. It happened again and Lanson swore. He held his breath as he watched the HUD and tried his best to commit the Ixtar positions to memory.

Then, the dots disappeared again, and this time they didn't return.

"Sergeant, we've lost our intel," said Lanson. "Private Wolf, check your connection to the comms AI."

"The connection is lost, Captain," said Wolf. "I'm trying to re-establish...damnit, no response."

"Well that's a kick in the balls," said Private Davison offhand, as if he didn't care in the slightest.

"We've got a real fight on our hands now," said Gabriel, ignoring the comment. "When we exit this lift, I reckon the closest Ixtar troops will be about a thousand metres north of our position. That puts them only four hundred metres beyond the authenticating station."

"We'll have to be real careful when we get closer," said Corporal Hennessey.

Lanson checked his HUD map again. While possessing a copy of the map was still advantageous, it was much less of a benefit when it wasn't showing the enemy positions.

"The authentication shouldn't take long," he said. "Once it's done, we can vanish deeper into the space station. The enemy have the numbers, but each time we take a left or a right, they have to halve their forces to keep on our tails."

The lift's descent continued and Lanson considered what he'd just said. While there was truth to his words, they would mean nothing if the Ixtar managed to subvert the Dalvaron security systems. Lanson's main hope was that the space station's various onboard systems contained plenty of redundancy and were isolated in such a way that a breach into one wouldn't allow easy access to the others.

A feeling of deceleration warned Lanson that the lift was almost at its destination. He readied himself for a quick exit from the car and the soldiers crowded around him shifted in anticipation.

"I'll exit first," said Gabriel. "Chan, Davison, Teague, you follow in that order, so we're not falling over each other. The rest of you wait for the all-clear."

The lift came to a halt and the door opened. Gabriel exploded into motion, dashing into a room which appeared identical to the one above. The moment he was out, Chan followed, then went Davison and Teague.

"Clear," said Gabriel.

Lanson exited the lift along with the remainder of the squad. He looked around, confirming this was indeed an identical space to the upper lift access room.

"Let's go," said Gabriel, who was already twenty metres along the single exit corridor and looking around a corner where the passage turned north.

The soldiers got moving. Lanson followed the corridor west and then it joined a much wider passage heading south to north. Intersections lay in both directions and, about two hundred metres north, Lanson could see another open space corresponding to the one on his HUD map.

Signs hung from the ceiling, offering directions to places Lanson didn't recognize and certainly didn't want to go, but what caught his eye were the windows in the passage walls.

Spaced every twenty-five metres, with the closest being a short distance along the corridor, these weren't windows in the truest sense of the word. Rather, they were viewscreens which received a feed from the exterior of Dalvaron.

Gabriel was already looking outside and, when Lanson stepped up close he could see not only space and stars, but the curving shape of the space station's main hull section. Then, the *Ghiotor* slid into view, impossibly vast and terrible in its technological superiority. Lanson could only stare, not even trying to deny the hatred he felt for this Ixtar construction.

"We should go, Captain," said Gabriel at last.

"You're right," said Lanson backing away from the view screen. "We already know what we're facing."

"Once we're done here, we'll have to escape from that warship," said Ziegler.

"One step at a time, Corporal," said Lanson.

The squad resumed their journey north. Soon, they'd near the authenticating station and that would be when the chance of encountering the Ixtar soldiers would be at its highest. Lanson glanced at the ammunition readout on his gauss rifle. An AR-50 magazine could hold fifty slugs and that was the number showing on the display.

Lanson hoped he and his squad could finish the mission without a single shot being fired. Somehow, he didn't think he was going to be that lucky.

SEVEN

Halfway towards the room ahead, Lanson called for a halt when his eyes picked out one of the words on a sign overhead.

"What it is, Captain?" asked Gabriel.

"Transportation," said Lanson, pointing at what he'd seen.

"That's how we escaped from Scalos," said Gabriel, narrowing his eyes as he stared upwards. "Damn I shouldn't have missed that."

The sign was at an intersection and it didn't indicate which way the transportation room was located. Lanson looked first east and then west. To the east, the passage continued for twenty metres before coming to another intersection with no signs. West, the passage was longer and then turned south, again with no signs.

Quickly checking his HUD map, Lanson determined that heading east and then north would lead to a dead-end room, and he informed Sergeant Gabriel of his findings.

"That sounds like it could be a transportation node," said Gabriel. He pursed his lips, clearly undecided on whether he should investigate further before proceeding to the mission goal. "Private Chan, with me," he said. "The rest of you wait here, and stay out of sight."

With that, Gabriel sprinted east and Chan went with him. At the corner, the two soldiers halted.

"Another transportation room," Gabriel declared a moment later. He headed back, again at a run. "Looks like the Captain found us an escape route."

The squad continued north once again and they soon arrived at the room which Lanson had seen from way back at the window.

"Stay low and head to that northern exit," said Gabriel. "We're approaching the danger zone."

Lanson dropped low, but not before he'd taken in the details. This space was huge and square, and its ceiling was arched like the room the squad had discovered not far from the docking bay. Consoles in all shapes and sizes were positioned around a much larger, circular console and screens were attached to all the walls, none of them showing data.

An image adorned the ceiling, depicting a solar system of ten planets, with binary stars each trapped in the gravitational field of the other. In the corner of the image, a huge black hole, made visible by its accretion disk, threatened the destruction of everything.

As he crept north, darting from console to console, Lanson kept looking up, wondering at the perfect detail of the scene. The same as had happened earlier, he felt himself being pulled in. Fear rose at the thought of what might happen if he gazed too long and he snapped his vision away quickly. Immediately, he felt a sense of loss.

I wonder if that solar system was once colonized by the Aral. Maybe the images I've seen here on Dalvaron are imbued with the collective emotions of an entire species.

It was a strange thought and Lanson couldn't help thinking he may have stumbled onto the truth. He put the idea from his head and continued his progress.

Sergeant Gabriel was a short distance farther on, and he'd stopped at the central console, staying low and watchful.

"This is like the consoles we found on Scalos, except those ones had pillars rising out of them," said Gabriel, tapping the butt of his rifle gently against the front panel of the device. "Maybe if we find another like it after the authentication is complete, it'll be a good place for you to give us access to the external comms and to find those answers you were looking for, Captain."

"Sounds like a plan," said Lanson, halting next to Gabriel. He cast his eye over the console, but he wasn't even tempted to bring it online. "But a plan for later."

"Yes, sir," said Gabriel.

"Captain, the northern entrance door just opened," said Ziegler urgently on the comms. "I'm crouched down so I can't see what's coming through."

"I've got a view," said Private Davison. "I counted four Ixtar. The door has closed again, so that might be the last in this party."

Gabriel didn't waste his breath on curses. He looked straight at Lanson. "Quantity over quality, Captain. Put as many bullets into these bastards as you can, and as quickly as you can."

He gave a hand motion to indicate that Lanson should head counter-clockwise around the console and Lanson nodded in response.

Staying low enough to remain out of sight slowed him down significantly and before Lanson had gained a position from which he could see the Ixtar, he heard Corporal Ziegler give an order to open fire. The thumping discharge of a RAHD came from the west and was followed by the rapid whining of gauss coils.

Lanson didn't want to miss out on the fun, and he poked his head and his rifle over the edge of the console. He saw a thickset figure dressed in dark combat armour drop out of sight behind a console less than ten metres away, and then he heard the Ixtar soldier crawling rapidly along the floor.

"One Ixtar down," said Ziegler, as the gunfire continued. "Grenade out."

"Make it two," said Davison.

Lanson didn't see where the second grenade went, but the first arced over the console behind which the Ixtar soldier had taken cover. He heard a scrabble of movement and the alien rose from cover. The creature was tall at seven feet, but it was massive too, like it could bench press eight hundred pounds a dozen times without breaking a sweat.

Without hesitation, Lanson aimed and fired. He held down the trigger and his AR-50 spat out a stream of projectiles. The Ixtar's energy shield lit up, absorbing the impact energy of the first few shots.

At first, Lanson didn't know if he scored the kill. The grenade detonated in a burst of light and heat, and the alien stumbled, falling out of sight behind the console.

Having checked that no other enemies were in view, Lanson darted from cover towards the place the enemy had fallen. The second grenade had already gone off somewhere east, and he could hear the continued discharge of both gauss rifles and RAHD guns. If the Ixtar were still alive to return fire, he couldn't distinguish the sound of their weapons from those of Gabriel's squad.

Once he'd gained cover behind the end face of the console, Lanson halted, listening. Aside from the sounds of gunfire, he heard nothing, though he caught the scent of burning flesh. As rapidly as he was able from his crouching position, Lanson advanced around the edge of the console, with his rifle held tightly. The Ixtar was flat on the floor a couple of metres away, its exposed back smoking from the grenade blast.

Even as Lanson's brain was registering the bullet holes in the enemy's torso, and the pooling blood, his finger pulled the trigger on his rifle a couple of times, just to be sure. The first slug crumpled the material of the alien's suit helmet, and deflected away somewhere, but the second projectile smashed clean through the Ixtar's skull.

Lanson suddenly realised that the gunfire had ended and the room was in silence.

"Got one dead over here," he said.

"That makes four out of four," said Gabriel. "We have to get out of here – this area will soon be crawling with Ixtar."

Coming to his feet, Lanson looked around at the splattered blood and the rising smoke. In warship combat, his mind always stayed calm and in control, but here, he reckoned he'd failed to keep a clear head. Certainly, there'd been no fear, but he'd tuned out everything apart from himself and the lone alien he'd killed. Next time, he needed to do better. Much better.

Gabriel was already over by the north exit, and as he hurried over, Lanson checked the HUD map once more. The authenticating station wasn't far – not much more than two hundred metres – and it was a little way to the west of here.

"Maybe we should take the western exit, Sergeant," said Lanson. "If the enemy head directly south this way, they'll bypass the authenticating station. Perhaps we'll have a chance to finish up before they notice we've slipped past them."

Gabriel was clearly torn. The squad were in cover, with their guns aimed towards the northern door, and his hand reached hesitantly towards the access panel.

"I'm not sure we can think our way out of this one, Captain," he said. He withdrew the hand. "But we'll go west."

The squad emerged from cover and hurried across the room, turning often to check the other exits. Gabriel ordered them into cover near the closed door and Lanson found himself a position behind a console where he'd have a straight view west into the passage.

Corporal Hennessey was next to him, hunched over her rifle. "I'd swap these Ixtar for Sagh'eld any day of the week," she said.

Standing to the left of the door, Gabriel gave a warning that he was about to open it. He touched his hand gently on the panel and the door vanished into its left-hand recess.

"Looks clear," said Ziegler.

Lanson stared along the revealed passage. He saw a couple of closed doors not far along, followed by a north-south intersection, and father yet, the passage north which would take the squad almost to the authenticating station.

The squad stayed in place for several seconds longer and no Ixtar appeared. Lanson felt the weight of approaching combat and he glanced over his shoulder for the dozenth time.

"Let's move," said Gabriel.

The soldier broke from cover and entered the passage, with Corporal Ziegler a couple of paces behind. The corridor wasn't wide enough for three to travel abreast, and the rest of the squad stayed in a line near the right-hand wall.

Gabriel halted at the first intersection, looked quickly around the corner and then swore loudly into the squad channel.

"There's another intersection about thirty metres north," he said. "A couple of Ixtar ran past, heading west. I don't think they saw me."

"Does that west passage connect with the northern passage we're aiming for?" asked Private Castle.

"Not directly," said Gabriel. "But if the Ixtar pick lucky for a couple of turnings, we might run into them." He watched north for another few seconds. "Let's go," he said.

Without further delay, Gabriel dashed across the passage and stopped at the far side, in order to look north again. He beckoned the soldiers into movement without taking a hand off his rifle.

The soldiers sprinted across the opening and continued past Gabriel. When it was his turn, Lanson took a quick look around the corner and then broke into a run. Barely had he managed a single stride when he saw movement north.

"Shit!" said Gabriel.

The soldier's gauss rifle whined with rapid discharge. Lanson saw the hulking figure of an Ixtar trooper, its energy shield lit up in red. Then, the shield collapsed and the alien staggered sideways.

Lanson didn't slow and he continued after the others. Corporal Ziegler was already nearing the next turning north.

"Move, move, move!" Gabriel urged.

No more shots erupted, though Lanson was sure he and the rest of the mission personnel would soon be overrun if the Ixtar got their act together.

"Clear north," said Corporal Ziegler, ahead at the turning.

"Go!" yelled Gabriel.

Ziegler didn't hesitate and he vanished around the corner, with Chan right behind him. Lanson wasn't far behind and he joined the others in the sprint north. A branching corridor went west not too far away, and, from memory, Lanson knew it would lead to another north turning and then into the authenticating room.

The mission was on a knife edge, and even if the authentication was successful, escape was already looking borderline impossible.

Lanson wasn't about to give up. He ran hard, and embraced his growing anger.

EIGHT

The west turning came and Corporal Ziegler declared no sign of hostiles. He disappeared around the corner and the other soldiers followed. Lanson threw a glance over his shoulder to reassure himself that Gabriel and the remainder of the squad were still close by. They were.

At the corner, Lanson enacted a rapid change of direction, the high-grip soles of his combat boots squealing on the alloy floor. The Aral had installed a couple more viewscreen windows here and Lanson looked through one as he sprinted past. He saw no sign of the *Ghiotor*, though he had no doubt the enemy vessel was simply out of sight rather than gone.

"There's a door at the end of this passage," said Ziegler, who'd halted at the next corner and was leaning out. "Twenty metres away."

The squad bunched up behind Ziegler as they waited to find out what approach Gabriel would decide on.

"I'll open the door," said Gabriel, muscling his way to the front. "Corporal Ziegler, Private Davison, you're with me.

Private Damico, deploy your repeater in case the Ixtar are already in the authenticating station."

"Yes, sir," said Damico, snapping open the bipod on his Karn-3.

"I'll head back east to the last turning and keep watch, Sergeant," said Corporal Hennessey. She patted Private Galvan on the shoulder and indicated he should come with her.

From his position at the corner, Lanson watched Gabriel and the other two soldiers sprint north. The moment they came to the door, Gabriel pressed himself to the left, next to the access panel, while Chan and Davison stayed right. By now, Damico was prone behind his repeater and he'd have a clear sight into the authenticating room once the door was open.

"Here we go," said Gabriel, darting out his hand and placing it on the access panel.

The door opened and Lanson saw shapes of tech beyond. He held his breath in anticipation of gunfire. None came and Gabriel dashed into the room.

"Clear," he said. "Everyone move up!"

Lanson reached out a hand and hauled Private Damico to his feet. Then, he ran north and straight through the door into the authenticating station.

Looking around, Lanson absorbed the details. The space he'd entered was thirty-five metres square, with four exits, and a single console in each corner. In the centre of the floorspace was a circular dais with a diameter of four metres and a height of less than one. Through the ceiling above the dais, the bottom of a dark metal cylinder protruded. This cylinder appeared to have the same diameter as the dais and its lower face was about three metres above the platform.

"Captain, that's got to be the place," said Gabriel, indicating towards the dais with his gun barrel. "We'll secure the room while you complete the authentication."

Lanson nodded his agreement and he ran across the floor towards the dais, while the squad headed towards their chosen positions. Unfortunately, there was no cover between the doors and the raised platform, which would make Lanson exceptionally vulnerable should the Ixtar launch an attack.

Pushing the thought from his mind, he leapt onto the dais. Immediately his feet came down, Lanson could feel a buzzing vibration, and he could hear it too.

What the hell am I supposed to do?

Light from above caused him to look up, where he found the bottom of the cylinder was glowing faintly, like a viewscreen coming out of sleep. As Lanson was watching, text appeared directly above his head.

Authentication request received: Tier 1 to Tier 0.

Awaiting.

"Shit," said Lanson. "Awaiting what?"

New words appeared.

Galos modifications identified.

Awaiting.

"Come on, come on," muttered Lanson, looking around the room. The soldiers were in position, but they looked few in comparison to the size of the room and the number of entrances.

Tier 1 to Tier 0. Security elevation complete.

"Done!" said Lanson.

He stood on the platform a moment longer, in case any new text would appear. The confirmation response didn't change and Lanson jumped down onto the floor. At that moment, he had an idea.

"Sergeant Gabriel, get onto this platform," said Lanson.

"Let's see if it'll elevate you to Tier o as well. If I get killed on the way out, everything will have been wasted."

"Yes, sir," said Gabriel, breaking away from the south-west corner console and sprinting over.

The soldier sprang onto the platform, just as the northern entrance opened. Lanson's gaze was already that way and he saw at least two Ixtar beyond the opening. The lead alien's face was visible through its visor and he could see its grey eyes and dark red skin.

Even as his brain was registering these details, Lanson was taking aim with his rifle. Before he could fire, bullets from Private Damico's Karn-3 tore straight through the alien's energy shield and punched numerous holes in the creature's stomach. Lanson pulled the trigger on his rifle and fired a dozen shots into the passage.

The first Ixtar crumpled, its body mangled by repeater fire, and the creature behind it went down too. Three other soldiers, including Sergeant Gabriel, were now shooting into the corridor and Lanson fired another burst. His magazine readout fell to zero and he cursed that he hadn't reloaded after the last gunfight. Crouching behind the dais, Lanson ejected the empty magazine and used the palm of his hand to drive a new one into place. Before he could stand once more, Private Damico called out that the passage was clear.

"Captain, the authentication has failed," said Gabriel.

Lanson looked up at the bottom of the overhead cylinder.

Unexpected event. Tier elevation request denied.

"Damnit," said Lanson. "I wonder if this station was only instructed to allow one tier elevation. Maybe it needs approval to perform another."

Gabriel stepped off the dais. "What if the *Ghiotor* has disabled some of the Dalvaron security systems?"

"That's a possibility too," said Lanson angrily. "It might be that I could perform a manual elevation using one of these corner consoles, but we can't afford to stick around and experiment."

"We're leaving?" asked Gabriel.

"Yes, Sergeant. We should head to the transportation room."

Nodding in response, Gabriel began giving orders to the squad. The soldiers backed away towards the southern exit, their weapons ready to fire should any more of the Ixtar attempt entry into the authenticating station.

"You should stay in the middle of the pack, Captain," said Gabriel.

"I will," said Lanson, wishing once again that he was in full GK-3 armour and able to take a greater part in the combat.

Gabriel opened the southern door and the passage beyond was empty.

"Let's get...shit! Incoming! East!"

Lanson spun round and saw that the eastern door was open. An Ixtar was using the corner as cover and the barrel of its rifle protruded into the room. Lanson heard a snapping sound which he realised was the weapon's gauss coils. He fired a few shots towards the doorway, hoping to force the alien into a retreat.

"Damnit, I'm hit!" said Davison, sounding angry, rather than hurt.

"Best get down," said Castle. "Rocket out."

Lanson dropped low and the rocket sped across the room. It entered the passage at an angle and detonated with a whump not far along. Plasma spilled into the authenticating room and all Lanson could do was curl up and hope his spacesuit would keep him alive.

He felt the shockwave and then came the heat. An alarm chimed in his earpiece to warn him his suit was close to its operational limits. Then, the light faded and the temperature began to fall.

Lanson was on his feet in moments. A fleeting dizziness threatened his balance and informed him that his suit hadn't soaked all the blast energy. Baring his teeth, Lanson steadied himself and turned towards the south exit.

Private Davison had taken a shot in the leg and another in the shoulder, and he was struggling to his feet with the assistance of Corporal Ziegler. Blood had leaked out from the bullet holes before the gel layer beneath the metal plating on the soldier's GK-3 could seal up the wounds. Lanson spotted another couple of impact marks near the first penetration on the shoulder, indicating that the combat suit had deflected at least two other gauss slugs.

"We have to move," said Gabriel. "Private Chan, help Corporal Ziegler."

"I'll do that, Sergeant," said Lanson, stepping towards Davison.

"Go ahead, sir," Gabriel agreed.

Lanson hooked Davison's left arm around his shoulder and held it there. The soldier hissed with the pain.

"Have you taken the suit drugs yet, Private?" asked Lanson.

"Yes, sir. There's no sign of them working yet."

Gabriel led the way south from the room, evidently keen to check the next turning was clear of Ixtar. Meanwhile, Lanson and Ziegler manhandled Private Davison from the room. The soldier was in a bad way and he wasn't able to put much pressure on his injured left leg. In combination with the weight of his combat suit, he was difficult to hold upright and even harder to keep heading in the right direction with any kind of speed.

While Lanson and Ziegler did the heavy lifting, Private Teague stayed a pace ahead, with her med-box in one hand. From the look of concern on her face, she was eager to begin treatment. Unfortunately, the situation didn't allow the squad to stop even for a moment and Teague's expression became progressively more frustrated.

"It's only a couple of flesh wounds," Davison protested.

"The angle of entry into your shoulder makes me wonder if the bullet cut right through your chest cavity," said Teague. "I need to check it out."

"The pain's going away," said Davison. "I'm feeling better already."

"That's how the drugs are designed to make you feel," said Teague. "And you damn well know it, Private."

During the short conversation, Gabriel and Chan arrived at the turning and then vanished east out of sight. The three soldiers at the rear were easily able to keep pace with Lanson, Davison and Ziegler while walking backwards, in order that they could keep their guns trained on the authenticating room door.

"I'd like to say you judged that rocket shot well, Private Castle," said Wolf. "But sometimes I'm just not sure where your skill and luck overlap."

"I didn't kill anyone apart from aliens, did I?" said Castle. "Hopefully I wiped out twenty of the bastards with that one shot. That'd be a good ratio."

Lanson and Ziegler helped Davison around the corner and into the passage leading east. Already, Gabriel and Chan were out of sight, having headed south at the next turning.

Despite the weight, Lanson didn't feel any fatigue, though his body never did since his encounter with the Galos module on Cornerstone. Regardless, the going was slow and it was clear the squad weren't likely to escape if they had to bring Private Davison all the way to the transportation room at this current speed. Looking over at Ziegler, Lanson could tell the soldier had come to the same realisation.

"I think we're going to have to rig you up with explosives and leave you as a trap for the enemy, Private," said Ziegler.

"Aw damn, Corporal, you wouldn't do a thing like that, would you?"

"Not until I'd stripped you of spare ammo, soldier."

Davison sounded surprisingly cheerful and Lanson wondered if he'd taken a double dose of the suit drugs. He twisted so he could see into the soldier's visor and the man's gaze was clear, rather than dull with painkillers. Then, Lanson noticed that the soldier seemed to weigh less than before, as if he wasn't leaning so heavily.

"I think Private Davison is healing," said Lanson.

Ziegler looked puzzled for a moment, as if he thought Lanson was playing along with Davison's claims of feeling better. Then, he raised his eyebrows. "The Galos modifications?"

"Maybe," said Lanson.

"How's your leg, Private Davison?" asked Ziegler. "Can you put more weight on it?"

Davison limped for a couple of paces, more as if he were expecting to experience pain than because any existed. After five paces, he was walking almost normally. Pulling his arm from around Lanson's shoulder, Davison flexed his injured shoulder with a grimace.

"I don't feel good as new, but I reckon I can keep up without help," he said.

"Those painkillers can make a dead man think he's ready to climb a mountain," said Teague.

"We don't have any choice but to let Private Davison look after himself," said Lanson. "He's slowing us up too much."

"Not anymore," said Davison, striding ahead.

Teague didn't say anything else, and it was clear she was desperate to believe in the power of the Galos.

With Private Davison seemingly hauled back from the threshold of death's door, Lanson knew the squad's chances of survival had increased tenfold. Perhaps a hundredfold.

Still, the transportation room was a distance away and Lanson doubted he'd seen the last of the Ixtar. Staying alert and listening carefully for sounds of pursuit, he hurried to keep up with the others.

NINE

The squad made rapid progress south and then east. Wherever the Ixtar were searching, it wasn't here, and Lanson's hopes rose that the mission personnel would make it to the transportation room without another encounter.

Where the transportation system would take them, he couldn't begin to guess. Maybe he and the soldiers would arrive elsewhere on Dalvaron, or perhaps the alien hardware would deposit them within another facility on another planet lightyears from here. Whatever the outcome, Lanson's overriding preference was to escape from the *Ghiotor* and from the Ixtar soldiers which were hunting through the space station's interior.

Not far from the turning leading to the transportation room, Lanson heard a distant rumble, which was closely followed by a noticeable shudder through the metals of the floor. He planted a hand on the wall, trying to obtain a greater sense of the cause. The vibrations were already fading.

"What the hell was that?" asked Private Davison, who was

quite clearly as good as new again and only a few minutes after being struck by a couple of enemy gauss shots.

"Either an explosion – and a big one – or a collision with Dalvaron," said Lanson.

"Does that mean the *Ghiotor* is attacking the space station?" asked Gabriel.

"I don't know, Sergeant. I can't think of a reason why the Ixtar would want to attack this place."

"Because they gained access to the security systems and discovered that you were elevated to Security Tier 0," said Corporal Hennessey.

Lanson snapped his gaze towards her, wondering what was feeding her intuition.

Hennessey shrugged. "Seems obvious to me."

Deep down, Lanson believed it, since Hennessey always managed to guess right in situations like this. He didn't know what to say, so he kept his mouth shut.

"If we had access to the Dalvaron sensor arrays we could find out what's going on," said Gabriel.

"Maybe once we're at the next transportation node, we'll find somewhere I can try and gain access to the external sensors," said Lanson. "And I'll see if I can add all of you to the higher security tier as well."

The squad really needed a break in order to discuss tactics, rather than doing it on the move. At the moment, the mission personnel were simply running for their lives, rather than thinking of ways to turn the situation around.

"It's not far to the transportation room," said Gabriel.

A short time later, the squad arrived at the turning which Lanson remembered from before. They headed west and from there, a short corridor north led to a closed door. The word *Transportation* was etched on the door in red alien script, leaving no doubt about what lay on the far side.

As Gabriel approached the door, the soldiers held their weapons in readiness, in case the Ixtar were on the far side. Meanwhile, two other members of the squad watched the main passage, in case any of the aliens were coming this way.

"Shit, Ixtar! Six in total," said Corporal Hennessey, backing suddenly away from the corner. "They ran past the last turning we took."

By now, Gabriel had the transportation room door open, and he urged the soldiers inside. Lanson walked rapidly backwards along with Hennessey and Davison. The air temperature was already dropping rapidly, doubtless because of the floating Galos cube powering the transportation network.

"Want me to seal this door with some explosives, Sergeant?" asked Private Galvan.

"Not with this Galos so close," said Gabriel. "We'll rely on speed to get us away once we're on the far side."

Before Lanson made it into the transportation room, he felt the same shuddering run through the structure of Dalvaron as before. The shockwave made the floor and walls shake and he tried to picture how deep inside the station he and the soldiers were.

"If the *Ghiotor* accidentally hits a Galos cube with one of its weapons, we're all going to be killed," said Castle. "And it'll take the station out at the same time."

"Maybe that's the intention," said Hennessey.

"Won't a Galos detonation destroy the *Ghiotor* as well?" asked Teague.

"Only if the warship is near enough to be affected," said Lanson. "But I reckon it'll be fitted with an energy shield capable of absorbing at least one detonation. The *Tyrantor* survived the *New Beginning*'s proximity explosion."

Despite the talk, the mission personnel were now all inside the transportation room and Gabriel had closed the outer door.

Lanson took a quick look around, though there wasn't much to see. A one-metre cube hovered in the room's centre and a panel on one wall displayed the word *Operate* and nothing else.

"Captain?" said Gabriel.

"Do it," Lanson confirmed.

Gabriel touched the panel.

Straightaway, Lanson felt the pressure in the room increase and he heard a rumbling sound from all around, as if he were in a room surrounded by Rodos modules. The already dim light lessened and in moments it had vanished entirely.

Having spoken to Gabriel about his experiences with the transportation network on Scalos, Lanson wasn't surprised by what was happening, but it was nevertheless both strange and threatening, particularly when his body began to feel as if it were being stretched in every direction by invisible forces.

After a time, the sensation faded and the light returned. The single door into the room – which had previously entered from the south – was now gone, and replaced by a single door exiting to the north.

"Let's go, Sergeant," said Lanson.

Gabriel touched the access panel for the door, which opened and revealed a passage leading into another room. Advancing rapidly, the soldiers entered the new space ahead, which was absent of hostiles.

"We're still on Dalvaron," said Lanson.

The map on his HUD had updated to show his new position as approximately one hundred kilometres from the first transportation room. It was cumbersome to read the map, given the huge size of Dalvaron and the smallness of the HUD screen, but Lanson reckoned he and the soldiers were within another of the rectangular protrusions.

"Yes, sir," said Gabriel. "And we should move out at once."

"Pick a direction, Sergeant," said Lanson. "We should keep

going for long enough that it's safe to stop and interrogate one of the consoles."

"We'll go north, sir," said Gabriel, indicating one of the three exits from the room.

The squad got going at once, and with no lessening of their guard. While everyone assumed there were no Ixtar in this part of Dalvaron, watchfulness cost nothing, and nobody wanted to discover if their Galos-modified bodies would recover from a headshot.

A short passage led from the northern exit and opened into another room, almost identical in appearance to the first. From here, Gabriel chose to go east. This way led to a mess area, with benches and a couple of replicators made familiar to Lanson by his time on the *Ragnar-3*. His suit was keeping him sustained, though it wasn't the kind of sustenance that entirely stopped the feelings of hunger. In his head, Lanson pictured a tray holding a pile of green mush, along with a cup of ice-cold alien fruit juice.

This wasn't a good moment to eat and the soldiers exited the room without slowing, heading east again. The passage led to another of the console rooms, and Lanson suspected the transportation network had deposited the mission personnel into one of the Dalvaron main control areas.

"Let's go north," said Gabriel on the comms.

The squad progressed in this manner for another ten minutes, without encountering the Ixtar. By this point, Lanson was beginning to think they might have escaped – if perhaps only temporarily.

Then, the mission personnel entered a corridor with more of the viewscreen windows, all of which offered the same view of the outside.

Calling a halt, Lanson stood and watched for a time. For nearly a minute, there was no sign of movement, and then the

Ghiotor appeared at the extreme edge of the window's view. Rapidly, the Ixtar warship approached, and then it decelerated before coming to a halt at what seemed to be directly opposite where Lanson was standing.

"Oh crap," said Davison. "Does it know we're here?"

A coldness sank into Lanson. "It can't do," he said, without believing the certainty of his words.

"What if the *Ghiotor* has accessed the Dalvaron internal monitors, Captain?" asked Gabriel.

"Then we're screwed, Sergeant."

Lanson stared for a short time longer, wondering if the enemy had indeed breached the security of the Dalvaron systems. Just as he was pulling away from the window, he felt the shudder of a distant explosion.

Stepping quickly closer to the window, Lanson looked to see if he could spot a visible sign of the weapon being employed by the enemy. There was no sign of explosive light, but a vast cloud of grey dust was expanding into view from a place which the window suggested was below the place he was standing, though for all Lanson knew it could be somewhere else on Dalvaron entirely.

"They're using a disintegration weapon," said Lanson, turning from the window once more.

"Would that destroy a Galos cube without setting it off, Captain?" asked Gabriel.

"I don't know, Sergeant," said Lanson. "The Human Confederation is decades away from having a viable warship-scale disintegration weapon, and we hardly understand what the Galos devices are capable of. If I had to guess, I'd say the Ixtar know far more about the Galos cubes than we do, and if they thought their disintegration attacks posed any threat to the *Ghiotor*, they'd find another way to kill us."

The enemy warship fired its disintegration weapon again,

and this time, the rumble it produced seemed closer than last time.

"We can't escape something like that," said Corporal Ziegler. "Maybe if we were in another acceleration field."

"Even then, the *Ghiotor* would get us eventually," said Hennessey.

"Its crew would be killing Ixtar soldiers at the same time," said Ziegler.

"What's your opinion, Sergeant - would the crew on the *Ghiotor* kill their own troops?" asked Lanson.

Gabriel furrowed his brow for a moment. "I have a feeling that the Ixtar are arrogant, sir. They have their warships and they have their energy shields. They think they're better than other species. They won't take casualties well, and I don't reckon they'll willingly inflict any on their own side."

"In that case, the Ixtar soldiers won't head through the transportation network while the *Ghiotor* is trying to kill us with its disintegration weapon," said Lanson. "We'll keep going until we locate a console that has high-level access to the Dalvaron systems and I'll see if I can do anything to prevent the *Ghiotor* from detecting us."

Gabriel nodded, his expression showing concern at the situation, but no sign of fear. "I'll lead the way, sir."

"Go ahead," said Lanson.

Gabriel sprinted to the end of the corridor and positioned himself at the access panel. Another rumbling vibration swept through the walls and floors, producing a few curses from the soldiers.

Once the soldiers were in position, Gabriel opened the door. Beyond, was a console room and it contained no Ixtar.

"Here's that hardware you were looking for, Captain," said Gabriel, evidently relieved to have found some Aral consoles so quickly.

Lanson entered the room and made his way over to the nearest station. Despite his relative lack of experience, it was clear this hardware was much less advanced than what was installed on the *Ragnar-3*. Undeterred, Lanson brought the console out of sleep and drummed his fingers as he waited for the logon prompt to appear.

As soon as the prompt appeared, Lanson placed his fingertips on the authentication panel. His credentials were accepted at once, and a top-level menu appeared on the screen. For a short time, Lanson went through the different options, and it soon became clear that, while his security tier was at maximum, the console itself was not capable of accessing the highest-level functions on the space station. On the plus side, it was able to provide the location of a console with the necessary level of access.

Unfortunately, this console was a long distance away - perhaps ten minutes or longer on foot.

Stepping back, Lanson was tempted to give the device a kick. Instead, he told Gabriel the mixed news.

"If it's ten minutes, then it's ten minutes," said Gabriel, turning his head to survey the room's three exits. "Which way is it, sir?"

"We have to go north, Sergeant."

"North it is, sir."

Seconds later, the soldiers were on their way. Lanson kept himself to the middle of the squad, while his mind hunted relentlessly for ideas. The Ixtar were holding all the aces and they had another few hundred pushed up their sleeves, but Lanson was determined to find a way to screw up what the aliens doubtless thought was a guaranteed victory.

If he was able to have a few minutes uninterrupted at the top-tier console, maybe he'd be able to come up with something.

TEN

The sprint took the soldiers through many console rooms, mess areas, inexplicably empty spaces, and along corridors which passed in a blur of grey. Lanson breathed deeply as he ran, though his body didn't feel the exertion in the way it would have done before his visit to Cornerstone.

Twice more during the short journey, Dalvaron was struck by the *Ghiotor*'s disintegration weapon. Lanson didn't know the reason for the delay between each discharge and all he could imagine was that the hardware had a cooldown period before it could be fired again.

However, the enemy had fired the weapon in quick succession in the recent past, and Lanson wondered if the *Ghiotor* was fitted with more than one. Now the Ixtar were firing with longer intervals he guessed it was possible they were in no great hurry, but more likely they were continuing to interrogate the Dalvaron station's data arrays and were choosing their firing locations carefully in case they destroyed some of the hardware they hoped to plunder.

After what seemed like an age, the soldiers emerged into a

room much larger than most of the others they'd traversed so far. Having crossed the threshold, Lanson paused a moment to take in the details. Dozens of the standard-design Aral consoles were arranged in rows, all facing a much larger and circular console of a type which he'd seen previously on Dalvaron. A black pillar rose from the centre of the console, and disappeared into the ceiling, ten metres above.

Turning his gaze elsewhere, Lanson saw that many huge viewscreens were fitted to the walls, such that they covered most of the space between floor and ceiling. The majority of these screens displayed readouts in a red text that left little doubt they were reporting on the damage to the space station.

Other screens, however, were showing feeds from the Dalvaron external sensors. Lanson shifted his gaze from one to the other, as he built up an overall picture of what damage the *Ghiotor* had inflicted so far.

Several of the feeds were directed at the rectangular protrusion at which Lanson and the others had first arrived. Plasma damage was visible across an extensive area around the docking bay entrance, from where the *Ghiotor* had first attempted to destroy the mission shuttle.

Elsewhere, Lanson saw ragged holes in the space station's hull, each about four hundred metres across. Entirely by chance, one of the sensor arrays from a different area of Dalvaron was pointing almost directly into one of the holes, allowing him to see that it went deep, but without him being able to accurately estimate exactly how far it had penetrated.

"Look at that, Sergeant," said Lanson, pointing at the screen. "The disintegration weapon affects a cylinder or a cone, instead of a sphere. It's almost like the *Ghiotor* is making incisions so that it doesn't have to wreck the entire space station to reach us."

"Why not deploy another few thousand troops to do the job?" asked Gabriel.

Lanson didn't know for sure, but he ventured a possibility. "Because the Ixtar think they can neutralise us quicker with the disintegration weapon than with their troops."

"Which would suggest they believe we can do some real harm to their interests while we're here on Dalvaron."

"You could be right, Sergeant," said Lanson. He turned from the feeds. "I'm going to take a look at this console over here and see what I can find out from it."

"I'll leave you to it, sir," said Gabriel. He strode off to make sure the positions of his soldiers were to his liking.

As Lanson approached the console, he became aware of a continuous, high-pitched whining - a noise he thought more likely to come from the pillar than the hardware. Circling once, he chose what he believed to be the command station on a console designed to be operated by eight or ten personnel at a time.

Placing his hand on the authentication pad, Lanson pretended to himself he wasn't concerned the process would fail. To his relief, the logon prompt disappeared and was replaced by a series of menus which differed significantly to those on the console he'd logged onto earlier. Fortunately, Lanson's time in command of the *Ragnar-3* meant he was able to quickly understand the organization of the software.

"First things first," he muttered. "Let's stop those alien bastards from locating us."

Lanson accessed the Dalvaron security systems and discovered them to be still operational. Calling up the list of personnel with high level access, he found only three had Tier 0 authority, all of whom were represented by long strings of characters and digits, which he guessed were encrypted identification data for each officer. Lanson was one of the three, and, though he didn't know which, at the moment it wasn't important enough to spend any time investigating.

Below this list of three, was another entry in a different format.

"G-1591," read Lanson.

After this entry, were numerous others all in the same format, and presumably representing the officers with Tier 1 access. Adding two and two together, Lanson guessed that the *Ghiotor*'s breach into the Dalvaron security systems had allowed it to elevate itself to Tier 1, but that a failsafe prevented an elevation to Tier 0. Maybe.

Smiling thinly, Lanson used his superior access level to delete the *Ghiotor* from the Dalvaron security network. With that done, he placed a lock on the security systems so they would no longer accept remote requests for access.

"We should now be invisible to the *Ghiotor*," he said on the squad comms. "I reckon the enemy might find a way to circumvent the changes I've made, but with any luck, we'll have those bastards off our backs for a while."

A shudder through the control room floor and through the console itself reminded Lanson that the *Ghiotor*'s crew knew the coordinates of his position before their security access was revoked. If the enemy could bring any greater firepower to bear on this area of Dalvaron, now was the time they'd do it.

"That one sounded real close, Captain," said Gabriel.

"I need to make more changes to the security systems, but there'll be other consoles like this on Dalvaron," said Lanson. "We should get away from here and locate another one."

"Yes, sir."

Despite his words, Lanson was itching to enter another few commands into the console while he had the chance. However, he knew that any delay would vastly increase the chance of the *Ghiotor*'s weaponry penetrating this control room, and that would spell the end of the mission. Already Lanson was doubtful that he and the squad could escape, given how much volume the enemy weaponry could disintegrate.

Once again, a discharge from the *Ghiotor*'s disintegration weapon produced a shockwave, and Lanson could feel from its intensity that the origin point wasn't far. He pointed to the room's northern exit and sprinted towards it.

Corporal Ziegler was first to the door. He opened it and then dashed into the passage beyond, closely followed by the rest of the mission personnel. At the end of the corridor, a second door opened into another large room. A circular console which might have provided some useful intel was positioned centrally, but Lanson wasn't nearly ready to call a halt.

"North again!" he said on the squad comms, thinking this would be the quickest route away from the area of Dalvaron currently being targeted by the *Ghiotor*. Lanson was sure the enemy would fire the disintegration weapon soon, and he cursed beneath his breath in anticipation of the coming strike.

We're not going to make it.

Lanson was halfway to the northern exit, when his body was struck by an agonising expulsion of bass energy. At the same moment, the wall and floor directly ahead crumbled into dust. The air in the room whooshed out, causing the particles to billow and swirl.

"What the hell just happened?" said Private Castle on the squad comms.

"We missed being disintegrated by about two metres," said Lanson, glad that the pain was already fading.

"We're alive, but our way forward is cut off," said Corporal Ziegler. "What's the effect area of that disintegration cannon?"

"About four hundred metres across near the point of discharge," said Lanson. "I have no estimate for the range."

"Going around is going to add plenty of time to our journey, Captain," said Gabriel. "And it'll give the Ixtar more chances to track us down, or for the *Ghiotor* to get lucky with a disintegration attack."

Lanson grimaced at the difficulties. A diversion around the disintegration area would cost the mission significant time, and substantially increase the risk of failure.

"Is anyone carrying a line?" he asked.

"It's not standard kit, sir," said Corporal Hennessey.

"I thought you might say that," said Lanson. He smiled grimly. "You've all done space walks, right?"

"What are you suggesting, Captain?" asked Gabriel, his tone indicating he knew exactly what Lanson had in mind.

"We could jump this gap," Lanson said. "Once we're outside Dalvaron, there'll be no gravity, so the distance won't matter – we aren't going to fall."

By now, dust particles were drifting into the room, making the disintegrated edges progressively harder to distinguish.

"Caught between a rock and hard place," said Gabriel.

"We can't stick around here, Sergeant," said Lanson. As the senior officer, this was his choice to make. "We're going for the jump."

"Yes, sir," said Gabriel, his response not giving much away about his feelings on the matter.

"I'll go first," said Lanson.

He strode towards the edge and felt the metal crumbling beneath his feet. Taking a final step, he launched himself into the dust.

"Here I go," said Private Davison.

A shape – faint in the grey – went speeding past Lanson. In ones and twos, the rest of the squad announced their jumps into the unknown. Lanson saw a second shape go by, but the rest were beyond his visual range. Fortunately, through means of suit-to-suit pings, the mission personnel were visible on his HUD, and the green dots representing their positions were all travelling much faster than Lanson.

He cursed inwardly – he'd been too cautious on his launch and now he was drifting at a slower rate than he'd intended.

"Listen up," said Lanson, his voice sounding distant and hollow within the confines of his helmet. "This dust and the insulation in our suits are keeping us hidden from the *Ghiotor*. Once the dust thins enough, we'll be visible to the enemy sensors. As soon as you're back inside Dalvaron, get out of sight."

Already, Lanson was concerned that his comparative lack of velocity would make him vulnerable to detection by the *Ghiotor*. His only method of propulsion was his gun and he decided to make use of it.

Since he had no manoeuvrability in the vacuum, and because he was facing north, Lanson was forced to grip his gauss rifle tightly between his arm and his flank, with the barrel aimed south. Nobody was behind, so he pulled the trigger once, safe in the knowledge that he wasn't going to kill anyone. With no air to carry sound, the discharge happened in silence, but Lanson felt the tiniest acceleration. The readout on his HUD indicated he was now travelling slightly faster than before.

Having tested the outcome of a single shot, he fired his rifle several times in rapid succession, paused a moment and then fired again. Lanson's velocity increased once again. Still dissatisfied, he fired ten more shots, leaving him with twenty-seven slugs in the magazine. By the time the ammunition readout was down to eight, Lanson was travelling at a velocity approaching that of a slow jog, though he hadn't closed the gap on the others.

Emptying his gun, he executed a rapid magazine change, leaving the empty one to drift. Since he didn't want to risk impacting with a solid object in a way that would cause him injury, Lanson then held fire and kept a close watch to the north. The disintegrated particles were noticeably dissipating, either because the rush of air escaping Dalvaron had imparted them with velocity, or because the initial expulsion of the Ixtar weapon had caused this behaviour. Whatever the truth, Lanson was sure he and the others didn't have long left before the *Ghiotor's* sensor operators located them.

A sudden swirling of the particles offered a glimpse of solidity ahead, though at the same time keeping most of the details maddeningly hidden - except for the distance, which was much farther than Lanson was expecting. Cursing to himself, he emptied half of his magazine to the south, and his velocity increased.

"I've got my feet on solid," said Private Damico, a short time later. "I'm in a passage and there's a closed door at the end of it."

"Don't open that door yet, Private," said Lanson. "The escaping air might push someone in the wrong direction."

"Yes, sir, I'll leave the door alone."

Corporal Ziegler was the next to report that his feet were on the ground. "I'm looking out for the rest of y'all, and I've got my eyes on three."

One-by-one, the soldiers reported they'd made it back onto the Dalvaron station. Lanson was last man, but by now he had sight of a wall straight ahead, and he was approaching fast.

Quickly slinging his rifle, Lanson put out his arms and legs in preparation for the impact. He struck the alloy surface in such a way that he suffered no injury and also didn't bounce off back into space. However, he was unable to see a way to re-enter the space station. Craning his neck, Lanson looked around, though all he could see was more of the wall.

"I don't know where I am," he said on the comms.

"Everyone, look for the Captain," said Gabriel.

"I can't see him," said Castle. "Maybe if I threw a grenade out, the direction of the flash would let him know which way to go."

"That's a bad idea on so many levels, Private," said Corporal Hennessey.

"Just trying to think of a plan, Corporal."

"I'm going to climb until I find a way into the space station," said Lanson.

"Should we hold where we are, Captain?" asked Gabriel.

Lanson's eyes searched his surroundings, and didn't see anything other than grey wall and dust. He reckoned he was far enough away that the air escaping when the soldiers opened the doors into the space station shouldn't dislodge him.

"Negative, Sergeant. Get to safety."

"Yes, sir."

Digging his fingertips carefully into the wall, Lanson put himself into gradual motion upwards, with upwards in this case being the direction of his head. He'd expected the movement to push him away from Dalvaron, but instead, he stayed planted to the wall. The station was possessed of huge mass, and he guessed that was helping to prevent him from drifting away.

On Lanson went, scrabbling with his feet and clawing with his hands. Each contact with the surface created furrows in the alloy, as though the metals at the extremes of the disintegration weapon's effect zone had been weakened by the attack.

Lanson hadn't climbed much farther than twenty metres when he came to an opening, little more than a metre square. He hadn't seen it from below, and assumed it had been hidden in the dust.

Without hesitation, Lanson hauled himself inside, unsure where he was, or whether he'd be able to rendezvous with the soldiers anytime soon.

The mission had seen its mixture of highs and lows, and Lanson hoped he'd reached the bottom of this current downward slope.

ELEVEN

The opening had taken Lanson into a duct, which was doubtless part of the space station's HVAC system. Having activated his night vision enhancement, he saw that it continued for fifty metres or more, before ending at an east-west intersection.

"I'm inside Dalvaron," said Lanson on the comms. "In a duct."

"How are we planning to rendezvous, Captain?" asked Gabriel, his voice crackling and difficult to understand. "The walls of Dalvaron are blocking my pings to your suit, and my connection strength is down to ten percent."

"Another twenty seconds at the control console and I'd have been able to give us access to the internal monitors," said Lanson, trying not to curse over something he couldn't go back and change.

"At least we're alive, sir."

"Best of all, the *Ghiotor* hasn't taken another shot at us," said Corporal Ziegler, his connection also on the verge of failure. "Its crew must think we're dead."

"That would be a good outcome," Lanson agreed.

While he was talking, he crawled rapidly along the duct, his knees cushioned by his spacesuit. At the turning, Lanson checked in both directions. Emergency vacuum seals had dropped into place along each of the turnings, though fortunately, tiny operation panels fitted to the walls would allow him to override the lockdown.

Lanson instructed the first vacuum seal to disengage, which it did by retracting into the floor of the duct. Air rushed out, but he was braced against it. When the airflow diminished to zero, Lanson stared along the newly revealed section of duct. To his annoyance, there was no obvious exit - just more duct, and more turnings.

Having opened the seal across the second turning, Lanson found no better visual clues as to which way he should be going.

"Captain, a bunch of us entered Dalvaron in about the same place," said Gabriel. "There're five of us together in one of the Aral mess rooms, but the rest of us are scattered. Private Wolf reckons the ping strength from her comms pack will be enough determine our locations."

"That would be the best solution," said Lanson. "How widely scattered are we?"

"One moment, sir, I'll check." Gabriel went quiet for a short time before he re-entered the channel. "Most of us are within a hundred metres of each other," he said. "But Private Wolf estimates you're more like two hundred metres away, and she believes you're on a lower level than the rest of us."

"I'll try and find a way out of this duct, then you'll have a better idea where to find me," said Lanson. "In the meantime, do your best to rendezvous with the rest of your squad."

"Yes, sir." Gabriel hesitated. "What about the Ixtar, Captain?" he asked. "If the *Ghiotor*'s crew believe we're dead, they'll no longer have a reason to destroy Dalvaron. They might land more of their troops."

"That's a possibility, Sergeant," said Lanson, though he wasn't in a good position to start considering the ramifications. "But there's nothing we can do to influence the enemy's behaviour."

"True enough," Gabriel conceded. "However, I'll feel a damn sight better once we've rendezvoused and better still once we've located another one of those security consoles."

"Me too, Sergeant."

Having chosen the eastern turning at random, Lanson crawled inside, pausing only to touch the operation panel and bring the vacuum seal back into place. As soon as he did so, he heard a distant thrumming and he found himself crawling into a breeze of warm air as the Dalvaron life support attempted to stabilise the interior.

The walls of this section of duct were utterly solid, which made Lanson sure they were running through the middle of a propulsion module, or perhaps a reinforced internal bulkhead. He pressed on.

Lanson didn't have far to travel. Having crawled another thirty metres, he arrived at a grille plate on the left-hand wall. He peered through the narrow gaps into a corridor. The lights were on, but the illumination was now red instead of blue. Listening carefully, Lanson heard no alarm. In fact, everything was quiet.

The grille plate was attached to its mounting by the low-tech means of thumb screws. In less than a minute, Lanson had removed all twelve screws. The plate fell inwards and he slid it to one side.

Poking his head into the corridor, Lanson could see an intersection north, while south, the passage turned east out of sight.

The lower edge of the duct opening was about two metres above the floor, and Lanson opted for safety by climbing out backwards, so he could lower his feet down without risking an injury.

Once in the passage, he walked a few paces north. The connection strength improved to twenty percent, which he took as a hopeful sign. Turning south, Lanson headed a few metres that way, but the connection strength didn't improve any further.

"I'm going to wait here for you, Sergeant," he said on the comms.

"That would be for the best, Captain," said Gabriel. "Private Wolf has a ping on your location, and we're trying to figure out the quickest way to reach you."

Since he didn't know how long it would take the squad to arrive, Lanson was tempted to explore, even if only a short distance. Instead, he occupied himself by pacing back and forth along the corridor into which the duct exited. Not for the first time, he wished he could make comms contact with the *Ragnar*-3, to hear about his crew's situation. It was unlikely there'd been any significant change, but it would have to been good to know.

As he waited, Lanson took the opportunity to ponder recent events. Assuming Corporal Hennessey had guessed right that the *Ghiotor*'s crew would have preferred to destroy Dalvaron, rather than allow somebody with Tier o access to escape from the space station, then it was an indication that Tier o personnel were capable of ruining the Ixtar plans.

In Lanson's mind, he likely had the authority to trigger a response from the Aral hardware of a kind the Ixtar feared. Whether that response could be triggered from here on Dalvaron, or somewhere else within the seemingly extensive network of Aral planets and installations, Lanson couldn't begin to guess.

After a few minutes of fruitless thought, Lanson's mood was improved by the arrival of Sergeant Gabriel and the rest of the squad, who came from the south.

"What took you?" asked Lanson.

"We had a bit of a party in the mess area, Captain," said Corporal Hennessey. "Didn't think you'd mind."

Lanson smiled. "We should get moving." His eyes sought out Private Wolf. "I guess we'd be lost without you, Private."

"I'm the glue that binds the team together, sir."

A few of the soldiers offered up their own opinions on the matter, but Gabriel brought them quickly to silence. "Like the Captain said, we should get moving." He turned towards Lanson. "We didn't find any of these bigger consoles on our way here, which leaves only north."

"North it is," said Lanson. "Lead on, Sergeant."

"Yes, sir."

The squad set off, and Lanson kept himself away from the front, in case any Ixtar were on the loose in this area of Dalvaron. At the first intersection, Gabriel paused only for a moment, before indicating that the squad would be heading east.

A series of short passages linked numerous rooms, many of which appeared to be monitoring stations where the Aral technicians would have checked status reports for whatever equipment the consoles were linked to. Every door was closed - presumably as a result of the enormous hull breaches - but they opened readily enough when their access panels were activated.

After twenty minutes of journeying north from the duct, the mission personnel finally stumbled upon one of the circular security consoles. The console was in the centre of a large, square room, and the ceiling overhead was decorated in a scene depicting a moody grey ocean, with cloudy skies and birds flying overhead.

"The Aral on Dalvaron must have missed their home world," said Teague.

"Can't say I blame them," said Lanson, striding towards the circular console. "Not everyone wants their life defined by alloy walls and viewscreens."

He stopped at the console and located the biometric authenticator. Having placed his hand on the pad, Lanson waited for the hardware to come out of sleep. His logon request was accepted, and a line of text appeared confirming his Tier o access level.

"Let's add the enemy positions to our HUD maps again," Lanson said.

It took only a few seconds, and when he was done, he could see that not only were the Ixtar still present in the last protruding section of Dalvaron, they were in this one too, albeit about three thousand metres away and just within the space station's hull.

"Sergeant, the enemy have deployed more troops," said Lanson. "You should be able to check out their positions now. There are no Ixtar close to this room."

"The enemy positions are now visible, Captain," Gabriel confirmed.

Next on Lanson's list was to restore the comms connection to the *Ragnar-3*. First, he gave everyone access to the Dalvaron internal comms, and then to the external antennae. Lanson wanted to test it for himself and he requested a channel to the *Ragnar-3*.

The channel request was accepted at once. "We thought we'd lost you, Captain," said Lieutenant Perry.

"You're not getting rid of me that easily," said Lanson. "What's your situation?"

"We're watching Dalvaron from two hundred million klicks as ordered, Captain," said Perry. "The details aren't perfect from this range, but we saw the *Ghiotor* launch an attack on the space station."

"Is that attack ongoing?" asked Lanson.

"No, sir. Not as far as we can tell."

"That's good," said Lanson. He quickly explained recent events.

"So you're at Tier 0, but also trapped on Dalvaron," said Perry.

"That's about the long and short of it, Lieutenant."

"Can you upgrade the rest of us to Tier 0 via the space station's comms, sir?" asked Perry.

"I don't know," said Lanson. "That was my hope, but since Sergeant Gabriel was denied a tier upgrade, I have a feeling something's wrong." He looked down at the console panel. "I need to do some digging first."

"Is there anything we can do to assist, Captain?"

"Not that I can think of," said Lanson. "Keep the *Ragnar-3* at a safe distance and watch."

"How're you going to escape, sir?" asked Perry. "If the *Ghiotor*'s crew resume their attack on Dalvaron, you'll have to get out of there."

"I'm working on a plan, Lieutenant," said Lanson.

"Does that mean there's no plan, sir?"

"That's exactly what it means," said Lanson. "We're taking this as it comes. If an opportunity presents itself, we'll be ready."

"Yes, sir."

Lanson cut the channel and stared for a moment at the console in front of him. The options for escape were seemingly non-existent and, though he and the soldiers might be able to evade the Ixtar troops for a time, eventually matters would come to a head.

How he was going to avoid that happening, Lanson didn't know.

TWELVE

For the next few minutes, Lanson remained at the security console, hunting for information. After a time, he discovered that the Dalvaron systems had a hard cap on how many personnel they could elevate to Security Tier o. Lanson guessed this was intended to prevent abuse by corrupt officers and he wondered if every facility had its own independent Tier o cap, or if an overall cap existed and was shared throughout the Aral military.

If it was the latter, Lanson might well be unable to elevate the other members of his crew, and that would leave him as the sole officer able to access the Singularity option on the *Ragnar-3*'s weapons panel. He could handle the responsibility, but Lanson would prefer it if his life wasn't so precious.

"Captain, is there anything more to find here?" asked Sergeant Gabriel after a time. "The Ixtar have landed another bunch of their troops – if they get a sniff that we're still alive, they have the numbers to make things tough."

"I'm checking out the transportation network, Sergeant,"

said Lanson. He called up a top-level map of Dalvaron on one of the console's viewscreens. "See these blue dots?"

"Yes, sir," said Gabriel. "Are they transportation nodes?"

"They are," Lanson confirmed. "Watch when I add the destination overlays."

"Most of the transportation nodes are linked to other nodes within Dalvaron," said Gabriel, staring at the new overlays. He pointed at several different locations on the screen. "Except for these ones, which have no given destination."

"I believe those nodes link to installations on other planets," said Lanson. "I'm trying to find where exactly they go, since our chances of escaping this space station by shuttle are close to zero."

"We'll need to go somewhere the *Ragnar-3* can pick us up," said Gabriel. His face twisted with another thought. "Will the Infinity Lens register our passage across the transportation network?"

"I don't know," Lanson admitted. "Even if it doesn't, it's possible the *Ghiotor* will be able to extract the data it needs from the Dalvaron security system – given enough time."

"I'll leave you to it, sir," said Gabriel, stepping away.

Lanson resumed his search through the menus of the security console. Although it seemed likely the crew on the *Ghiotor* believed the mission personnel were dead, he nonetheless felt the weight of passing time. The Ixtar weren't finished with Dalvaron and the longer it took Lanson to identify an escape route, the more of their troops the enemy would deploy. Despite the overwhelming size of the space station, the Ixtar were possessed of a knack that ensured they were always in the places they were least wanted.

After a few more minutes – during which the soldiers became increasingly agitated – Lanson thought he'd located a node on the transportation network which would take the mission personnel to another primary Aral facility in a solar system far from here. Unfortunately, the target node was almost eighty kilometres away, and would require two internal transits to reach.

In addition, the *Ragnar*-3 would need to travel by light-speed to the new facility, and, despite the warship's ability to disguise its trail, it was possible the Ixtar would be able to plunder the most likely destinations from the Dalvaron data arrays and thereby make an educated guess as to where the *Ragnar*-3 was headed – assuming they were of a mind to follow.

Cursing at the uncertainties, Lanson logged himself out of the security console and strode across to where Sergeant Gabriel was waiting nearby.

"We have to make two transits on the internal network, and then a third will take us off Dalvaron and to another primary Aral facility," said Lanson.

"What will we find at this new facility, Captain?" asked Gabriel.

"I don't know, but it's a place called Ravrol," said Lanson. He gestured towards the console. "We've been here too long, and what I'm looking for now is a mission reset – we've achieved our goals at Dalvaron, and I want to return to the *Ragnar*-3 to consider the next steps."

Gabriel nodded his understanding. "Can you provide me and my squad with the route details for the transportation nodes, sir?"

"Yes, I'll do that now," said Lanson.

It took him only a minute to make the route data available, and, when he was finished, he stared for a moment at the blue line overlaid upon his HUD map. The first node was more than two thousand metres away, and required the mission personnel to pass near where the Ixtar were currently deploying their troops.

Alternative routes were likely available, but Lanson wasn't familiar enough with Dalvaron to start tinkering with the computer-generated instructions. It seemed best to move fast and rely on the real-time positional data for the enemy soldiers, to avoid becoming bogged down in unnecessary and possibly fatal combat.

"Let's get on our way," said Lanson. "I'll inform the crew of the *Ragnar-3* while we're moving."

Gabriel barked out some brief instructions on the comms and then he headed for the north exit.

As he followed, Lanson requested a comms channel to the *Ragnar-3*. Once the channel request was accepted, he spoke to Lieutenant Turner.

"I've transmitted the coordinates of our intended destination," he said. "The facility or the planet is named Ravrol – check it out and see if there's anything about it in the *Ragnar-3*'s data arrays."

"Yes, sir, I'll do that," said Turner. "I assume you don't want the *Ragnar-3* to make the journey to Ravrol immediately?"

"Hold your current position until I give the order," said Lanson. "Despite the lightspeed scatter, it feels as if the Ixtar are never far behind. I don't want them figuring out where we're going and then turning up at just the wrong time." He had another thought. "Tell me the *Ragnar-3*'s travel time to Ravrol."

"I'll ask Lieutenant Abrams to enter the details into the navigation system, Captain," said Turner. "One moment."

Lanson wasn't left waiting long.

"The travel time is almost exactly twenty-three hours, Captain."

"Acknowledged."

Lanson cut the channel and focused on the run. He was halfway along a wide corridor leading north. Other passages branched off and closed doors prevented him from seeing the contents of several rooms.

"The Ixtar are on the move," said Gabriel on the comms. "It's hard to be sure, but I'd say that a bunch of them are heading in the direction of our destination node on the transportation network."

"There's plenty of time for them to go elsewhere," said Corporal Hennessey.

"And more just landed," said Gabriel in disgust. "The internal monitors are tracking more than three thousand enemy soldiers north of us in total."

"We were never going to fight our way out of this one, Sergeant," said Lanson.

"True," said Gabriel, though he didn't sound as if he liked the reality too much.

The passage opened into another console-filled room, little different to the others Lanson had already seen on Dalvaron. Gabriel didn't hesitate and made straight for the northern exit. A short passage led into a second room, this one containing three airlifts.

Stepping up to the centre activation panel, Gabriel thumped his palm impatiently on the dull surface. The lift's double doors opened immediately to reveal a car with ample room for everyone.

"Inside," Gabriel ordered.

Once the mission personnel had entered the lift car, the soldier touched the inner activation panel.

"We're going down twenty levels," said Gabriel. "But there's still plenty of running to do when we get to the bottom."

The journey was short and soon, Lanson was out of the car and continuing north with the others. Every few seconds, he checked the HUD overlay. The Ixtar troops were spreading out rapidly from their deployment point in one of the Dalvaron bays, and several of their squads were unmistakeably heading towards the transportation node location. Whether this was by accident or design, Lanson didn't know, but it was galling to watch it happen.

"The Ixtar have deployed another three hundred soldiers way to the north of here," said Gabriel a short time later. "What the hell are they playing at?"

"If the crew of the *Ghiotor* thought we were still alive, the warship would have continued its attack on Dalvaron," said Lanson. "So I don't know why they need to land more personnel."

Although he didn't fully understand the enemy's motives, Lanson had a good idea the Ixtar were here to either gain themselves Tier 0 security access, or to obtain more control over the Infinity Lens. Perhaps they needed the former to achieve the latter.

On the basis of this understanding, Lanson had no difficulty in accepting the Ixtar's current behaviour, even if he didn't know the specifics. He put the unexplained elements from his mind – his own goals were clear and the obstacles to achieving them were equally clear.

"Twelve hundred metres to the target node," said Corporal Hennessey. "I don't think we're going to make it there first."

"We have to, damnit," snapped Gabriel with surprising venom.

The journey continued, through long-deserted corridors, and rooms filled with abandoned tech. Despite the situation, Lanson's mind wandered and he couldn't help but wonder what events had taken place which could have led the Aral to seemingly leave everything behind. So far, he'd seen no sign of a conflict which might have driven them away or indeed wiped out this mysterious species. The lack of answers gnawed at Lanson and he longed to know more.

"Eight hundred metres to the target node," said Hennessey. "I count nearly fifty Ixtar at a similar distance to our destination and heading there fast."

It wasn't just the Ixtar heading for the transportation node which were the worry. The enemy continued landing their troops in bays all along the length of Dalvaron. Already, they'd deployed thousands and the numbers kept on growing. Although the space station was an easy place to get lost in, that defence wasn't so applicable when the target destinations of the opponents were shared.

At four hundred metres from the transportation node, it was still unclear to Lanson if he and the others would arrive ahead of the Ixtar. The aliens were approaching from the north-east and they showed no signs of deviation in their course. Lanson scanned the HUD map with increasing desperation, looking for an alternative route through the transportation network which would take him and the soldiers to Ravrol. Unfortunately, the HUD map showed only limited data and a full re-calculation of the route would require another stop at one of the security consoles.

A hundred metres farther and it was clear the Ixtar would be first to the transportation node. With a growl of anger, Sergeant Gabriel called a halt, with the squad halfway across a dingy storage area filled with locked crates.

"We're not going to make it," he said. "And there's no backup plan."

"We can track the enemy movements, so they're not likely to catch us anytime soon, Sergeant," said Private Wolf. "Why don't we back off and wait for the Ixtar to lose interest in the transportation node?"

"Because they might not lose interest," said Gabriel. "And

because with each passing moment, they're landing more of their soldiers."

"Eventually, the *Ghiotor* will gain control over the internal security systems again," said Lanson. "When that happens, we'll lose every advantage we have. Hell, the enemy warship might resume its bombardment of Dalvaron instead."

"There's got to be something we can do," said Corporal Ziegler. "Something better than sticking around here until the enemy discovers we aren't as dead as they thought we were."

Lanson hated to think that he might be out of options, but with the way to the transportation network effectively blocked, he couldn't see a way to make it to the second node on the journey.

Unless...

"Sergeant Gabriel, if we were to cross from one side of the nearest docking bay to the other, that would cut about three thousand metres from our journey to the second transportation node," said Lanson. "We could skip the first node entirely."

"Yes, sir," said Gabriel. "But I reckon the Ixtar must have docked at least half a dozen of their shuttles in that bay. I count thirty of their soldiers on the internal monitors in that location, plus however many others are invisible to the monitors because they're out of sight onboard those shuttles."

"Point taken," said Lanson. "However, the map shows airlifts leading up to one of the higher docking platforms. If we could board an Aral transport out of the enemy's sight, we could be across the bay before the Ixtar have time to respond."

Gabriel chewed his lip in thought. "We're going to find it tough just making it to the first transportation node," he said. "Even if we make it through, the Ixtar will follow."

"While if we cross the bay quickly enough, we'll be able to lose the enemy in the corridors of Dalvaron," said Lanson.

"They'll know that we're alive, but they won't know our destination."

"Let's go with your plan, Captain," said Gabriel.

The way to the docking bay required a short re-trace of the route already taken. Lanson didn't mind too much, since the Ixtar, having closed to within two hundred metres of the transportation node, were now spreading out in a way which indicated they were intending to secure this area of Dalvaron. Either that, or they had orders to continue the search for the mission personnel.

As Lanson sprinted through the enclosing passages of the space station, he kept focus on the near future. Escaping Dalvaron was only one step on the road, but right now, it felt as if a vast canyon lay in his path.

THIRTEEN

"The airlifts should be just ahead," said Lanson, with one eye on his HUD map and the other on the floor of a room cluttered with seats and tables. A mural of swirling green and blue patterns covered one wall, but he couldn't spare it more than a glance.

"And those lifts will take us to any of three entrances into the docking bay," said Gabriel. "Depending on which we choose."

"Let's decide when we get there," said Lanson.

The mission personnel headed for the eastern door. The passage beyond continued for fifty metres, before turning north. According to the map, the cold dark of space was less than five hundred metres east – a distance which seemed less than reassuring given the colossal penetration of the *Ghiotor*'s disintegration weapons.

Exiting the passage into the airlift room, Lanson slowed to a walk. He breathed the chill air deeply through his nostrils, his heart rate hardly elevated and his body feeling no strain whatsoever from the journey so far.

Gabriel touched the activation panel for the centre of the three airlifts. "The enemy soldiers are mostly on our current level, with fewer on the two levels above us," he said. "Are we going for the middle or the top, Captain?"

Lanson, studied the map on his HUD, trying to hold back his frustration. The Ixtar soldiers were clearly marked, but the detail of the map, combined with the clustering of the enemy troops, made it difficult to be sure exactly how many of them were on which level. Given time, Lanson could have figured out the specifics, but for now, he went with his gut.

"Let's go for the topmost level, Sergeant," he said. "The lift exit there takes us into a room joining the docking bay, and I can't see any Ixtar troops within a hundred metres."

"The top level it is," Gabriel confirmed.

The lift doors opened and the soldiers pressed inside. Lanson joined them, and kept to the left-hand side of the car.

"Going up," said Gabriel.

Lanson told himself he was calm, but his jaw muscles were tight. Crossing the bay was gambling time the mission personnel didn't have against the risk of exposing themselves to combat with a superior enemy force.

The lift journey was short and the car stopped with a faint whine of its hidden motors. As soon as the door opened, Lanson surged out with the others into a room which was larger than he'd expected, and which contained yet more crates, some of which were two metres high and five in length. An eerie green light from the security panels on the crates illuminated the room, and, when he stood on his toes, Lanson could see exits north, east, and west, all sealed behind doors.

Gabriel headed at once for the northern exit. As he followed, Lanson read the text on the security displays of the crates he passed. Two of the readouts were nothing but numbers – doubtless codes for the contents – while the third display simply showed the word *Ammunition.*

The northern door opened onto a fifteen-metre tunnel which ended at another door – a door which led into the docking bay. A red light glowed on the access panel at the far end.

"The bay must be in vacuum," said Lanson. "We'll have to wait for this airlock to cycle."

In moments, the soldiers were inside the airlock. Corporal Hennessey closed the first door and the Dalvaron onboard systems ejected the air from the space with a quiet hissing sound. Once the tunnel was in a vacuum, the red light on the exit panel changed to green.

"The closest enemy haven't moved more than a couple of metres since we entered the airlift," said Gabriel. "When I open this door, we'll take stock. If it's feasible, we'll shoot every alien bastard we see, and then steal ourselves a shuttle."

As plans went, the details were lacking. This would be all about the execution and, Lanson freely admitted to himself, good old-fashioned luck. He gave the HUD map one more check – the docking platform outside ran east-to-west across the doorway and it appeared that a squad of between five and seven enemy soldiers was stationed approximately eighty metres east.

The soldiers were in position, with Gabriel at the access panel on the eastern side of the door, Private Davison at the opposite side, and Private Damico ready to deploy his Karn-3. With any luck, the repeater would cut down the enemy soldiers before they had a chance to return fire or to call for backup.

"Ready," said Gabriel, his eyes wide and his hand poised over the access panel.

Without further delay, the soldier activated the panel and the door opened. From his position in the tunnel, Lanson was able to see right across the bay. This was another enormous space, lit dimly, but well enough that he could see the various Aral shuttles docked against the far wall, perhaps twelve hundred metres away. Straight outside the door was an alloy platform, though no transport was visible upon it – at least not from Lanson's current vantage.

Gabriel glanced quickly around the corner and then withdrew his head. "The enemy soldiers are just where they're showing on the map," he said. "Seven in total, and they're standing next to one of their shuttles." His face twisted. "The outer bay doors are open, but there's no sign of the *Ghiotor*."

"What about a transport for us, Sergeant?" asked Corporal Ziegler.

"There's one parked right next to the enemy shuttle," said Gabriel. By the curl of his lip, he'd been hoping for something more favourable.

"What's your feeling, Sergeant?" asked Lanson. "Are we going with this, or are we better off descending to the mid level?"

"I think we should play this hand, Captain," said Gabriel, after a moment's hesitation.

"Then let's do it," said Lanson.

Gabriel nodded and then gave orders to the soldiers. Private Damico stepped rapidly out of the tunnel and dropped prone behind his Kahn-3. He started firing at once, though the pulse of the repeater's discharge was inaudible in the vacuum.

The other soldiers didn't expose too much of themselves. Instead, Private Davison, Private Chan and Sergeant Gabriel fired from the cover of the passage. Standing a few paces back, Lanson bit down on his frustration at having to stay out of the action. It was for the best, he knew, but that didn't make it any easier.

In a few short seconds, the engagement was over.

"Enemy down," said Gabriel. "Let's move, in case there're any Ixtar hiding in their shuttle."

Gabriel hauled Private Damico to his feet, and the squad dashed from the passage. When he emerged fully into the bay, Lanson fixed his gaze east to where the Ixtar shuttle was parked. The vessel was landed so that its stern was facing him, and he estimated the transport was perhaps fifty metres in length, with the space to carry hundreds of troops.

Parallel to the Ixtar shuttle, and closer to the wall, was an Aral transport of similar dimensions. Two thousand metres beyond, the open bay doors offered a glimpse into space. All Lanson could see was darkness.

The sprint was executed in near silence, as the squad members focused their energy on covering the distance as rapidly as possible. Through the gaps in the soldiers ahead of him, Lanson saw the bloody, crumpled remains of the Ixtar which had been slaughtered in the surprise attack. The corpses weren't far from the open flank door to the Ixtar shuttle, though so far, no additional aliens had emerged.

Suddenly, and with the squad still more than forty metres away, the Ixtar transport lifted off. It rose on a sharp upward diagonal, clearly under maximum thrust.

"Private Castle!" snarled Gabriel.

"Yes, sir," said Castle, bringing his rocket tube smoothly up onto his shoulder. The aiming took only a moment. "Rocket out."

The missile sped across the intervening space and struck the fast-accelerating transport on its stern. Straightaway, the shuttle banked hard to the north, with a large section of its hull wreathed in plasma flame.

"No kill," said Castle.

As damaged as it was, with its rear plating punched inwards by the rocket strike, the Ixtar shuttle remained operational. As it banked, the transport's pilot threw the vessel downwards, clearly aiming to gain cover below the level of the docking platform. Had the enemy crew known that Castle's rocket tube had a recharge period, they could have simply rotated the shuttle and cut down the squad with their underside repeaters.

Instead, the ignorance of the Ixtar allowed the mission personnel to reach the Aral shuttle. The midsection entrance was at the top of a short ramp, and closed. Gabriel was first up, and he crashed his hand onto the access panel.

"Inside!" he yelled.

The soldiers scrambled through the opening, Lanson amongst them. He muscled his way past the others and dashed along one of the aisles between the seats in the passenger bay. Soon, he was in the cockpit, along with Sergeant Gabriel and Private Wolf.

"Private Castle's launcher is ready for another shot," said Gabriel. "He's holding in the entrance door."

"Acknowledged," said Lanson, as he checked the console in front of him. The shuttle was powered up and ready to go, which was a relief given that he didn't expect to have a long wait before the other Ixtar in the bay got their act together.

"Here we go," said Lanson tightly, as he hauled back on the control sticks.

The transport's interior wasn't yet pressurized, so he couldn't hear the propulsion, though he could feel the vibration in his palms. With a surge of acceleration, the shuttle rose from the platform.

"I've located our exit point, Captain," said Private Wolf. "It's north-west of here and one level down – it's the fastest way to the next node on the transportation network."

"I see it," Lanson confirmed, checking the feed on his screen.

The proposed exit was larger than a standard personnel door, and it was located on another of the many docking platforms. At the moment, it was closed. A couple of Aral shuttles were parked close by, though not so much that they would impede a landing.

Hoping that he might throw off the damaged Ixtar shuttle – and the others which he expected to appear in the next few seconds, Lanson piloted the Aral transport stern-first to the west, while keeping the vessel directly above the docking platform where it wouldn't be so easily seen from below.

After five hundred metres, the platform ended, allowing the underside sensors to gather a view of the bay's lower levels. Lanson spotted numerous shuttles – most of them Aral – along with a couple of the fighter-type warships which had defended him and the squad during the initial deployment onto Dalvaron. These warships, however, were stationary in the mid-point of the bay and this time, Lanson didn't think they were going to come to his aid.

"Enemy shuttle incoming," said Wolf. "Make that two."

The Ixtar transports were far below and they raced upwards. A thundering clatter of repeater slugs – sensed, rather than heard - against the hull of the Aral shuttle told Lanson that he was already in the enemy's sights. He kept on the same heading, meaning to take cover above the next docking platform which was lower and less than two hundred metres away.

"Targeting enemy shuttle," said Gabriel.

The Aral transport was fitted with twin underside repeaters. Lanson didn't hear them fire, but the guns sprayed out a torrent of projectiles, which smashed into the topside armour of the nearest enemy vessel, producing a visible distortion on the alloy.

"Rocket out," said Castle, calmly on the squad comms.

The soldier's second missile streaked from the flank door

where he was standing. Castle had aimed it well – sending the rocket above the incoming repeater fire and onto the cabin plating of the Ixtar shuttle. For a brief moment, the enemy vessel was concealed in superhot plasma, and when the light from the blast faded, Lanson could tell that the damage was severe.

Sergeant Gabriel didn't let up and he continued firing into the heat-softened hull of the failing transport, the repeater slugs plunging through the enemy's armour plating and into the cockpit. Either the Ixtar crew were killed or the shuttle itself had suffered too much, resulting in the transport veering off course and then thumping into the side wall of the bay with a crunching impact.

"Target one down," said Gabriel. "Targeting enemy shuttle two."

Made wary by the rocket attack, the second Ixtar transport also changed course, and headed for cover beneath one of the docking platforms. This suited Lanson fine – if the aliens wanted to play cat and mouse, that would make it easier to fool them with a rapid transit of the bay.

Taking his opportunity, Lanson banked away from the bay wall and aimed his shuttle directly for the exit platform. Another enemy shuttle was now on the sensors, but the short exchange with the other Ixtar transports had convinced him they lacked the firepower to wreck the Aral vessel in quick time.

That left the landing as the most perilous obstacle between success and failure, though Lanson reckoned he could set down close enough to the exit that he and the squad could escape the bay while using the Aral shuttle as cover.

The transport accelerated across the bay, while Gabriel directed repeater fire at the undamaged enemy craft. Where the first shuttle struck by Castle's shoulder launcher had gone, Lanson didn't know, but if it stayed out of sight, he'd be happy.

"Got two more incoming," said Wolf. "They're heading in through the bay entrance. Shit, make that four more incoming."

Lanson bared his teeth in anger at the sight of the Ixtar transports. They hadn't started firing yet, but it would happen soon. Although Lanson was sure the Aral shuttle was heavily armoured, it wouldn't hold out for long in a five-versus-one engagement.

"We're in the shit, folks," he said.

His words didn't describe the half of it. With inertia-defying ease, a vast grey shape accelerated into sight, not far outside the bay opening. It was the *Ghiotor*, and it came to a halt with its midsection sensors and weapons aimed directly into the bay.

That was when Lanson felt the crushing weight of failure. In moments, the *Ghiotor*'s weaponry would open up and the Aral shuttle would be pulverised in the blinking of an eye.

FOURTEEN

A desperate idea illuminated in Lanson's mind, and he acted upon it at once. The shuttle's portside flank door – the place where Private Castle was still standing and waiting with his shoulder launcher – was facing west, away from the main bay opening. Wrenching on the controls, Lanson rotated the transport rapidly around its vertical axis. The vessel was more agile than most other shuttles he'd piloted, and it responded eagerly.

At the same time, Lanson yelled an order on the squad comms. "Private Castle, hit the *Ghiotor* with your Galos launcher!"

In his mind, he pictured the weapon which the soldier had shown him earlier. With its two-inch bore and stubby barrel, surely the Galos launcher wouldn't have the punch to trouble the *Ghiotor*. Even if it had the impact, the travel time of the Galos cube would certainly be too high to reach the enemy warship before it fired its weapons. And yet, this untested launcher was the only hope of survival.

"Yes, sir," said Castle, so quickly it was as if he'd been waiting for the instruction. "Galos launcher: fired!"

The result of the discharge was both more rapid and more dramatic than Lanson's wildest expectations. A sphere of complete darkness appeared almost before Castle had confirmed the launch. It filled the portside feeds, hiding everything from sight for a split second.

Then, the darkness vanished and Lanson's jaw nearly dropped open at the extent of the destruction. The Galos detonation had gouged a vast, incredible hole in the side of the Dalvaron station, obliterating half of the bay and the surrounding areas, and almost killing Lanson and everyone else at the same time.

The detonation had produced no dust, nor indeed any other debris, as if the Galos cube had turned the affected section of Dalvaron into motes so tiny they were invisible to the sensors. Either that, or the Aral had figured out a way to completely unmake matter. Only a few weeks ago, Lanson would have considered that an impossibility. Now, he wasn't so sure.

"The *Ghiotor* is gone!" said Private Wolf. "Do you think it's...?"

"Not a chance," said Lanson.

He felt it in his bones. The enemy warship wasn't destroyed. Its energy shield had absorbed the blast, but its crew had seen enough to convince them it wasn't a good time to gamble a capital warship against the might of an unknown weapon.

Over the next few minutes, the Ixtar would run the calculations, figure out the drain on the shield, and then they'd come back. Since the Galos launcher only carried a single projectile, there'd be no second shot.

Despite this, Lanson was ecstatic at the outcome of this surprise attack on the enemy warship. Not only had the *Ghiotor* been driven away, but the four shuttles which had most recently entered the bay were no more, having been utterly destroyed by the Galos detonation.

That left only the one shuttle left to contend with, but even as Lanson watched, the vessel's pilot guided it beneath one of the docking platforms, while Sergeant Gabriel directed a stream of repeater fire into its topside plating.

"These Ixtar are used to winning," said Lanson. "And it makes them go to ground when things get tough."

"That's what happens when you have too much warship backup," said Wolf, with a hint of mischief in her voice. "It makes you soft."

"I'll need to know a lot more about these bastards before I'm willing to call them soft," said Gabriel. "I reckon they're mean enough."

Lanson didn't want to continue the discussion, particularly not in the circumstances, and he held the Aral shuttle on course for the far side of the bay. The vessel was still travelling stern-first because of his rotation to bring the portside door into line with the bay entrance, and Lanson brought it around so that its nose was once more pointing north.

Every second or two, he glanced at the starboard feeds, still hardly able to comprehend the devastation created by the Galos launcher. He wondered if the Aral really, truly under-stood the technology they'd created, or if they'd been too greedy or too curious to stop themselves travelling a road which could lead seemingly only to damnation.

"Be ready to get the hell off this shuttle," said Lanson on the comms. "We're leaving by the portside exit." He turned towards Gabriel. "Join the others in the passenger bay, Sergeant."

"Yes, sir."

"You too, Private Wolf."

"On my way," said Wolf, rising easily from her seat.

As the two soldiers headed down the narrow steps leading from the cockpit, Lanson began the final positioning of the shuttle, so that he could set it down directly between the two Aral transports which were already parked, and with its portside flank as close to the exit door as he could manage.

When Lanson was only a few seconds from landing, he spotted first one, then a second Ixtar shuttle climbing into view on the starboard sensors. The feed was clear enough for him to see their multi-barrel repeaters spin in a blur, and once more, he felt the impacts against his shuttle.

"Shit, we've got incoming," said Lanson on the squad comms. "This will have to be a damn fast exit."

"That's the only kind I know, sir," said Gabriel.

"Hold on tight," said Lanson, flying the shuttle in rapidly with its portside flank parallel to the bay wall.

To save a few precious fractions of a second, Lanson left the deceleration too late, and allowed the transport to crash into the wall. As he'd intended, the life support unit cushioned the impact, and Lanson immediately dumped the shuttle vertically down onto the docking platform.

"Time to go," he said.

In moments, he was out of his seat and into the passenger bay. The portside flank door was open and, for a split-second, Lanson thought he might have landed so close to the wall that the squad's exit was hampered by the proximity.

The soldiers didn't seem to be suffering any difficulty and they dropped to the ground rapidly, before sprinting west towards the bay exit door. Corporal Hennessey was last to go and she waved urgently for Lanson to follow.

"Ah shit," she said, her eyes widening.

Lanson threw a glance over his shoulder, and saw that the passenger bay's starboard wall was crumpling inwards as it was pounded by repeater fire from the two approaching Ixtar shuttles.

It was encouragement he didn't need, and he hurtled towards the exit. Hennessey jumped out just before Lanson arrived and dashed west after the others. Unable to help himself, Lanson checked once more behind him, just as a jagged tear appeared in the Aral shuttle's armour plating.

Projectiles ricocheted through, smashing up the seats and throwing debris everywhere. A piece of metal – a flattened slug or a shard of metal broken from the passenger bay, Lanson wasn't sure – flashed by his head, thudded into the main bay wall, and then fell to the ground.

By this point, Lanson's body was pumping adrenaline. He scarcely looked at the object which had nearly killed him as he sprang from the shuttle onto the ground. The soles of his combat boots gripped the alloy and he accelerated towards the exit through which every member of the squad had already passed, barring Corporal Hennessey, who waited outside, waving with the same urgency as before.

The gap between the shuttle and the bay wall was only two metres, but it was enough for Lanson to swing his arms, and he hared it towards the exit passage. When he was close to the turning, Hennessey spun on her heels and vanished around the corner. Less than two seconds later, Lanson made it as well, and his relief at not being struck by a ricocheting repeater slug was immense.

However, he and the squad weren't yet safe. The exit passage was fifty metres in length and opened into a room at the end. In order to escape the certain pursuit, the squad would need to lose themselves in the depths of Dalvaron, and that wouldn't be so easily accomplished in the large spaces of a storage area.

A quick reminder check of his HUD map informed Lanson

that the room ahead was indeed large, and it linked to several others of equivalent size. However, there was a clear route to an area of labyrinthine corridors, of a type which had characterised the space station's interior for most the mission so far. It was those passages which offered the best chance of escape.

"Do you know which way we're going, Sergeant?" asked Lanson.

Sergeant Gabriel was out of sight, having already entered the storage area ahead. "Yes, sir. We're going straight for those passages to the north. There're a few Ixtar between us and the transportation node, but we might be able to avoid them."

By the time this short conversation was over, Lanson was approaching the entrance to the storage area. The space was larger than it appeared on the map, and the floorspace was filled with stacked crates of many dimensions. Aisles ran between them, like gloomy alleys in a bleak city of grey, and the high ceiling was faint in the near darkness.

"This way," said Gabriel, indicating a gap between the crates which was offset from the entrance.

"If those Ixtar want a fight, they'll be off their shuttles any moment, Sergeant," said Private Galvan.

"That's why we're not hanging around," said Gabriel, setting off along the aisle.

Picking up his feet, Lanson ran with the others, his gauss rifle clutched in a tight grip. He kept an eye on his HUD and, after a few seconds, several red dots appeared on the map of the main docking bay.

"We've got company," said Lanson.

"I see them," said Gabriel.

The numbers of red dots increased until they were more than Lanson could easily count. Those dots didn't remain still for long and they swarmed the landing platform where he'd set the shuttle down. In his mind, Lanson could picture the Ixtar searching the transport, looking for corpses. It wouldn't take them long before they realised the mission personnel had made their escape, and then the chase would begin.

At the end of the first aisle, Gabriel cut west and then turned north again as soon as he was able. The vacuum ensured the sprint was enacted in silence and Lanson felt a peculiar sense of isolation from it. However, his experience of space and its near infinity allowed him to embrace the feeling of loneliness as more of a comfort than a thing to be feared.

"Here they come," said Corporal Hennessey.

Sure enough, the Ixtar in the docking bay were now entering the passage leading to the storage area. The aliens were coming fast and their numbers had grown yet further, to the extent that Lanson estimated more than two hundred of the enemy were heading this way. Not only that, the Ixtar throughout Dalvaron were now showing signs they'd received new orders that would doubtless lead them to converge on this area of the space station. The hunt was on.

After another turning west, the next aisle north led to the far wall of the storage area. From there, the closed exit door was another few metres east. Gabriel struck the access panel at once and the door opened.

"Airlock," he said.

The passage leading from the storage bay was twenty metres long, four wide, and with a high ceiling. A tall loading vehicle with a strong resemblance to a Human Confederation forklift had been abandoned here, and it hovered silently on its gravity engine.

"Activating the airlock cycle," said Gabriel, already at the far access panel.

The passage entrance door closed, and the exit remained shut. After a few seconds, Lanson heard the faint hissing of pressurization and his spacesuit's environmental sensor told him the air was now breathable, albeit far too cold to do so in comfort.

Once the pressurization was complete, the exit door opened, revealing another storage room. The external temperature fell sharply, and, as he entered the space along with the rest of the squad, Lanson discovered the reason for it.

FIFTEEN

"Galos cubes," said Corporal Ziegler, in a reverent whisper.

Lanson nodded, as he looked across the floorspace. This storage area was approximately the same dimensions as the previous one, but the contents were incomprehensibly deadlier. Dozens of one-metre Galos cubes floated above the surface, evenly spaced with five metres between each.

The devices exuded cold and threat in equal measure, and Lanson experienced a shiver of fear at the sight of them. Why the Aral had left these cubes here on Dalvaron, he couldn't begin to guess, though it seemed like an act of extreme recklessness.

"What if the *Ghiotor* hits this area with its disintegration weapons?" asked Private Davison nervously.

"Then we're dead either way," snapped Gabriel, making his way between the closest of the two cubes.

"Want me to plant a charge on one of these, Sergeant?" asked Private Galvan. "We have access to the internal comms, so I could trigger the detonation remotely, wherever we are on Dalvaron."

"You just spelled out the problem right there, soldier," said Gabriel, without breaking stride. "Wherever we are *on Dalvaron*. We don't want to be anywhere within a million klicks of these Galos cubes when they explode, implode, or whatever the hell the outcome will be. And we can't guarantee that Ravrol will be in comms range to trigger the pack charge once we've passed through the transportation node."

"Yes, Sergeant, but what if—"

"Just plant the charge, Private," said Gabriel. "But keep it out of sight and do it quickly."

"Yes, sir," said Galvan, already fishing in his pack.

"And best make it a big charge," said Corporal Ziegler, tapping his knuckles on the dark plating of the nearest Galos cube. "The armour on these things is tough."

"I remember," said Galvan. He pulled out an explosive about the size of two fists side-by-side, dropped into a crouch and stuck the device onto the underside of one of the cubes. "Done."

"If we get cornered, we'll have the last laugh when we set off those Galos cubes," said Private Wolf.

"I don't want any talk of defeat," Gabriel warned. "Let's focus on getting out of here and nothing else."

The squad hurried across the room, and Lanson found it hard not to stare at the potential destruction stored within this one place. Then, he remembered the ten-metre Galos cubes – thousands of them – which Sergeant Gabriel had discovered in the underground Scalos facility, and suddenly, the devices here seemed like mere toys in comparison.

A fast run across the floor soon brought the mission personnel to the room's northern exit. By now, the pursuing Ixtar were spilling through the previous storage area, and yet more were following from the docking bay. It was an indication of how keen the Ixtar were to prevent any further interference with the space station's onboard systems.

The moment Gabriel had the exit door open, he sprinted into the next passage. Lanson went after, glancing over his shoulder as he did so. He half expected to hear the bone deep rumble of the *Ghiotor*'s disintegration cannons, but no attack came.

For fifty metres, the passage ran straight. Doorways in opposite walls midway along led into compact rooms holding tech which Lanson didn't recognize in the brief glimpses he obtained as he sprinted by. Then, the corridor turned west, where it continued for a hundred metres or more.

Each stride carried the mission personnel farther from the outer hull of Dalvaron, though Lanson was under no illusion that they were anywhere close to outranging the *Ghiotor*'s weapons.

When the corridor finally turned north once more, another storage room was visible not far away. The northern exit from here would lead into the warren of passages in which Lanson hoped to lose the pursuing Ixtar. His eyes went to his HUD again. The enemy were already in the Galos storage room, and Lanson was pleased to see they were splitting into groups in order to search each of the different exits.

Upon entering the storage room, he looked around and saw nothing that was unusual. Yet more crates were stacked, though not so high and not so numerous that his vision was completely impeded. Lanson spotted a couple of gravity-engined forklifts like the one which had been left in the linking tunnel earlier, but aside from that, there was little here of note. Although he was interested to search within the crates, it wasn't the time or the place to assuage his curiosity.

The northern exit was easily located, and, shortly after, the mission personnel were once more within an area of Dalvaron which was made up from smaller rooms and linking corridors. Several minutes of running in a direction that was a mixture of north and west was enough to raise hope within Lanson that the Ixtar would be shaken from their pursuit. At the very least, he felt a lessening of the pressure – a pressure which had been bearing down upon him ever since he'd first landed on Dalvaron.

Not for the first time, Lanson found himself longing to be back onboard his warship, where he could exert a greater control over his own fate. He hated this endless running, always at the mercy of the *Ghiotor* as it stalked him and the others through this vast, unbelievable construction of alloy.

After another ten minutes, Gabriel finally called a halt in a room of consoles and wall screens, where the air felt strangely charged and the tangy scent of metal mixed with the industrial odours of advanced polymers.

Overhead, the flat ceiling was decorated in a starscape, which seemed to shimmer faintly when Lanson stared upwards. Wary of his losing himself to the void, he dragged his gaze away.

"We're less than twelve hundred metres from the transportation node," said Gabriel. "The Ixtar which followed us from the docking bay aren't going to find us except by luck, but we've got some groups in front of us which might cause problems if we aren't careful."

"Are we taking the direct route, Sergeant?" asked Corporal Ziegler.

"I'm not about to start guessing the future movement of the enemy troops, so yes, we're heading straight for the goal," said Gabriel.

"Ten-to-one says Ravrol is going to be another shithole," said Private Castle.

"I wouldn't lay a day's wage on that if you were offering a hundred to one, Private," said Gabriel. "Now, let's go."

The journey resumed, along drab corridors which twisted and turned through the Dalvaron interior. Lanson had spent much of his adult life within the confines of Human Confederation warships, but even he felt assailed by the unremitting greyness of this place.

Even so, he didn't allow the surroundings to sap his mental strength and he switched his attention between the enemy movements on his HUD and the sights around him. Many closed doors kept their secrets, while others which were open offered views into rooms of tech, or into passages which stretched into the endless depths of the space station. Had circumstances been different, Lanson could have happily spent days or weeks exploring and learning.

"Eight hundred metres," said Corporal Hennessey.

"The Ixtar ahead of us aren't showing any signs they know our destination," said Gabriel. "We might yet—" He cut himself off with a curse. "No predictions."

Six hundred metres from the transportation node, the squad passed through a blast door almost three metres thick. On the far side, a vast open space contained hundreds of dull metal pillars, arranged in offset rows, which emerged from the floor and vanished into the ceiling. The air was heavy, and it felt to Lanson as if he was wading through it.

"Power conduits," he said. "Don't touch anything."

The squad proceeded and, as Lanson passed near one of the pillars, he noticed that it was wrapped in thousands of thin, criss-crossed strands of metal, so tightly entwined that the individual strands were not visible from farther away. Here, the denseness of the air was greater – stifling, almost – and Lanson thought he heard a high-pitched whining at the extremes of his hearing.

A few metres in front, Gabriel maintained the same rapid pace, keeping his distance as he zig-zagged through the pillars.

"The northern exit is straight ahead of us," he said. "Then we go west."

Once the far blast door was open, Lanson entered another passage that turned west a short distance ahead. He was relieved to have left the power conduits behind, though he wasn't quite sure why. Perhaps it was a primal fear of alien constructs which channelled such vast power, though Lanson wasn't convinced by his explanation. He was usually a man with an appreciation of tech, even when it was being used for the purposes of depriving him of his life – such as with the *Ghiotor*.

Lanson didn't overanalyse and turned his attention back to the job at hand. The transportation node was now fewer than five hundred metres away. During the transit of the conduits room, several of the Ixtar squads had begun to spread out deeper into the space station. So far, their intended destinations were not clear, and Lanson wasn't happy with this new unpredictability.

Sergeant Gabriel also wasn't pleased, and he cursed a few times, before pausing briefly and then cursing twice more for good measure.

"A couple of those Ixtar squads are heading away from the transportation node, Sergeant," said Corporal Ziegler

"Yes, they are," Gabriel nodded. Abruptly, he reduced pace to a fast walk. The western passage was narrow, and he indicated the soldiers should stay close to the left-hand wall. "But their movements make me think they've been ordered to step up the search for us."

As he was speaking, several dozen additional Ixtar squads began moving rapidly south and south-west, along with a few larger platoons of thirty to forty soldiers and two companies, each numbering more than a hundred Ixtar troops. As the enemy spilled through the interior, others – hundreds in total – remained stationary. Then, and much to Lanson's chagrin, new dots began appearing on his HUD, about four hundred metres from the location of the transportation node.

"The Ixtar are unloading more troops," said Lanson.

"And they're heading in our direction," said Gabriel angrily. "With all these other enemy soldiers to dodge, we're going to have a hard time beating the new arrivals to the transportation node, assuming that's the area they're planning to flood."

"We should get our asses in gear, Sergeant," said Corporal Ziegler. "I reckon if we're quick enough on our feet we can break through to the transportation node without encountering more than one or two enemy squads. Maybe we'll get lucky and —" He finished with a shrug, unwilling to tempt the gods of fate any more than he already had.

Gabriel didn't answer at once, which meant he was deciding how best to proceed. The soldier could act on instinct when he needed to, but at times like this, he preferred to think. Lanson had his own thoughts, but he waited to see what the other man would choose.

"The longer we take, the more of their troops the Ixtar are going to land," said Gabriel. "We can't kill them all, so let's stick with Plan A and head for the transportation node as quickly as possible."

He accelerated to a run and the soldiers went after. Lanson kept pace, while most of his attention was on the HUD map. The Ixtar continued pouring from their shuttle like they would never stop. Not for a moment did they hesitate, and they rapidly exited the docking bay before sprinting both south and south-west. It appeared increasingly unlikely these troops had landed soon enough to pose a threat to the mission personnel, but even a short delay in the dash for the transportation node might prove fatal.

Gabriel was clearly aware of the urgency and he pushed the mission personnel to ever greater speeds, such that Lanson didn't have any more pace left in him. The western passage soon offered a turning north and the soles of Lanson's combat boots squealed at his rapid change of direction.

"We're damn well going to make this," said Private Castle, running just ahead of Lanson, with his rocket tube slung across his back.

"Damn right," said Lanson.

The nearest enemy squad wasn't far away, though the Ixtar were travelling fast enough that it was difficult to predict if an engagement was unavoidable. Lanson became more aware of the rifle in his hand, and he readied himself to use it.

Mere moments later, disaster struck. While Lanson was watching his HUD screen, the red dots showing the position of the Ixtar troops vanished all at once, leaving only the space station map on the tiny screen.

Lanson swore loudly. "The *Ghiotor* must have cracked the Dalvaron security again," he said.

"Is there any way to kick those alien bastards out, Captain?" asked Gabriel. "Like you did before."

"Maybe if we could find another of those master consoles," said Lanson. "But if we go looking for one, we might be giving up our best chance to reach the transportation node."

"I agree," said Gabriel. "Let's keep going."

With the space station's internal monitors no longer providing data on the Ixtar positions, the outcome of the run to the Ravrol transportation node had suddenly become even less certain than it was only moments before.

The situation was not about to get any better. When Lanson requested a channel to the *Ragnar*-3, his suit comms unit detected no receptors. He checked the reason for the failure and discovered he was no longer connected to the Dalvaron comms network. A request for reconnection failed.

"Sergeant Gabriel, I've been kicked off the local comms," said Lanson.

"Damnit, me too," said Gabriel, without breaking stride. He cursed loudly. "And I'm unable to re-join."

"The *Ghiotor* must have subverted the Dalvaron comms network," said Lanson. He grimaced at the extent of the problem. "I told my crew to hold position until I gave the order for them to initiate the journey to Ravrol," said Lanson. "Now, they'll be reduced to guessing."

Gritting his teeth, Lanson mentally cursed the enemy. The Ixtar were not only ruthless, but the alien assholes were holding all the aces. Sooner or later, they'd lay down the winning hand and it didn't seem like there was a damn thing he could do to stop them.

SIXTEEN

"There's an open space just ahead of us," said Corporal Hennessey. "If we cross straight over it, we'll end up 350 metres from the transportation node. Or we can cut west and stick to the passages, which I reckon will add a hundred metres to the journey."

"We're taking the shortest route," said Gabriel. "We have to push through before the enemy coordinates a response."

"North it is, Sergeant."

The open space was approximately a hundred metres away, and Lanson could see the closed entrance door at the end of the passage. What lay on the far side of the door he didn't know, and the HUD map offered no clues. The room had a total of four exits and based on his memory of the last known Ixtar movements, Lanson reckoned the enemy could potentially enter the space from either the east, west, or north. Or all three if luck was bad.

After completing the sprint towards the closed door, Lanson halted, his breathing and the muscles in his legs untroubled by the expenditure of energy. Nearby, Sergeant Gabriel had positioned himself at the control panel, his eyes sweeping across the squad to ensure everyone was ready for whatever they might find on the far side of the door. On other occasions, the soldiers would have doubtless exercised much greater caution – or taken another route entirely – but this wasn't the time for circumspection.

"Let's get this done," said Gabriel, crashing his hand onto the access panel with venom.

The door slid open and a wave of sub-zero air washed out.

"Ah crap," said Ziegler. "More Galos cubes."

Sure enough, the room contained a multitude of the familiar dark cubes, equally spaced - with five metres between each - and all of them floating a metre above the surface.

"No hostiles sighted," said Gabriel. Then, he dropped low to the ground so that he could see beneath the cubes. "We're clear," he said, pushing himself upright and breaking into an immediate run for the opposite door, which was less than seventy metres away.

Lanson went with the others and he straightaway felt vulnerable in a way that wasn't entirely explained by the presence of the Galos cubes. Although the devices had been placed in a grid pattern – meaning he had a clear sight along the aisles which divided them - he couldn't yet see the east or west exits. If the Ixtar entered from either of those directions and engaged the squad, the fighting would be dirty and unpredictable. Lanson didn't much like the idea of exchanging fire beneath the Galos cubes, and explosives would be out of the question.

The fast pace soon ensured that Lanson gained a view to both the east and west exits. To his relief, the doors were closed and he turned his attention to the northern exit, which was also closed.

Not for long did the northern door remain in this state. As Lanson was watching, it slid open, revealing several Ixtar in the corridor outside. The aisle between the Galos cubes was wide and Lanson's firing line was not impeded by the other soldiers. Although he lacked extensive experience with ground fighting, his reactions were there with the best, and he aimed and fired even before Sergeant Gabriel had unleashed his first shot.

Holding down the trigger, Lanson directed a stream of automatic gauss fire into the corridor. His rifle whined and the stock punched into his shoulder. In the passage, the light of the closest Ixtar's energy shield cast a crimson pool on the floor and walls, while the ammunition readout on Lanson's gun plummeted.

Only moments after he'd opened fire, Lanson heard the discharge of a RAHD, and then a second shot from Private Galvan nearby. Then came the softer sound of gauss rifles as the squad unloaded their guns into the enemy squad.

With no time to scatter and no reliable cover, the soldiers knew instinctively that they had to kill the Ixtar before they recovered from their surprise. The quantity of bullets entering the passage quickly overcame the enemy shields, before tearing into flesh and bone alike. In a few short seconds, the Ixtar squad had been reduced to grisly, bloody lumps.

"Cease fire!" ordered Gabriel loudly on the comms. "Any casualties?"

As he spoke, he ejected the magazine from his rifle and stowed it in one of his leg pockets to recover the few remaining slugs later. Then, he snapped in a full magazine while glancing over his shoulder towards his squad, as if he wasn't expecting anyone to answer his question in the affirmative.

"I took one in the guts, Sergeant," said Private Davison.

"You let yourself get shot again?" asked Gabriel. "You're becoming a liability, soldier."

"I did it for the team, sir," said Davison.

"Shit," said Gabriel. "How do you feel, Private? Can you keep up?"

"Those painkillers I took earlier are still in my system, Sergeant. I can hardly feel a thing."

"I'm not sure we should—" began Private Teague. She cursed and shook her head. "Damnit, what choice do we have?"

"Not much," said Gabriel, setting off again. "Corporal Ziegler, keep an eye on Private Davison. Make sure he doesn't fall behind."

"Yes, sir."

By now, Lanson had seen the fist-sized patch of blood in the middle of Davison's stomach. The soldier's combat suit had sealed over the wound quickly and there was no sign the bullet had exited the man's body. There'd be a slug to remove at some point, though given how the Galos modifications made everyone affected heal at a vastly increased rate, maybe the bullet wouldn't ever need to be cut out.

The exit wasn't much more than twenty-five metres ahead, and Lanson hurried after the others, his own magazine change executed with steady hands. Movement from the extremes of his periphery caused him to snap his head towards the east. A small grey cylinder was tumbling through the air as it arced towards the squad. From where he was standing, Lanson could see a tiny red light on the surface of the device.

"Grenade!" he yelled.

The grenade – which had been hurled from the western door – did not land where it was intended. Instead, it detonated in the adjacent row with a dull thump. The plasma flames didn't reach the mission personnel, but Lanson felt his suit absorb the blast wave and his environmental sensor registered a spike in the air temperature.

Shit. If any of those Galos cubes detonate...

"Move, move, move!" yelled Gabriel.

Engaging the enemy here would be suicidal – either a Galos device would explode, or the delay would give the Ixtar time to flood this room with troops – so the mission personnel sprinted hard for the north exit.

Looking west as he ran, Lanson saw shapes darting between the cubes, but the angle was such that he couldn't gather an estimate on the enemy numbers. No more grenades came sailing across the room, which made him think the first one had been thrown in error by an over-eager member of the attacking group. On the plus side, Lanson saw no indication that the damaged Galos cubes were on the verge of detonation.

With the exit less than ten metres away, Lanson felt something thud into his upper left leg. He nearly stumbled, but managed to right himself, though his leg felt suddenly weak. Glancing down, Lanson saw a red patch on his outer thigh, midway between his knee and his hip, and another – the exit wound of the bullet which had struck him – at about the same height on the opposite side.

As quickly as Lanson instructed his suit to inject him with a painkilling shot, the searing agony reached his brain first. He clenched his teeth and focused on making it to the exit. Escape wasn't far and Lanson followed the others into a passage. Sergeant Gabriel was waiting at the access panel near the storage room's exit, while the squad ran on towards a west turning a short distance away.

"I'm hit," said Lanson. He tried to maintain his pace, but the weakness in his leg had increased, such that it wanted to collapse beneath him, and every time he put his left foot on the floor, it felt as if white-hot jagged spikes were being driven cruelly into his thigh.

Having closed the storage room door, Gabriel hurried to catch up with Lanson.

"Put your left hand over my shoulder, sir," said Gabriel. "We can't slow down."

Lanson did as he was asked and gripped tightly to ensure he wouldn't fall over. Once he was supported by the soldier, Lanson discovered he was able to move faster, though not at a pace that was much above a walk.

"You took painkillers, Captain?" asked Gabriel, after he'd informed the rest of the squad about Lanson's injury.

"Yes."

The suit drugs were fast acting and already the agony in Lanson's leg had diminished to a deep ache that, while intrusive enough to occupy much of his attention, was far easier to handle. He found he was able to put more weight on his left leg, and thereby move faster than before. In addition, Lanson could feel a peculiar sensation at the site of the injury, like his blood was frothing. Accompanying the sensation was an itching deep within his flesh, that he had no way to scratch, even were he of a mind to do so.

By the time Lanson – with Gabriel's support – had made it around the western turning, the pain had become so remote that, while he knew it was still there, it was no longer occupying his attention. He increased his pace as much as he was able and the limiting factor became the weakness in his leg rather than the pain. However, the itching hadn't gone anywhere, nor had the feeling that the blood in his leg was being carbonated.

The rest of the squad had slowed and three of the soldiers had fallen to the rear. Directly in front of Lanson, Corporal Ziegler was jogging alongside Private Davison but without offering any direct support.

"How're you doing, Private Davison?" asked Lanson.

"My guts are itching like crazy, which I reckon means I'll be good as new in no time."

Lanson tried to remember how long it had taken Davison to recover from being shot last time. He couldn't be sure, but it hadn't been more than a few minutes. Given that escape was hanging in the balance, Lanson knew he couldn't afford to hold the squad up for much longer.

"Keep watching our six," said Gabriel, checking over his shoulder.

"Roger that, Sergeant," said Corporal Hennessey, who was one of the three soldiers at the rear.

The pursuing Ixtar would surely be close behind, and the soldiers couldn't afford to fight a rear-guard action, particularly given the high chance of running into other squads of aliens approaching from the front. Lanson's eyes went to his HUD map. This western passage headed north again in about fifty metres, and from then on it was all corridors and compact rooms on the way to the transportation node.

With the northern turning only a dozen metres away, Lanson's scant hopes of a clear run to the goal were dashed.

"Incoming!" yelled Hennessey.

The muffled thump of a RAHD discharge was accompanied by the rapid whining of Human Federation gauss rifles firing on fully automatic. Lanson didn't dare twist around to look in case he lost his footing. Instead, he fixed his gaze on the northern turning. Private Castle had stopped just inside the passage and was holding his rocket tube over his shoulder. The soldier's eyes were wide – either from the pressure or the proximity of death – but his expression was almost serene.

"You'd best keep moving, Captain," said Castle. "The explosion from this next rocket is going to be hungry when it comes up this tunnel and it won't care who it burns."

Sergeant Gabriel didn't even question the wisdom of launching a rocket at the approaching enemy, which spoke volumes about his confidence in Castle's ability.

"Make sure you're pointing that tube the right way, soldier," he said.

"I read the manual just this morning, sir."

By now, Lanson and Gabriel were several metres into the north tunnel. Footsteps indicated that Corporal Hennessey and the two soldiers with her were not far behind.

"Hell, Sergeant, we've got some real heat coming our way."

"You've got it the wrong way around, Corporal," said Castle. "Rocket out."

Lanson heard the whumping sound of the missile as it exited the tube, and then he felt Gabriel almost dragging him along the passage. Doing his best to quicken his pace, Lanson didn't yet feel confident enough to relinquish his grip on the soldier.

"Boom," said Castle, just as the rocket detonated.

The passage lit up briefly in white, and then Lanson was struck by a wave of overpressured air. His suit absorbed the worst of it, and he hardly felt anything. The blast wave transitioned into a howling wind, which pushed Lanson forward like a powerful, invisible hand. He didn't stumble and he didn't fall, and he didn't look back.

After only two or three seconds, the wind abated and then the air became once more still. Gabriel turned to check on the squad members who were behind, and then faced forward again, evidently satisfied that nobody was injured.

"We're less than 250 metres from the transportation node," said Hennessey.

"Private Castle has bought us some time," said Gabriel. "I don't think the enemy behind will be so eager now."

"I burned them good," said Castle.

"Sometimes I worry about you, Castle," said Chan. "Did you escape the asylum by torching it?"

"Enough!" snapped Gabriel. "Don't lose focus."

With the pursuing Ixtar served up a main course of plasma incineration, Lanson felt confident that any survivors would have learned a valuable lesson in the pitfalls of being too keen in their pursuit. With any luck, the pressure from the south would reduce for a time, allowing the mission personnel to focus on what lay before them.

The transportation node wasn't far, and, with a short command, Sergeant Gabriel ordered the soldiers to resume what remained of the journey.

SEVENTEEN

A branch from the northern passage took the mission personnel west, then a northern turning ended at a door a short distance ahead.

"Think you can stand, Captain?" asked Gabriel.

Lanson took his arm from the other man's shoulder and tested his injured leg. The pain was gone – or at least it was at such a low level that he hardly noticed it – but the leg itself was still weak. However, it was noticeably stronger than when Lanson had first taken the bullet.

"I can stand. I'm not sure if I can run," he said.

Gabriel nodded. "What about you, Private Davison? You've been running well enough."

"Yes, sir. I don't sprint with my guts."

Something akin to a smile flickered briefly on Gabriel's face, and then it was gone. "Private Hennessey – open that door," he said.

Hennessey touched a hand on the access panel, but the door didn't open. She tried again, with the same result.

"Red light, no access," she said.

"The *Ghiotor* must have subverted the door controls," said Lanson. He limped towards the door panel. After a couple of paces, he realised he didn't need to favour his leg so much, and he put more weight on it. "Let me give it a go."

Pressing himself against the wall, Lanson touched the access panel, knowing that if the door failed to open, this was likely the end of the road.

Lanson need not have worried. His Tier 0 access was enough to overcome whatever security blocks the *Ghiotor*'s crew had imposed, and the door opened. The soldiers didn't open fire. Instead, Gabriel and Chan darted into the room.

"Clear," said Gabriel after a moment.

The room wasn't large, and contained a half-dozen generic consoles of the type Lanson had seen many times before. A metal cup rested on the top panel of the nearest console and when he glanced inside on the way past, he saw a thin layer of dark-coloured matter – type unknown, but more than likely the residue of an Aral beverage.

"We have 175 metres to go," said Hennessey.

"North, west, and then north again," said Gabriel, approaching the exit door. "The transportation node is accessed from that final passage." He half turned. "Captain, there's a red light on this panel."

Lanson had already guessed that he'd be required to open the doors between here and the node and he hurried across the room. His leg was getting stronger by the second, such that he could now walk normally without fear of it crumpling beneath his weight.

The soldiers were in position. Some crouched behind the Aral consoles, with their guns trained on the northern door, while others were keeping an eye on the two additional exits – one of which was south and the other east. Lanson placed his hand on the access panel and the door opened with only the faintest hum of its motors.

"Move!" ordered Gabriel, dashing past Lanson and into the passage.

Having allowed two additional soldiers to precede him, Lanson followed. His leg didn't fail, and he was able to keep up without difficulty. He informed Gabriel on the squad comms, so the soldier wouldn't feel obliged to limit his pace.

The west turning wasn't far, and the passage continued north for some distance, with other branches visible. Gabriel came to a halt at the corner. Although speed was of the essence, he hadn't thrown caution entirely to the wind and he looked carefully west. Almost at once, he withdrew his head rapidly.

"Ixtar," he said. "They're coming from the north and turning west away from us."

"A fifty-fifty and it came out in our favour," said Corporal Ziegler.

"I don't want to keep flipping the coin," said Gabriel. He looked around the corner again. "I'd estimate their numbers at twenty, near enough."

"Is it safe to go?" asked Ziegler. He checked over his shoulder and then to the north. "We're in a real bad position here."

"Sergeant, the door to the room we just exited opened and then closed," said Private Wolf, who was near the back of the pack. She had her rifle aimed south.

Gabriel didn't hide his anger and he swore. "Follow me!" he snarled. "And stay quiet!"

With that, he vanished around the corner. The other soldiers didn't hang about and they went after in double-quick time. Lanson was still near the front, and when he emerged into the western passage, he saw the nearest Ixtar about eighty

metres away, and approximately thirty metres past the final
turning north.

Lanson hadn't gone far when he heard the whine of Private
Wolf's gauss rifle firing on automatic. He couldn't help but look
over his shoulder, just as Wolf sprinted into the passage. Then,
Lanson turned west again, wondering if the Ixtar had heard the
gunfire. Not one of the aliens looked behind, so he guessed the
noise had been covered up by their footfall. However, he was
sure that sooner or later, one of the Ixtar would look over its
shoulder, or perhaps the enemy in the southern room would
communicate the location of the mission personnel.

Not far in front, Gabriel was moving rapidly, yet not so
much that his feet or his kit made excessive noise. The other
soldiers were equally aware, though the combination of eleven
people running produced a volume level that sounded uncomfortably loud to Lanson's ears.

Given the circumstances, the mission personnel couldn't
afford to slow down. It wouldn't be long before the Ixtar to the
south discovered that the soldiers were no longer in the passage,
while the aliens to the west might look behind at any moment.

The distance to the northern turning fell. Sergeant Gabriel
gave only the quickest of glances around the corner and then he
entered the passage. Had there been any Ixtar inbound from
this direction, the mission personnel would have been in real
trouble, so Lanson sighed with relief at what he took to be a
lucky break.

That lucky break was soon over. Just as Lanson was turning
into the north passage, he saw the rearmost Ixtar to the west
look around, as if it had caught a sense of something. A moment
later, he was out of sight, but it was clear the enemy had spotted
the soldiers. Lanson gave a warning on the comms, a split
second before a mixture of gauss rifle and RAHD fire erupted
in the western passage.

"Grenade out," said Private Galvan.

"Keep moving!" yelled Sergeant Gabriel.

Now that he was heading north, Lanson looked along the passage ahead of him. A turning east thirty metres away led to the transport node, but time was running out to enact the escape. It wouldn't take the Ixtar long to realise that the mission personnel had gone through the transportation network, and then the aliens would follow.

Halting briefly at the corner of the western corridor, Gabriel declared it clear and then he set off that way.

"Captain, move up!" he urged.

Lanson's injured leg had healed completely – or at least to the extent that it no longer felt any weaker than the other – and he sprinted past Corporal Ziegler before darting west. The passage went north again after a few metres and when Lanson turned the corner, he was confronted by a closed door a few metres away.

"Here, Captain," said Gabriel, gesturing at the access panel to the left-hand side of the door.

Without hesitation, Lanson stepped closer and thudded his hand onto the panel. The door opened, revealing the familiar node arrangement of a one-metre Galos cube, along with a rectangular panel on the left wall, which displayed a single word.

Operate

Hurrying inside and standing by the operation panel, Lanson waited anxiously for the rest of the squad to enter the room.

"Now that we're off the internal comms, I can't even send the detonation command to that charge I laid in the Galos room way back there," said Private Galvan.

"That was never going to be anything more than our shot at revenge," said Gabriel.

"What if we set a timed charge on this cube here?" asked Lanson. "The transit to Ravrol won't take long, so a sixty second countdown should do the job."

Gabriel lowered his brow, as if his mind was bombarding him with all the possible ways such a plan could go wrong. "Screw it," he said. "Private Galvan, set a charge – and keep it out of sight."

"Yes, sir."

"And the rest of you, watch that door."

As Galvan crouched next to the cube, with his open pack beside him, the other soldiers spread along the northern edge of the room and trained their guns on the door. Meanwhile, Lanson stood at the operation panel, his hand ready to activate it as soon as Galvan was done.

"I've set three of these smaller charges on the underside of the cube, with their timers synchronised to one minute," said Galvan, straightening and then shrugging into his pack. "I'll set the countdown away once I receive the order."

"Do it now, Private," said Gabriel.

"Yes, sir," said Galvan. "Sixty seconds and counting."

"Activating the transportation," said Lanson, touching the panel. "Let's see what Ravrol has in store for us."

The low light in the node room rapidly diminished into complete darkness. A rumbling sound came from all around, and then Lanson felt as though he were being pulled in every direction. Although he'd travelled the transportation network before, the sensation was still disconcerting.

The rumbling faded and the lights returned. Turning to check his surroundings, Lanson found the receiving node room was much larger than the one he'd recently departed, and this one held four Galos cubes, arranged with equal distances between each. A total of four operation panels were attached to the walls, each displaying the same word -

Operate. A single exit led from the room, and it was to the north.

Sergeant Gabriel didn't spend any time taking in the details. He barked orders, directing half of the soldiers towards the eastern wall. Realising the danger, Lanson stepped rapidly backwards towards the north-eastern corner, his gun raised and his eyes watching the room.

Without any warning, a squad of Ixtar soldiers materialised in the hub room. One appeared directly in front of Lanson, with its back to him. This was as close as he'd been to one of the aliens, and it was a fearful sight from up close. Not only did it loom above him, but its wide shoulders spoke of great strength, and both its legs and arms – clad in its black combat suit – looked proportionately muscular.

A cacophony of gunfire filled the room as the soldiers attacked. For his part, Lanson held down the trigger of his gauss rifle, and bullets poured out. The red light of the Ixtar's energy shield illuminated and, from this close range, he scented the metallic odour of technology.

Spinning with unexpected speed, the alien lashed out with one arm. Instinct and reactions saved Lanson from taking the blow. He leaned back, stumbled, and then thudded into the wall. With his aim disrupted, Lanson held fire, in case he accidentally hit one of the mission personnel.

In those few moments, the Ixtar had turned completely around, and Lanson saw its narrow grey eyes peering at him with hatred through the visor of its trapezoidal helmet. In its hand, the alien held a gun that wasn't much different in appearance to a Human Confederation gauss rifle, albeit larger in size. The barrel of that gun was swinging towards Lanson.

From close by came the thumping, muffled boom of a RAHD gun and the Ixtar's head vanished from its shoulders. A spray of bright red blood, along with chunks of bone and metal splattered messily on the eastern wall, as well as liberally coating Lanson's helmet and upper torso. Wiping his visor clear, he stayed low and tried to figure out what was happening so that he could pick his next target.

"Cease fire!" yelled Gabriel. "And keep watch for more coming!"

A comparative silence fell. Pushing himself upright, Lanson noted that all the Ixtar were down. Pieces of flesh were visible in many places, where they had been torn away by explosive RAHD shells, and blood was smeared so liberally that it seemed to Lanson as if it could have come from twenty Ixtar, rather that the six or seven who'd been killed. The smell of it was sharp and tangy, and not at all pleasant.

Sergeant Gabriel held the soldiers in position for a full five minutes. None of the mission personnel had been hurt, so complete had been the surprise. Still, Lanson thought it something of a miracle and he wondered if those travelling across the Aral transportation network arrived at their destination before their senses had fully recovered. If he was correct, it would be something for the squad to bear in mind for future transits, and Lanson mentioned it to Gabriel.

Eventually, Sergeant Gabriel accepted that no more Ixtar were about to cross the transportation network.

"These ones must have passed through the node before Private Galvan's explosive charge went off," he said, giving a nearby corpse a nudge with the toe of his boot.

"If the Galos cube in the node room went off, that means the whole of Dalvaron was destroyed," said Corporal Ziegler. "Damn."

"And if all those other cubes went up at the same time, the detonation radius could have been many times greater," said Lanson.

"Do you think the blast would have taken out the *Ghiotor*, Captain?" asked Private Teague.

"Maybe," said Lanson, unwilling to commit one way or another. "The cube detonations are massive, but I'm sure the *Ghiotor*'s energy shield was built to soak plenty of damage."

"Best not to guess, huh?" said Teague.

Lanson nodded and smiled. "I'd hate to set expectations."

"Well, we're here – presumably at Ravrol – and the destruction of Dalvaron means we should be safe from pursuit, for a while in any case," said Gabriel. "We need to get on with doing whatever we're going to do."

Having indicated that he required some time to think, Lanson pondered the next steps. The mission to Dalvaron had been a success, but much was yet to be revealed. A mystery surrounded the Aral and the purpose they intended for their technology.

More obvious were the motives of the Ixtar. This new enemy couldn't be permitted to take control of the Aral resources and unlock the full potential of the Infinity Lens. If they did so, they would soon locate the Human Confederation's worlds. Having seen the power of the *Tyrantor* and the *Ghiotor*, Lanson was sure an attack by the Ixtar would be short in duration and deadly in outcome.

He was determined to prevent it happening.

EIGHTEEN

"We're in a hub room," said Lanson, talking just to keep the mental oil lubricating his mind. He gestured at the Galos cubes and the wall panels. "With four destinations."

"And no signpost telling us where they lead," said Corporal Hennessey. "On the plus side, the air is breathable. However, if anyone takes their suit helmet off to find out what it tastes like, I'll fire a gauss slug up their ass."

"Our first move should be through that door over there," said Gabriel.

"I agree," said Lanson. "Private Wolf, can your comms pack boost a signal to the *Ragnar*-3, to let my crew know we've arrived at Ravrol?"

In anticipation of the question, Wolf already had her comms booster on the floor, with its protective cloth cover drawn back. She pushed a few buttons, stared at the tiny display and then pushed a few more buttons.

"The pack can't make a connection, sir," Wolf concluded.

Lanson didn't let the bad news get him down. "My crew

know where we're going and they might already be on their way here."

"What if the *Ghiotor* survived the Galos blast and is also on its way, sir?" asked Corporal Hennessey.

"That's a possibility," Lanson admitted. "I have no idea what's beyond that door, but it's likely we're somewhere within an Aral facility. If we can locate a comms station, I'll be able to send a transmission to the *Ragnar-3* and have them come pick us up."

"Then let's get out there and see what we can find," said Gabriel.

Lanson nodded his assent, and the soldier strode towards the door. Once everyone was in position, Gabriel placed his hand on the access panel. He exhaled in visible relief when the door opened for him.

"Looks clear, Sergeant," said Corporal Ziegler, standing at the other side of the door and leaning out.

Gabriel also leaned out, then nodded to Ziegler. The two men sprinted through the doorway, one going left and the other going right.

"Clear," Gabriel confirmed moments later.

When he passed through the doorway, Lanson found himself in a low-lit, fifteen-metre room, with bare concrete walls, a blue-tiled floor and a ceiling with many cable ducts running from one side to the other. Air thrummed quietly through high vents, and yet the stale odour of age hung heavily about the place, like the scent of a long-dead corpse.

"More Aral consoles," said Lanson.

A total of eight such devices were installed in the room and, while in appearance they were similar to those on Dalvaron, he thought they might be older in design. He approached one, which, like the others in this room, didn't show any sign that it was powered up. Lanson was tempted to find out if the console was only in a sleep state – which would give him an idea if Ravrol had operational power – but it seemed better to explore first, and hopefully establish how safe, or otherwise, it was in this place.

"Are we moving on, Captain?" asked Gabriel, his gaze intense.

"I don't think we'll find anything useful in these consoles," said Lanson. "Lead on, Sergeant."

"We're heading that way," said Gabriel, pointing at the exit directly opposite the one through which they'd entered. "From now on, we're calling that direction north, so calibrate your suit computers."

Standing at the access panel, Gabriel hesitated for only a moment before he activated it. The door opened, revealing a short passage which ended at some stairs leading up.

"Are we underground, or are those steps going to take us to the next level of a building?" wondered Corporal Hennessey.

"Only one way to find out," said Gabriel, entering the passage and approaching the stairs.

The squad climbed carefully, with Lanson three from the front. As soon as the door at the bottom closed – which happened automatically – it blocked out the seeping chill of the Galos cubes in the transportation node, and the temperature reading on his suit climbed rapidly before it settled at a warm twenty Celsius. The walls here were of the same stark concrete as the level below, and the footsteps of the soldiers echoed hollowly, no matter how much care they took to minimise the noise.

Six flights of stairs later, the squad emerged into a corridor, which went east and west. A door directly opposite was closed. Lanson peered in both directions, but each of the passages cut north, denying him a view of anything interesting. He was now certain the mission personnel were underground, though he had nothing to prove this conclusion.

"Let's try this door," said Lanson. "Who knows – we might be lucky and find a comms station on the other side."

"Nice joke, Captain," said Private Castle. "I can't remember the last time things went our way."

"What about when you shot the *Ghiotor* with that Galos launcher?" asked Wolf in disbelief. "That was the luckiest damn break we ever got!"

"Yeah, well, maybe I forgot about that one," said Castle lamely.

Sergeant Gabriel didn't interfere with the talk, since it wasn't distracting the soldiers from their state of readiness. He positioned himself at the door panel and then thumped it with his clenched fist. On the far side of the doorway, Corporal Ziegler leaned quickly out and back, then Gabriel did the same from the other side.

"Looks clear," said Ziegler.

Gabriel used his head to indicate he was about to enter the room, and then he sprinted through the doorway, with Ziegler straight behind. Meanwhile, the soldiers in the corridor kept a wary eye on the other approaches. This place was still a complete unknown.

"The rest of you – inside," Gabriel ordered, a couple of seconds later.

Lanson entered the room along with the rest of the soldiers. A quick look around was enough to tell him that he wasn't in a comms station. Consoles of the usual Aral kind were arranged in clusters of eight around the large floorspace. A few screens were attached to the wall, but otherwise, there wasn't anything to see.

This room made Lanson think of the soul-destroying administrative areas he'd visited on Human Confederation facilities, where nameless bean counters spent countless hours at their desks, drinking coffee and figuring out ways to shave fractions of pennies from the construction plans of multi-trillion-Fed warships.

"Any of these consoles of use to you, Captain?" asked Gabriel, his expression making it clear he knew the answer already.

"I could try powering one of these up and seeing if it'll let me remote link to the comms station," said Lanson, his tone of voice making it clear he knew the outcome already.

Gabriel gave a half-smile. "We'll go somewhere else, then."

"I'd like to find out where we've arrived, Sergeant," said Lanson. "A larger facility is more likely to hold data on what happened to the Aral."

"Is that a new goal, Captain?"

"More of a side-quest," said Lanson. "Perhaps if we learn about the Aral, we'll gain an understanding of what they hoped to achieve with their construction of the Galos cubes and the Infinity Lens."

Gabriel headed for the north door, but at the same time, he ordered Private Chan to check the eastern exit, and Private Davison to find out what lay through the western door.

"No obvious way out through here, Sergeant," said Chan, closing the door again. "A passage with some more rooms."

"Private Davison?" asked Gabriel, turning his head.

Davison had the door open and was staring at something. "There're some signs along this way, Sergeant. Room or area numbers, I think, but there's one that says *Way Up.*"

"Sounds promising," said Gabriel.

Even so, he activated the access panel on his own door and looked through the opening. "Another corridor, ending in a room." Gabriel touched the panel again and the door closed. "West it is."

The soldiers made their way between the consoles. Private Davison had backed out of the western doorway, and looked towards Gabriel, to see if he was going to be ordered outside first.

"I'll take point," said Gabriel.

The mission personnel walked rapidly along the corridor. After only a few metres, Lanson became aware of something at the extremes of his senses. "Hold up," he said.

"What's wrong, Captain?" asked Gabriel.

Lanson raised a finger to his visor to request silence. He turned his head, listening with a growing sense of unease. Then, he placed his hand palm first on the wall nearby and listened for a few seconds longer.

"Either there's a power generator close by - a big one - or —" Lanson hesitated. "Or it's a spaceship propulsion I can hear."

"I know where my money's going," said Corporal Hennessey.

"I'd planned to take us to the surface, Captain," said Gabriel.

"I don't think we should deviate from that plan," said Lanson. "If I'm right, and there's a spaceship here, I need to find out if it belongs to the Ixtar."

"It's not going to be one of ours," said Private Damico.

"Not likely," Lanson agreed.

The stairwell wasn't much farther along the corridor. Standing at the bottom, Sergeant Gabriel looked upwards. Outwardly, he was calm, but Lanson saw the tell-tale signs of agitation in the other man. The presence of a spaceship was a complication nobody wanted.

"I can hear it more clearly here," said Lanson, joining Gabriel in the stairwell. "Like the sound is being channelled down the shaft."

"That's not a power supply," said Gabriel, listening intently. "At least not like any I've heard before."

"It's a spaceship," said Lanson, now convinced. "One with high propulsion mass."

"Small, big, it probably doesn't matter either way," said Gabriel. "All we can do is hide from it."

"But only once we've confirmed what it is," said Lanson.

Gabriel nodded almost imperceptibly and then began his ascent. Acutely aware that he was the only one with top-level access to the Aral systems, Lanson allowed Corporal Ziegler and Private Chan to go ahead of him, before beginning his own climb.

Six more flights brought the mission personnel to another nondescript area of concrete and tiles. The readout on Lanson's HUD indicated the air temperature was twenty-eight degrees, when it had only been twenty Celsius on the level below. A climate control system wouldn't allow the variation, which made Lanson believe the hardware had failed and also that the temperature outside this building must be unpleasantly hot.

"There's another sign for the way up along here," said Gabriel, pointing west with his gun. He held his rifle in such a manner that it would only take a moment to bring it into a firing position. The presence of a spaceship vastly increased the likelihood of encountering ground-based troops, and Gabriel clearly didn't intend to be caught by surprise.

"Nothing much to the east," Ziegler remarked. "Passages and doors."

"Are we exploring, Captain?" asked Gabriel, not taking his gaze off the stairwell exit.

"Not yet," said Lanson. "We should find out what we're up against first."

Gabriel advanced cautiously along the corridor, ready to put a gauss slug into any aliens which ventured into his line of sight. None appeared, but the soldier didn't drop his guard, nor did any of the others.

Lanson too kept his focus at maximum. On this level, the propulsion sound was deeper and louder, such that it pressurised the air.

"Do you think it's the *Ghiotor* again, sir?" asked Gabriel.

"I don't know, Sergeant," said Lanson. "We only saw it directly when we were in the bay - when Private Castle hit it with the Galos launcher. Since everything was in vacuum, I don't know how its engines sounded."

Without another word, Gabriel began the climb. The stairs ended after six flights and exited into a corridor, much the same as on the lower levels. To the east, the lighting was the too-dim artificial illumination as elsewhere, but it was much brighter to the west.

"Natural light," said Lanson.

"We're on the ground level," said Gabriel.

"Let's hold here for a moment," said Lanson. "I need to listen."

He took a few paces west and then halted. Turning his head slowly, he listened to the propulsion, the volume of which was now enormously louder. With a sinking feeling, Lanson realised what he was hearing. The propulsion of the vessel outside had a distinct thrum underlying the main bass note – it was something he'd heard before.

"What is it, Captain?" asked Gabriel.

"Sagh'eld," said Lanson.

Gabriel's eyebrows rose. "Shit. How sure are you, sir?"

"Not one hundred percent, but near enough."

"What are those bastards doing here?"

"That's what we have to find out, Sergeant. Unfortunately, the bad news doesn't end there – I can hear more than one spaceship, but don't ask me to guess how many."

"This keeps getting better and better," said Gabriel in disgust. He cursed a few times, while pacing back and forth. "There's nothing we can do to change the situation, so let's just get on with it."

The Human Confederation needed more officers like Gabriel, and Lanson was glad he wasn't stuck out here with a bunch of complainers, instead of the get-the-job-done soldiers in this squad.

Regardless of the virtues of the personnel, they were still neck-deep in the mire. The Sagh'eld were enemies just as much as the Ixtar, and Lanson didn't want either species to lay their hands on the worst excesses of Aral technology.

Eleven soldiers against what might turn out to be a Sagh'eld war fleet wasn't a fair match, but Lanson had no plans to hide out underground and hope the danger passed.

He headed west with Sergeant Gabriel towards the daylight along the corridor.

NINETEEN

The corridor ended at a room, which neither Lanson nor Gabriel entered immediately. Instead, they stopped at opposite sides of the doorway in order to check the lay of the land. A short distance back, the rest of the soldiers were on guard for the unexpected.

Having taken a glance into the room, Lanson waited until Gabriel had done likewise and then he looked again, this time for longer.

"No sign of hostiles," said Lanson.

"There's plenty of tech to hide behind," said Gabriel, his head half-turned so that he could listen better. "But the Sagh'eld don't know we're here, so there's no reason for them to lay an ambush."

"Any sign of comms hardware, sir?" asked Private Wolf on the squad channel.

Lanson poked his head into the room for a third time. The space measured about twenty metres by twenty, with two exits south and two more to the west. North, there were no exits, but four large windows had been installed into the concrete wall.

Aral consoles filled much of the floorspace, along with a larger, circular console in the room's centre.

"There's some hardware in here with a different purpose to all the rest, but I'm sure it's not a comms station," said Lanson.

"Damn," said Wolf.

Lanson met Gabriel's eyes. "I'm going to take a look through those windows."

"I'll come with you, sir. We'll need to stay low."

Quickly, Gabriel gave the soldiers orders, which amounted to little more than *keep watch and shoot anything that moves*.

Maintaining a low crouch, Lanson set off into the room, his gaze jumping from window to window. All he could see through the apertures was the pristine blue of an alien sky, though his viewing angle was severely limited. The sound of warship propulsions created a throbbing in the air, which, along with the heat, would been stifling had Lanson not been wearing his combat suit.

Following a short, darting run between the Aral consoles, Lanson came to a halt adjacent to the left-hand window, still in a crouch so that he was below the level of the sill. Sergeant Gabriel was at the next window, also out of sight.

Cautiously, Lanson raised his head enough that he could see outside. He grimaced as he realised the depth of crap he and the mission personnel had waded into.

The window looked directly across a vast, flat area of grey alloy – a landing strip. Into the distance it went, to the north, east and west. In these latter two directions, Lanson could also see buildings, though the viewing angle was such that the details were unclear.

Approximately two thousand metres north, a spaceship was parked flank-facing on the landing field, the lowest part of its undersides no more than twenty metres from the ground. It was one of the strangest-looking vessels Lanson had ever seen – and this strangeness didn't come from the elaborateness of its shape, rather from the lack thereof.

From this vantage, the spaceship was little more than a cuboid of dark grey alloy, which his suit computer estimated to be almost 5500 metres from one end to the other and about 1200 metres from undersides to topsides. The depth of the spaceship couldn't be determined from Lanson's position at the window.

The few details on the vessel included Gradar turrets on the spaceship's topsides only – perhaps they were accompanied by other weapons, but he couldn't see them from ground level – and, more mysteriously, several rows of square protrusions which ran all the way along the spaceship's flanks, with others just visible at one end but not the other.

Lanson was more than intrigued, but there were other things to draw his attention. In the sky above the landing field, two identical, 4000-metre, Sagh'eld Ex'Kaminar battleships hovered motionless at an altitude of three thousand metres, their hulls parallel and their noses pointing north, directly towards the place where Lanson and Gabriel were hiding.

Ducking down out of sight, Lanson crouched with his left shoulder pressed against the cold concrete wall of the building.

"What the hell are they doing here?" asked Gabriel, sounding angry more than scared.

"That warship on the ground—" said Lanson, his mind working. "The Sagh'eld didn't construct it. I'm sure it was built by the Aral."

"Do you think it's what they came here for, Captain?"

"I don't know," said Lanson. "Maybe they didn't come to Ravrol for that exact reason, but now they're here, they found something they weren't looking for."

"I didn't see any Sagh'eld ground forces," said Gabriel.

"Either they already broke into that warship, or they're readying for an attempt."

"Perhaps they're not going to do either," Lanson mused.

"Sir?"

"That Aral spaceship would fit nicely into the cargo bay of a Sagh'eld superheavy lifter." Lanson rose carefully, so that his eyes were once again above the sill. "Let's see if there's anything we missed first time."

Poking his head above the parapet was a risk, but he doubted the sensor teams on the enemy battleships were on full alert. For thirty seconds, Lanson scanned the clear skies, using the zoom on his helmet sensor to look for other Sagh'eld vessels. Two moons were visible against the blue, one pale and distant, the other so huge that Lanson felt like he could almost reach out and touch its pocked surface.

Sinking down out of sight, Lanson looked over to Sergeant Gabriel, who was still searching for enemy vessels.

"I counted three in addition to the battleships," said Lanson. "At least one was a Tagha'an heavy, but the others were too far away for me to determine their vessel class."

"I saw three as well, Captain," said Gabriel, dropping low. "It may as well be a hundred for all the chance we have against them."

Lanson knew it too, though he wasn't about to give in to despair. "There are too many enemy warships for the *Ragnar-3* to handle, but if I can get back onboard, I should be able to unlock the Singularity function on the weapons panel," he said. "That might give us access to an attack that's powered by one of the Galos cubes still onboard the warship."

"How will we board the *Ragnar-3* with all those Sagh'eld warships overhead?" asked Gabriel.

"That's the question, isn't it?" said Lanson. He pursed his lips in thought. "Our top priority is still to find a comms station.

The *Ragnar-3* is heading into a shitstorm and we need to let the crew know what's waiting for them at Ravrol."

"If they're already at lightspeed—" Gabriel began.

"Then there's nothing we can do to alert them," said Lanson. "I trust my crew – they won't have targeted a light-speed exit within easy detection range of the planet. When they arrive, they'll run long-range scans and discover the Sagh'eld are already here."

"A base like this might have transportation nodes capable of taking us to places where the *Ragnar-3* can safely pick us up," said Gabriel.

"That's right," said Lanson. "So we need to locate a console that will show us the transportation network and where each of the nodes leads. But without comms to the *Ragnar-3*, any intel we find won't help us one little bit."

"We should find that comms station," said Gabriel. "And hope the *Ragnar-3* isn't already at lightspeed."

"No matter how cautious my crew are on the approach, they need a heads-up on what they're going to find here," said Lanson. "The travel time from Dalvaron is twenty-three hours, so whether the *Ragnar-3* is at lightspeed or not, we're going to be here on Ravrol for a while."

"I guess we've seen what we needed to see," said Gabriel. "We should get away from these windows."

"We'll go south," said Lanson.

He and Gabriel kept low and proceeded towards the room's southern exit. Meanwhile, the rest of the squad entered the room and headed the same way. Now that he knew what was outside, Lanson found himself glancing regularly over his shoulder, for all the good it would do. If the Sagh'eld had spotted them and decided to fire a couple of plasma missiles this way, death was guaranteed.

Corporal Ziegler was first to the exit and he held it open

until everyone was into the passage beyond. When the door closed, Lanson straightened and looked from face to face. His conversation with Gabriel had taken place in the squad comms, so the soldiers knew what they were up against. As a group, they looked on edge, but no more so than they normally did when danger loomed.

"We're likely to be stuck here for a time," said Lanson. "If the enemy gain sight of us, they'll either deploy troops or, more likely, incinerate us with missiles."

"Might the Sagh'eld have already deployed their soldiers, Captain?" asked Private Damico.

"That's the big unknown," said Lanson. "All we can do is act with caution and hope to surprise any aliens we run into."

Everyone knew the score, and nobody complained.

At the end of the passage south, a door barred the way until Sergeant Gabriel placed his hand on the access panel. A room was revealed, filled with more of the Aral consoles, though none which looked designed for a specialist function. For a short time, Gabriel watched and listened, before advancing into the room and shortly thereafter declaring it clear.

"South again, Captain?" the soldier asked.

Lanson doubted his own guess would be any better than Gabriel's. "South it is, Sergeant."

Working on the basis that it would be many hours before the *Ragnar-3* showed up, Gabriel erred on the side of caution and he crossed the room watchfully, despite having announced the lack of hostiles.

As he stepped between the consoles, Lanson sighed inwardly. This building appeared to have been designated to low-level tasks and he was already becoming doubtful that he'd find either a comms station or any other hardware of use. If he was correct, that meant the mission personnel would have to travel elsewhere and with the Sagh'eld warships being so close, the risks would be great unless an underground way existed.

"We should search for a map of this facility as well," said Lanson. "Which we're not going to find in any of these consoles here."

"Let's hope we get lucky sometime in the next twenty-three hours," said Corporal Hennessey.

The south exit brought the mission personnel into another short passage, which in turn gave access to a room of almost identical dimensions to the previous one. This room contained more consoles, and several huge viewscreens were attached to the walls, none of them displaying any data.

Before Lanson could feel any irritation at the mundanity of the room, he caught sight of a ceiling-hung sign above the western exit.

Comms Station.

"What were you saying about luck, Corporal Hennessey?" asked Lanson, bringing everyone's attention to the sign.

"I said we were due some any time now, Captain."

"And there it is," said Lanson.

Gabriel strode towards the western exit, with no discernible change in his demeanour. For his part, Lanson felt excited at the thought of making progress. He fervently hoped that the *Ragnar-3* was still at Dalvaron, so that he could warn his crew. However, Commander Matlock wasn't one to shy away from bold action, and that made Lanson believe that he'd be unable to contact the warship.

There was only one way to find out.

TWENTY

A short time later, and having traversed two additional rooms – neither of which contained the necessary equipment to fulfil the role of a comms station – the mission personnel arrived at a much smaller room containing a single airlift.

"No more signs," said Gabriel angrily. "How do we know which level the comms station is located?"

"Beats me, Sergeant," said Davison.

"I wasn't expecting an answer, Private," said Gabriel, sounding as if he were squeezing the words through gritted teeth.

He called the airlift, which arrived immediately. The car was large enough to accommodate everyone, but Gabriel ordered his squad to wait.

"Maybe the operation panel will tell us which level to select," he said, stepping into the car. Gabriel peered at something out of sight. "Only one other level," he grunted. "And it's down." He raised his head. "You all better get your asses inside."

The soldiers entered the car and Lanson went with them.

Gabriel activated the lift panel. A moment later, the car doors closed.

For a long time, the lift descended, prompting Lanson to wonder if the car was travelling with exceptional slowness, or if the lower level was thousands of metres below.

At last, a sense of deceleration gave sign that the journey would shortly end. The car came to a halt and the doors opened automatically. Lanson exited into a room similar to the one above, though it was much colder here and the single exit – a solid-looking door of alloy in the western wall – was closed.

"Damnit," muttered Gabriel, this single word encapsulating the feelings of everyone.

The soldier approached the door and, having taken only a single glance over his shoulder to reassure himself that his squad were suitably positioned, he touched his hand against the access panel.

After a split-second delay, the door opened with a whine of motors. Through the opening, Lanson saw a long corridor of grim concrete, sporadically lit in dim blue. In the distance, he spotted several darker patches on each of the side walls, which he took to be intersections. A ping from his suit helmet informed him the end of the corridor was nearly eight hundred metres away.

Gabriel refrained from further profanity, though the tension was obvious in his stance. "This is not a good place to run into aliens," he said.

Having little choice other than to proceed, Gabriel entered the passage and then accelerated to a jog that wouldn't interfere with his aim should the worst happen.

Lanson stayed four from the front and kept pace. Not only was it cold in the passage, but the air was stale. Not for the first time, he wondered what had become of the Aral and how long ago.

The mission personnel approached the first turning and Gabriel reduced pace. Halting just before the corner, he pointed at a sign on the wall.

"*Engineering C3 1-P,*" he read. "The comms station must be farther along."

Advancing the short distance to the opening, Gabriel checked for danger.

"Steps," he said. "And no sign of hostiles."

Resuming the journey, Gabriel stopped at each of the following two turnings. In both cases, wall-mounted placards gave no mention of a comms station.

By this time, the mission personnel were more than five hundred metres along the passage, and two more turnings were visible, both in the left-hand wall. A door blocked the way at the corridor's end. Steps led down from the first turning to an area signed as *Engineering Research 5*. Gabriel moved quickly on.

The placard adjacent to the final turning read *Comms Station*, leading Gabriel to call another halt. "Looks like this is the place," he said, stepping warily towards the opening.

As soon as he poked his head around the corner, Gabriel swore. "Shit, Sagh'eld!" he said.

Even as he was speaking, the soldier took three rapid shots with his gauss rifle and then sprang across to the far corner. With the reactions of a cat, Private Chan took Gabriel's place at the near corner and fired a single shot from his RAHD. The thumping discharge was heavily muffled, as though the close walls sought to crush the sound.

For several long moments, Gabriel and Chan directed gunfire up unseen steps. When the two soldiers stopped firing, Gabriel shouted out an order.

"Get clear!" he barked, urging the soldiers back along the passage. "In case there are others with explosives."

Despite his words, he didn't move. Instead, he held stock-still at the corner, with his rifle aimed up the steps. Gabriel held that position, while the others – including Chan - sprinted back along the passage. At the turning for Engineering Research 5, Corporal Ziegler darted right onto the steps, which he descended to a switchback landing about fifteen metres below and then climbed down another few steps before coming to a halt.

"This should be far enough," said Ziegler.

For more than a full minute, the soldiers stood quietly, everyone listening intently to the squad channel. Then, Gabriel spoke on the comms.

"No more sightings," he said. "And I don't want to wait around here any longer, in case those alien bastards got out a comms warning."

Corporal Hennessey had been at the rear on the way down and now she was at the front. She led the soldiers upwards and then sprinted towards the place where Gabriel remained frozen, with the barrel of his rifle unwavering.

"Five Sagh'eld down," he said, lowering his gun partway.

"It's messy on those steps," said Hennessey, gazing upwards. "Plenty of entrails to slip on."

"Not if we're careful," said Gabriel. Finally, he looked away from the opening. "Private Davison, are you hit?"

"No, Sergeant," said Davison, not fazed by the unspoken and part-humorous accusation. "I must've got lucky this time."

Gabriel didn't delay any longer. He began the ascent, indicating that Corporal Ziegler should stay at his side. An AR-50 gauss rifle was a great all-rounder, but it lacked the stopping power of a RAHD in close-quarters combat.

When he started upwards, Lanson struggled to see the top, owing to the soldiers in front of him. After about twenty steps, the pace slowed as the mission personnel trod carefully across the shredded spacesuits, the lumps of flesh and the ruptured organs which had once been Sagh'eld. Steam rose from the still-warm bodies and the smell of butchery made Lanson wrinkle his nose.

The steps made two switchbacks before they exited onto a corridor. Sergeant Gabriel was clearly losing patience. He swore loudly and with feeling.

"This is beginning to feel like a wild goose chase," he said.

During this short pause, Lanson had made his way into a position where he could better see his surroundings. The new passage headed east and west, with doors and side-turnings along both ways. Once again, the light was dim, but Lanson could just make out another sign for the comms station, about thirty metres west.

"We need to go that way, Sergeant Gabriel," he said.

"Yes, Captain, I saw. However, I'm starting to ask myself if those Sagh'eld we killed on the steps came from the comms station."

"You might be right," said Lanson. "But there's no reason the enemy should be interested in the Aral comms. Maybe they were searching for a security station."

"Maybe," said Gabriel noncommittally.

"We should keep heading for the comms station, Sergeant."

Gabriel gave a nod. He beckoned the others to follow and set off west, soon arriving at the turning north. A short passage led to steps and Gabriel began the climb without hesitation.

With his body charged by Galos energy, Lanson kept up without effort. His breathing was steady and his muscles didn't complain at all, nor did his recently injured leg. Absently, he asked himself what would happen were his body to be completely incinerated by a missile, or smashed beyond all recognition by gunfire. It was an interesting question, though Lanson wasn't keen to learn the answer.

After a lengthy climb, the mission personnel emerged from the stairs and entered a ten-metre room with three other exits. Four basic Aral consoles faced each other in the room's centre, and to Lanson's eye, the hardware looked older than what he'd seen elsewhere. Doubtless an installation like this one had plenty of history. Perhaps, he thought, the creation of these underground levels preceded the construction of the main topside base. Ultimately it didn't matter, but Lanson's brain nevertheless craved the knowing.

"The comms station is west," said Gabriel, using his rifle to point that way.

"Lead on, Sergeant," said Lanson.

The exit west brought the soldiers, a short distance later, to an airlift room with only a single lift. Gabriel summoned the car, and, when the doors opened, he stepped inside to check the inner panel.

"You've got to be shitting me," he said. "There's only one other stop, and it's up. The comms station is probably only a few hundred metres west from where we first saw the Sagh'eld fleet."

"Beats crossing the street with those battleships overhead, huh?" said Private Wolf.

"Yeah," said Gabriel reluctantly. "I can't beat your logic on that one, Private."

He waved everyone into the lift and then struck the activation panel a vicious blow with the side of his fist. The doors closed and the ascent began.

Lanson fully expected the lift to go all the way to the surface and he was sure the journey would take many seconds. Here in the car, the tension had lifted a notch. The encounter with the Sagh'eld had put everyone on edge, and the exit from a confined space like this lift could be deadly if the enemy were anywhere close by when the doors opened.

"Slowing down," muttered Private Teague when the feeling of deceleration began.

When the lift car stopped and the doors opened, the mission personnel exited at speed into a room that was a mirror of the one at the bottom of the lift shaft, albeit many degrees warmer. The droning vibration of warship engines came from everywhere, muffled, yet still intrusively loud. It was all the confirmation needed that the lift had taken everyone back to ground level.

No Sagh'eld were waiting in ambush and Sergeant Gabriel strode towards the single exit passage. About fifteen metres ahead, a closed door blocked the way.

"I'll open that door," said Gabriel. "Private Chan, you're coming with me. Everyone else, be quiet."

Slowly and carefully, the two soldiers advanced. In the airlift room, Private Damico deployed his Kahn-3 repeater, though the gun would be of limited use if the Aral had installed consoles near the far side of the door. Standing next to Lanson, Private Castle drummed his fingers softly on the metal tube of his shoulder launcher.

"Let's get this done," said Gabriel, his extra caution making it clear his instinct alarms were ringing.

He touched the activation panel and the door slid aside. A room was revealed, and, when Gabriel gave the all-clear, Lanson let out the breath he'd been holding.

"More consoles," said Gabriel. "Damned alien shit." The soldier peered into the room for a time, before he pointed west. "The comms station is that way."

Lanson entered the room – which was almost twenty metres by twenty - and looked around. He got the distinct impression that the hardware in here was many generations in advance of that which had been installed on the lower level. In addition, when he breathed deeply through his nostrils, Lanson sensed a metallic charge in the air, which made him think these consoles were merely in sleep mode, rather than powered down completely.

"Anything we can use here, Captain?" asked Gabriel, having noted Lanson's interest.

"Maybe," said Lanson, approaching a larger, circular console in the centre of the room. "This terminal might have higher level access to the facility databanks."

"What are you hoping to find, sir?"

"A base map would be a good start," said Lanson. "I doubt this console has control over the security systems, but it would be useful if we knew how to access the internal monitors." He stepped away. "It's not the right time for distractions. We should come back here once we're done in the comms station."

"Yes, sir," said Gabriel, trying to hide his relief.

The soldier headed for the room's western exit and paused until he was satisfied his squad were suitably positioned. Then, Gabriel brushed his fingers against the access panel.

A moment after the door opened, revealing a passage that went west for a short distance and then turned north. Gabriel motioned for silence and he turned his head to listen.

"Shit," he said. "I can't hear a damn thing over those battle-ship engines."

"We're expecting to find Sagh'eld, but they aren't expecting to find us, Sergeant," said Corporal Ziegler. "If we play it right, we'll have the advantage of surprise, whether we can hear the enemy or not."

Gabriel didn't offer a response, and set off west into the passage, the butt of his gauss rifle tucked into his shoulder and the business end of the gun aimed at chest height. Stopping at the northern turning, he leaned out and then back.

"There are two Sagh'eld in a room ahead," he said. "They've got their backs to us."

"Are you sure there aren't any more?" asked Corporal Hennessey.

"No, I'm not sure, but we're going to kill these two anyway. When they're down, I'll make a run for the room." Gabriel pointed at Private Davison. "And you're coming with me."

"Yes, sir," said Davison, making his way to the front.

The deaths of the Sagh'eld were enacted quickly and quietly. Gabriel gave a signal, and then both he and Davison stepped out of cover. Each soldier fired three shots and then they sprinted north.

"Clear," said Gabriel, almost thirty seconds later. "Move up." He was silent for a moment before he spoke again. "This might be the place we're looking for."

Lanson dashed around the corner and sprinted along the passage north. Once he entered the room – which turned out to be a huge space, with a high ceiling – he looked around eagerly.

Dozens of Aral consoles were neatly installed here, with wide aisles running between them. The two dead Sagh'eld had fallen onto the floor next to a circular station that was larger than all the others. Nearby, a metre-sized cube of grey hovered above the floor and was connected to the console by several thick cables.

"A Sagh'eld security breaker," said Lanson.

"It doesn't look as if it cracked the hardware yet, Captain," said Gabriel, waving his arms as he directed the squad into defensive positions. The comms station had numerous entrances and watching them all would be a challenge.

"This is definitely the place," said Lanson.

The circular console was powered up, though the top panel backlighting glowed only dimly. Lanson was already familiar with Aral hardware and he knew he could send a transmission from here to the *Ragnar-3*. Unfortunately, when he unlocked the console's security, the Sagh'eld breaker would gain access as well.

"I'll have to disconnect this," he said, giving the cube a kick. "And once I do that, it might send a transmission to those warships up there."

"It won't be long before the Sagh'eld realise we've killed a few of their soldiers, anyway, Captain," said Gabriel. "Once you've contacted the *Ragnar-3*, we'll have to leave this area of the facility quickly."

"It feels like we're always running," said Private Castle. "What we need is a bunch of those Galos launchers. Then we'd kick some ass."

"Keep dreaming," said Damico. "I reckon that launcher was a one-off."

Lanson didn't pay much attention to the talk. One-by-one, he pulled the security breaker's cables out from the ports on the comms console. Each time he extracted one, the cable retracted smoothly into the breaker's outer shell.

When he was done, Lanson logged into the console. Private Wolf was close by and clearly interested, but she couldn't spare too much attention.

Once he was into the top-level menu of the comms console, Lanson ran a search for active Aral resources. The list contained thousands of entries, and, though he was only interested in the *Ragnar-3*, he found more than he'd bargained for.

"That's the *Ragnar-2* out there on the landing field," he said.

"Which is good news," said Gabriel.

"Only if we can steal it."

Lanson had already briefly wondered if the Aral warship on the base landing field was a Ragnar class, but the vessel's wildly different appearance had made him dismiss the idea.

Here was proof that he was wrong. How it changed the mission, he had no idea.

Pushing his thoughts on the *Ragnar-2* to one side for the moment, Lanson turned his attention to the most immediate task – getting in touch with his crew on the *Ragnar-3*.

He had a good idea what the outcome would be.

TWENTY-ONE

Having located the *Ragnar-3* on the comms system, Lanson requested a connection. Nothing happened for several seconds after he'd sent the command, and then an error appeared.

Connection attempt failed. Error 31.

Lanson cursed under his breath as he ran a search for the error code. The answer, when he found it, was disappointing, but no surprise.

"The *Ragnar-3* is at lightspeed," he said.

"Is there anything more we can do here, Captain?" asked Gabriel. "Can you connect to the *Ragnar-2* and take control of it remotely?"

"Let's give that a go," said Lanson, acutely aware of the passing time.

"I was more thinking you should try the connection from elsewhere, sir. Somewhere far from these dead Sagh'eld."

"This'll just take a moment, Sergeant."

It wouldn't be long before the Sagh'eld realised that something was up, and Lanson didn't want to be here when that happened. Operating the Aral hardware was rapidly becoming second nature and it only took him a few seconds to request a connection to the *Ragnar-2*.

Connection attempt failed. Error 93.

"Damnit, comms lock down," said Lanson once he'd looked up the code. "This station isn't on a high enough security tier to transmit to the *Ragnar-2*." He looked up at Gabriel. The other man was clearly desperate to leave. "We should go at once."

"Yes, sir," said Gabriel.

He snapped out an order and then turned for the comm's station's south exit. The mission personnel sprinted from the room and into the corridor. Lanson was gripped by the feeling that he'd pushed too hard and that, at any moment, a Sagh'eld plasma missile would puncture the roof somewhere nearby and turn everyone into carbon.

The missile didn't come, though Lanson wasn't nearly ready to believe the mission personnel had achieved safety. Across many rooms they dashed, and along many corridors. With the initial fear of death fading, Lanson's mind focused itself on other matters. He regretted that he hadn't extracted the map data when he had the chance, though he was hopeful he could correct that failing once everyone was far enough from the comms station that the Sagh'eld wouldn't easily find them.

Then there was the matter of the *Ragnar-2*. Although Lanson had neither the means to capture the vessel, nor the crew to pilot it, he knew it was imperative to deny the Ixtar and the Sagh'eld access to the warship - even though he wasn't sure quite why it was so important, other than the fact the enemy so clearly wanted to capture the Aral spaceship.

The building through which the mission personnel continued their flight was huge, but eventually it came to an end. A sign above a metal door in a ten-metre room displayed a single word – *Exit* – though the windows in the same western wall made that clear anyway, granting as they did a view onto the street outside.

Warily, Lanson approached the left-most window, in a crouch that maximised his visibility arc into the planet's sky. All he could see was blue and the upper stories of an alloy-clad building about forty metres away. On the opposite side of the room, Gabriel made his way to a different window.

"I can't see the enemy warships," said Lanson, trying to build a mental map of the where the members of the Sagh'eld fleet had been positioned. Wherever they were, they were out of sight.

"No sign of them here either," said Gabriel, crouched below the sill and peering upwards.

"We're not planning to leave this building, are we?" asked Corporal Hennessey. "With five Sagh'eld warships up there – and maybe more – there's going to be at least one with a view onto the street outside of here."

Lanson didn't answer. He rose from his crouch so that he could see over the windowsill at whatever was at ground level outside. A road of dark grey metal, without traffic markings, ran from south to north. This road was deserted for as far as Lanson could see in both directions.

However, two features caught his eye. The first was a large wall sign adjacent to a door in the building opposite.

"Security," Lanson read out loud.

Aside from the sign, he also spotted a grey arch a few metres west along the street. Steps descended into the pavement and out of sight. On the far side of the road, not far from the security building's entrance, was a second arch.

"An underpass," said Lanson. "We might be able to make it over the road." He glanced over at Gabriel. "What do you say, Sergeant?"

Gabriel knew the risks and his brow wrinkled in thought.

"If we gain entry to the security station, you'll be able to access the facility monitors," he said. "And download a base map."

"That's right," said Lanson. "I should also be able to override the comms block on the *Ragnar-2* and maybe gain remote control over the vessel. What options that'll give us, I don't know, but I'd rather have command of the warship than not."

"Won't this facility have ground-to-air batteries, Captain?" asked Corporal Ziegler.

"Almost certainly," said Lanson. "However, I reckon the defence systems have failed, else the Sagh'eld warships would have suffered damage when they first arrived. If I'm wrong, and the batteries are still operational, maybe I'll be able to activate them."

"It sounds like there aren't any downsides to crossing that street," said Private Chan. "Except for the possibility we're spotted and killed as we make a run for the underpass."

"Where's your sense of adventure, Chan?" asked Private Wolf. "Every day brings a new way to die and at the end of every day we're still alive."

"I've dodged death so many times I've stopped thinking about it," said Chan with a shrug.

"That's enough talk," said Gabriel without a trace of anger. "We're heading for the security building. We've always pushed on, even when the safest path lay elsewhere."

With that, Gabriel positioned himself at the access panel for the exit door. He paused for only a moment and then activated the panel.

The door opened and unexpectedly bright light flooded in from outside, causing Lanson to narrow his eyes, and making him realise that the windows were tinted. As well as the light, hot air filled the room, and the temperature readout on Lanson's HUD rose to forty Celsius and kept climbing. The sound pressure from the Ex'Kaminars' propulsion increased by many decibels.

"Ten metres to the underpass," said Gabriel. "We can do this."

"Maybe one of us should go first and get the security building open," said Private Davison. "And before anyone complains, I'll volunteer myself."

"Much appreciated, Private, but we're sticking together," said Gabriel. "Get ready to go."

He counted slowly down from three, giving the other personnel enough time to cluster around the door. When the count hit zero, Gabriel launched himself out of the doorway. One-by-one, the soldiers followed.

Lanson went third and he kept his eyes on the underpass entrance as he ran. Only once did he glance along the road, and he saw that it was entirely empty. Suddenly, he was struck by the lonely feeling of abandonment which clung to this place.

Almost before he knew it, Lanson was at the top of the underpass steps, which could accommodate three or four people side-by-side. Grabbing the left-hand rail, he descended rapidly. The searing brightness from outside diminished with each stride, to be replaced by the dedicated lighting within the underpass.

When he reached the bottom – some five metres or so beneath the road – Lanson continued his run after Gabriel and Chan. Behind, he heard the footsteps of whoever was coming after. No Sagh'eld missile detonated, though if the enemy launched an attack, Lanson knew he'd be dead before his senses registered the explosion.

By the time Lanson reached the steps upwards, Gabriel was already halfway to the top. He'd stopped where he had a limited view of the sky overhead and was clearly searching for the enemy warships.

"Nothing," he spat, as if the uncertainty offended him greatly.

Meanwhile, the rest of the squad had reached this end of the underpass and they waited without speaking for the inevitable moment when Gabriel would give them the order to go.

"Ready," said Gabriel. "Three...two...one..."

The soldier dashed up the steps, the pounding of his combat boots inaudible above the overlapping warship propulsions.

Straining his muscles, Lanson overtook Private Chan and emerged from the underpass. Sergeant Gabriel was almost at the security building entrance, and he covered the last two strides with his right hand stretched out towards the access panel. With a thumping blow, the soldier's palm connected with the panel, but the door didn't open.

"Shit!" said Gabriel, slowing to a halt and attempting to operate the panel again, with the same lack of success. "I'm not authorised."

Without ceremony, Lanson shouldered his way past the other man and struck the access panel himself. The two-metre-wide door slid open, just as Chan arrived. The soldier darted inside, followed by Private Davison. Keeping his hand pressed against the panel, Lanson swept his gaze anxiously across the skies. All he saw was the same beautiful blue, along with one of the planet's shimmering moons.

Suddenly, and with Lanson still at the control panel, the reverberations of the overhead propulsions changed in such a way that the volume increased along with the pressure in the desert-hot air.

Frantically, Lanson looked upwards, expecting to see an enemy warship appear over one of the buildings adjacent to the street. "Move!" he yelled.

The soldiers were already fully motivated and they dashed through the opening. When the last member of the squad was approaching the entrance, Sergeant Gabriel – with his eyes searching the skies - reached out a hand and tapped Lanson urgently on the shoulder.

"Time to go, Captain!"

By now, the propulsion sound was so pervasive that it seemed to Lanson as if the outline of the buildings around him were slightly blurred by the strength of the vibration. Then, the nose section of an Ex'Kaminar battleship drifted into view, almost directly overhead.

A surge of fear ran through Lanson, and adrenaline pumped into his body as he left his position at the access panel and sprinted through the doorway. The moment he was inside, he slowed in order to touch the inner panel. As soon as he did so, the door closed, blocking out much of the noise from outside.

Lanson's eyes had adjusted to the bright daylight of the planet, which made the dimly lit interior of the security building seem almost like full darkness. He saw moving shapes close by and walked towards them, while voices on the squad comms spoke mostly curses.

"This way, Captain," said Corporal Hennessey. "We need you to open this door."

Already, Lanson's eyes were adapting to the change in illumination, and he saw that he was in a short, wide passage. The soldiers had gathered near to the door which Hennessey had just mentioned, and the light on the access panel glowed a clear red.

"Let's get this open," said Lanson, hurrying past the soldiers and planting his hand on the panel. The door opened. "For those of you who were first inside and didn't see it coming, there's an Ex'Kaminar over the top of this building."

"Why aren't we dead yet?" asked Private Wolf.

"A question for later," snapped Gabriel. "We're alive and that's what matters."

The mission personnel entered a fifteen-metre room, containing metal chairs, a few tables, some offline wall screens and a replicator. Three exits led to places unknown, and their doors were all closed.

"We're heading west," said Lanson, gesturing towards the door opposite.

He crossed the room, with Sergeant Gabriel alongside. A chair had the temerity to be in the way, and Gabriel lashed out with a foot. Clattering loudly enough to be heard over the Ex'Kaminar's propulsion, the chair skittered across the floor and into the wall.

"We've got this, Sergeant," said Lanson. "One way or the other, we've got it."

"Yes, sir," said Gabriel, sounding suddenly tired.

Lanson stopped at the access panel and used it to open the door. When he looked into the revealed passageway, he felt a surge of excitement. At the end of the passage, another room could be seen, along with a large, circular console, with a dark pillar rising towards the ceiling.

"This looks like the place," said Lanson.

He let Gabriel and Ziegler go first – just to be on the safe side - and then followed. Once he was standing at the console, Lanson felt with certainty that he'd be able to achieve something positive with this hardware.

Assuming the Sagh'eld didn't get in the way.

TWENTY-TWO

The security console was large enough to accommodate four personnel and its front panel was scuffed, as if one of the former operators had spent every shift kicking the device. Lanson picked one of the seats at random and dropped into it. A hum from within the console indicated it was connected to a power supply, though the device was in sleep mode. Once Lanson had placed his hand on the authentication panel, the top panel lit up and the three screens in front of him did likewise.

While the console booted, Lanson took the opportunity to catch up with his thoughts. Had the Ex'Kaminar been actively hunting for him and the squad, he was sure the battleship's sensors would have detected the escape into this security building. A missile launch was the most likely outcome of the discovery.

Since the launch hadn't come, Lanson could only imagine that the Sagh'eld hadn't been looking for intruders, which meant the enemy hadn't yet learned that several of their soldiers had been killed. Such an oversight was sloppy in the extreme, but the Sagh'eld did tend towards overconfidence, presumably because the Human Confederation wasn't proving to be much of an opponent.

With a mental shrug, Lanson put the matter aside. A glance around the room told him that the soldiers were already in defensive positions, though they were too few to repel a concerted attack.

Speed was still of the essence, so the moment the prompt for input appeared on the middle screen, Lanson called up the map data for the facility. A heading at the top of the 3D model told him it was the base that was named Ravrol, rather than the planet itself.

The map was too large for him to study in any detail, but he zoomed out in order to see the security building's position in relation to everywhere else. Lanson had expected Ravrol to be extensive, but it turned out to cover an area much greater than he'd anticipated. In addition to the landing field north, there was a second to the south. The presence of eight parallel trenches on a level area to the west told Lanson that the Aral had once built many warships here at Ravrol.

Finding his curiosity drawing him in when he didn't have time to explore the map, Lanson closed out of the file. Saving a copy of the data to his suit computer, he then pushed the file to the other soldiers, so they could also view it on their HUDs.

With that done, Lanson gave the other mission personnel access to the Ravrol internal comms. This would ensure that if the squad were separated, they'd be able to communicate from places where transmissions would otherwise be blocked by solid objects, or active Sagh'eld jamming.

Feeling as if he was making good progress, Lanson then accessed the base monitors. To his relief, they were still active, and he added everyone to the permissions list, so they'd be able to see the enemy movements on their suit HUDs. A total of three hundred Sagh'eld soldiers were on the ground, in small groups and spread out mostly at the north end of the base. Whatever they were looking for – if anything – wasn't clear.

The base monitors were also tracking the warships overhead, and they had visibility on five enemy vessels in total. It was possible that other Sagh'eld warships were out of sensor sight, but Lanson had no way to confirm.

Before he could access the feeds targeted on the enemy vessels, Lanson saw four red dots detach themselves from the much larger red dot representing the Ex'Kaminar which was currently stationary over the security building. These smaller dots – shuttles – descended rapidly and Lanson judged that all four were planning to set down on the street outside.

Cursing at the sight, he beckoned Gabriel over. "Sergeant, there're no enemy soldiers within four hundred metres of our position, but that's about to change real soon."

Gabriel peered at the screen, and he also swore. "There could be thousands of Sagh'eld troopers on those shuttles."

"It looks like the enemy have become aware that they've lost a few soldiers," said Lanson. "The good news is, they probably don't know where we are, else they'd have killed us with missiles instead of sending down a bunch of troops to flush us out."

"Is it time to run, Captain?"

"I reckon so," said Lanson. "I just have one more thing to do."

Calling up a new menu, he gave Sergeant Gabriel and the other soldiers facility-wide access to operate the doors. When that task was completed, Lanson locked down the Ravrol doors and airlifts, so they would only respond to personnel on a high enough security tier.

Rising from his seat, Lanson explained what he'd done. "The Sagh'eld will find it tough to follow us now."

"Won't that push the enemy into using incendiaries, Captain?"

"It might," said Lanson. "However, I suspect the Sagh'eld have big plans to extract every technological secret from Ravrol. If they burn this place to the ground, there'll be nothing left for them."

Gabriel looked reassured by the response. "Which direction, sir?"

"Let's go west," said Lanson. "I haven't had a chance to study the base map in any detail, but I'd like to find somewhere I can access the live feeds from the Ravrol monitors. I want to keep a close eye on those Sagh'eld warships to see if I can figure out what they're planning."

"We can view those feeds on our HUDs now, sir."

"It's not the same as sitting in front of a big screen," said Lanson. "Besides, we're going to need a place to hole up until the *Ragnar-3* arrives."

"Yes, sir," said Gabriel. "West it is."

The Sagh'eld transports had come in at speed and already troops were exiting onto the street outside. Lanson was uncomfortably aware that only two doors separated him and the enemy – two doors that would succumb quickly to explosives, assuming the Sagh'eld decided to search the security building first.

With the confidence of a man who knew his enemy was in front and not behind, Lanson ran for the western exit. He stopped in front of the door and indicated that Sergeant Gabriel should attempt to operate the panel, to ensure that that his newly elevated access authority had been applied across the Ravrol network.

The door opened at Gabriel's command and Lanson dashed first into the next passage. At the end was a second door, which he opened at once. From there, he traversed another room, which contained a second of the main security consoles. Lanson didn't slow to check it out and he kept on going west. He kept the facility map on his HUD and did his best to look at the route ahead, but it wasn't easy given the small size of the screen in his helmet.

Maintaining a high pace, Lanson crossed two more rooms, always heading west, before he came to a room from which the only exits were north and south. He slowed for a moment to study the HUD map. To his relief, the Sagh'eld troops were making no apparent effort to enter the security building. Instead, they were pouring into the structure east, doubtless planning to search the comms station and the interior areas nearby.

"The enemy aren't coming our way – yet," said Lanson. "Let's take a break here for a moment, so I can search for a monitoring room."

Sitting on the edge of the nearest console, Lanson zoomed in and out of the map, hunting for a place where he'd be able to access the Ravrol external sensors. He located such a place, which wasn't far. Unfortunately, the downsides were that the room was only two in from the northern landing strip, and it was perhaps not far enough from the Sagh'eld ground troops which had recently deployed. However, the next monitoring room was a long distance, and could only be accessed by exiting this security building and crossing one of the facility's many streets.

Lanson discussed the matter with Sergeant Gabriel, who agreed that venturing outside again would be a risk too far, particularly since the enemy were now aware they'd lost some troops and would therefore be far more vigilant than before.

"North and then west it is," said Lanson.

He pushed himself away from the console and walked rapidly towards the room's northern exit. Glancing around,

Lanson suddenly became aware of the mundanity of everything here, and he was glad that his duties offered him a variety of experiences beyond sitting in a windowless room, performing whatever tedious support tasks were required to keep a vast military machine – like this one – running smoothly.

The monitoring room wasn't far and Lanson was the first to enter. He gauged its dimensions at twelve metres by fifteen, with grey cladding on the walls, floor, and ceiling. The lights were dim, like everywhere else on Ravrol, and the air was warm. Two rows of advanced-looking consoles were positioned east-to-west, and a pair of semi-circular consoles had been installed in front of the south wall, positioned so that their operators were facing the personnel sitting at the two rows. The view through the west and northern exits was blocked by closed doors.

"Officer stations," said Lanson, pointing at the two larger consoles.

"Are we staying here, Captain?" asked Gabriel.

"I'll let you know in a moment, Sergeant."

Lanson strode to the nearest console. A single rotatable seat constructed from bare alloy was positioned in front of the operation panel. Dropping himself onto the seat, Lanson spent a short time studying the hardware, which closely resembled the sensor stations on the *Ragnar-3*. Above the buttons, touch panels and switches, a total of nine viewscreens gave the operator the option to watch dozens of the monitor feeds at the same time.

The console was in deep sleep, and Lanson touched one of the panels to authenticate himself. Dim lights brightened and a message appeared confirming that his credentials had been accepted. Once he'd called up two or three menus, Lanson was content that this console could do what he required of it.

"This is the right place, Sergeant," said Lanson.

"Yes, sir," Gabriel replied. "We'll secure the area and keep a close watch on the enemy movements."

"And be careful if you go through that door to the north," Lanson reminded him. "It leads to a room just inside the external wall. If there're more windows, there's a chance the enemy will detect us."

"Yes, sir."

As Gabriel turned away to deal with the organisation of the soldiers, Lanson accessed the Ravrol sensor feeds. The base was covered by thousands of external monitors, and it took him a short time to locate the relevant feeds. Soon, Lanson became familiar with the naming conventions for the sensor arrays, and he was able to quickly swap between the feeds which offered the best views of the Sagh'eld warships.

"Take a look at this, Sergeant," said Lanson, once he had a sensor lock on each of the enemy spaceships.

Gabriel came over and stared at each of the screens in turn. "Two Ex'Kaminars and three Tagha'an heavies," he said. "Those alien bastards must have known what they were going to find out here."

"Or maybe they didn't know what, only that it was important," said Lanson. He shrugged. "The big unknown is whether the *Ragnar-2* has access to the Infinity Lens. If it does and the Sagh'eld manage to pilot the vessel away from here, the Human Confederation will soon end up dealing with two warlike species, both with superior technology to our own."

"And all we can do here is watch, and hope the enemy aren't in a hurry," said Gabriel. "I reckon we won't see sign of the *Ragnar-3* for at least another twenty hours."

"Even then, the Sagh'eld are more than it can handle," Lanson reminded him. "Unless we can make it onboard the warship and unlock the Singularity menu."

"I don't know what hidden weapons systems the *Ragnar-*3 is fitted with, Captain, but I've seen enough of the Galos cubes to know that the outcome of a Singularity discharge isn't going to be subtle. We might take out the *Ragnar-*2 at the same time as we destroy the Sagh'eld warships."

"That's the problem," Lanson admitted. "And I've hardly had a chance to think of a solution – assuming there is one."

"You've got a chance now, sir," said Gabriel. "The Sagh'eld troopers are all to the east, so the pressure is off for now."

Lanson nodded, though it didn't feel as if his mind was on the brink of coming up with a plan, good or bad. He leaned back in the seat, cursing its lack of comfort and how its edges dug into his combat suit, and put himself to thinking up some ideas.

TWENTY-THREE

An hour went by, during which Lanson discovered that his console had access to the Ravrol automated defences. Those defences were extensive and included missiles, gauss cannons, a weapon which Lanson thought was designed to inflict wide-area disintegration on an attacking fleet, and finally, something listed as a Singularity Turret.

Lanson was exceptionally keen to activate these defences and use them against the Sagh'eld, but they were all offline. He attempted to bring them online, but whatever commands he entered into the console, they produced the same response.

> *Error#*

The response code was infuriatingly vague and, when Lanson searched through the list of errors, this one wasn't shown. After thirty minutes of failure, he queried when the defence systems had gone offline. This time, he received an answer, though one he could scarcely believe.

"The weapons systems were shut down almost five thousand years ago," said Lanson.

"Any idea why, sir?" asked Gabriel.

Lanson shook his head. "None. But this likely means Ravrol has been deserted for all that time."

"Can you find out where the Aral went, Captain?"

"I don't know, Sergeant. If the Sagh'eld keep to the east, I might have the time to find out."

After that, Lanson searched through the Ravrol databanks. Such was the quantity of information that it would have taken a dedicated forensics team weeks or months to sift through it all.

However, when Lanson checked the main audit file for Ravrol, he discovered one interesting fact – the last commands issued to the hardware five thousand years ago all had the same time stamp on them, down to the second. For this to be coincidence seemed remote in the extreme, and the only explanation Lanson could think of was that something had befallen Ravrol, and it had happened abruptly.

The more I learn, the less I know.

Lanson was intrigued, though his attempts to learn more came to nothing. Perhaps given the time he'd be able to unearth some additional clues, but he had more pressing matters to deal with than his curiosity.

So, Lanson kept an eye on the feeds, while his brain attempted to conjure up a plan that would thwart the Sagh'eld.

Three hours after their arrival in this security room, Sergeant Gabriel ordered the soldiers to get some shuteye, while he and Corporal Hennessey took first watch. With every surface a solid one, this wasn't a great place to rest, but the soldiers were accustomed to sleeping in their combat suits wherever and whenever the opportunity arose.

As he watched the soldiers put their heads down, Lanson realised his brain was in a fog, doubtless because he hadn't slept in so long, and the adrenaline keeping him going was a poor substitute for the rest his body needed.

"I'm going to take a break," he said, rising to his feet and stretching.

"The executive suite is free, Captain," said Corporal Hennessey pointing to the nearest corner.

"Thank you," said Lanson dryly. "Sergeant Gabriel, make sure there's always someone watching these feeds."

"Yes, sir."

Lanson lay down in the corner. Although the padding in his combat suit provided a layer between his body and the floor, it wasn't anything like comfortable. For several minutes, Lanson struggled to settle, and he wondered if he'd be better off sleeping in one of the seats.

Before he knew it, someone was shaking him gently. "Captain," said Corporal Ziegler. "It's time to wake up."

Gathering his thoughts, Lanson pushed himself into a sitting position, the action making his left shoulder and hip groan from the poor quality of the sleeping arrangements. The clock on his HUD told him he'd been asleep for almost five hours.

"Anything to report?" he asked.

"No, sir. The Sagh'eld warships are still overhead, and the enemy troops are still looking for us to the east."

Although the grogginess of sleep clung to Lanson, he knew his brain would soon feel much clearer than it had five hours ago. Standing, he looked around the room. A few of the soldiers – including Gabriel – were asleep, or hoping to achieve such a state, while the remainder were sitting near the main console and talking outside the squad channel.

Private Wolf had been chosen to watch the feeds and she looked up at Lanson's approach. "Nothing to report, Captain," she said. "Are you taking over?"

"Yes, Private," said Lanson, lowering himself into the seat as soon as Wolf had vacated it.

The feeds offered no surprises. One of the Ex'Kaminars was now a little farther east – presumably offering support to the Sagh'eld troopers on the ground – while the other was motionless to the north, and directly above the *Ragnar-2*. Elsewhere, the three Tagha'an heavies hadn't changed position either.

Lanson called up a sixth feed – this one aimed directly at the *Ragnar-2*. He saw no indication that the Sagh'eld were attempting to break into the warship. Switching to one of the perimeter feeds, he confirmed the enemy were also not present at the *Ragnar-2*'s opposite flank. The Sagh'eld were clearly at Ravrol for something important, but there was no apparent sense of urgency.

"Twelve more hours and the *Ragnar-3* might arrive," said Private Wolf, who hadn't gone very far.

Lanson grunted noncommittally. As the senior officer, the pressure was all on him to pluck a working plan out of thin air and he was beginning to feel as if he was in one of the Human Confederation training simulator scenarios where there was no way to achieve victory.

An hour slid by. Lanson watched the feeds and thought about what he might do. His brain was no longer afflicted by tiredness, but it couldn't come up with a method to defeat five Sagh'eld warships using only handheld weapons.

Handheld weapons...

The formation of an idea was interrupted by a crack like the loudest of thunder multiplied by ten. Before Lanson had even begun to gather his thoughts, the walls, floors – everything – shook violently. The shaking subsided rapidly, but now he could hear and feel a bone-deep grating sound coming from all around, producing a vibration of such intensity he felt sure it would have killed him were it not for the protection of his combat suit.

Then, he saw it on the screen in front of him. A sixth warship had been detected by the Ravrol sensors and it was vast, utterly dwarfing the two Ex'Kaminar battleships. It could be only one thing.

"The *Ghiotor*!" said Lanson.

Keeping his head down was the safest choice, but he had to see. Leaving his seat, Lanson dashed across the room towards the northern exit. The soldiers who'd been asleep were now on their feet and that single warning – *Ghiotor* – had been all the explanation they needed.

The room accessed through the north door, with its seats, tables, replicators, wall screens, and pictures, had presumably once been a relaxing place for the Aral personnel to spend some downtime as they looked out across the landing strip through the full-width window. The view now was anything but pleasant.

Having kept low as he sprinted to the window, Lanson dropped below the sill, but not so much that he couldn't watch the drama unfolding outside.

The planet's searingly-hot day was drawing to a close, and the deepening sky was no less pure, with both moons directly overhead, one bright with reflected light and the other so dark it was little more than an outline.

A few thousand metres north, the *Ghiotor* was stationary at a ten-thousand-metre altitude, its propulsion rumble completely overwhelming the sound pressure created by the Sagh'eld fleet. The Ixtar warship had somehow survived the Galos detonations at Dalvaron, though it hadn't come through unscathed.

Once indomitable in appearance, the enemy vessel's armour had been corroded so badly that it remained only in discoloured patches, while the dark matter beneath was revealed, and this too, continued breaking up. A heavy rain of particles created a growing cloud, and they were mixed with larger pieces of debris that tumbled towards the far end of the landing field.

Lower and closer, one of the Sagh'eld Ex'Kaminars was also visible, and against the vastness of the *Ghiotor* it looked almost like a toy. The battleship was already accelerating vertically, with such urgency that it seemed impossible an object of such incredible mass could overcome its inertia so easily.

Lanson's eyes were drawn by streaks of orange, crossing the blue at impossible speed. Suddenly, the *Ghiotor* became surrounded by a shimmering red ovoid, against which the incoming missiles detonated in a flash which made him avert his eyes.

A second salvo – this time coming from the south – struck the *Ghiotor*'s flank. Then came third, fourth and fifth missile strikes against the enemy warship. The Ixtar vessel's energy shield, the capability of which had clearly been reduced by the explosion at Dalvaron, dimmed so much that it was almost invisible.

Then, the *Ghiotor* unleashed its own weaponry. Missiles spilled from its remaining operational clusters and raced away. Fifteen or twenty of those missiles were aimed south and they crossed directly over where Lanson and Gabriel were crouched, disappearing from sight in the blinking of an eye.

The Sagh'eld activated their Kraal repeaters, and hundreds of bright streaks criss-crossed the sky as the gauss projectiles punched the Ixtar missiles into pieces. Additional waves of Zavon and Gorlan missiles added to the lightshow with their vivid propulsions leaving fading trails in their wake.

Hundreds of tiny interceptor missiles were ejected from the *Ghiotor*'s launchers. These interceptors sought out the Sagh'eld warheads, neutralising many.

"The *Ghiotor*'s lost too many of its emplacements," said Lanson, his eyes narrowed. "It's outgunned."

"Its crew wasn't expecting to find a bunch of Sagh'eld warships at Ravrol," said Gabriel. "Do you think the *Ghiotor* will make a run for it?"

"If it hasn't lost its instant lightspeed transit capability," said Lanson.

"The Ixtar haven't shown themselves willing to take big risks so far, Captain. If they can get out of here, they'll do it."

Lanson couldn't read the situation as well as he might have liked, so he didn't offer further comment. Outside, the *Ghiotor*'s energy shield was wreathed in flame, and it was clear that the Ixtar vessel's main defence would soon collapse. Even so, the huge warship was rotating and accelerating upwards.

How desperate are the Ixtar to kill me, and how much do they want the Ragnar-2?

By now, the propulsion of the *Ghiotor* was generating so much sound that Lanson could scarcely hear his own thoughts. Certainly, he didn't hear the approach of the second Ex'Kaminar as it sped two thousand metres directly overhead. The battleship had been struck by missiles several times on its starboard flank and, though the detonations hadn't penetrated its armour, the expanse of mangled alloy was proof enough that the *Ghiotor*'s warheads carried a huge payload.

Without warning, Lanson was gripped by an excruciating pain that made him feel as though he was being put through a wringer. The Sagh'eld battleship – the stern of which was now a few hundred metres north – suddenly exploded violently into dust, the vessel's destruction absolute.

A split-second after that, an eighteen-thousand-metre sphere of darkness engulfed the *Ghiotor*. When the sphere vanished, all that remained of the Ixtar warship was a few hundred metres of its nose section and nothing else. Lacking propulsion, the debris began the long fall to ground.

"What the hell—" said Lanson, his stunned disbelief over-coming the pain for a brief moment.

It wasn't only the Ex'Kaminar and the *Ghiotor* which had been affected by this cataclysmic destruction - the building in which the mission personnel had taken shelter began decaying rapidly. Before Lanson's eyes, the walls sagged inwards, flaking and crumbling as they did so. Even the windows became yellow and opaque, before turning into dust.

The ongoing agony of the disintegration attack made Lanson want to close his eyes, but he couldn't – what was happening here was too important to miss. Particles of metal from the levels above came down heavily, covering him in grey and piling at his feet. He wiped his visor clear, only for the continuing fall of dust to settle upon it once more.

Then came a vicious, strong wind, heading north. Its arrival took Lanson completely by surprise and he stumbled forward. He recovered his balance and the dust flew by him in a storm. Hunkering down, Lanson realised this was the movement of air being sucked into an eighteen-thousand-metre sphere of vacuum created by the destruction of the *Ghiotor*.

Almost as quickly as it came, the wind diminished into little more than a powerful breeze that whipped up the dust, before fading once more to nothingness.

"We're exposed, Captain!" yelled Gabriel from nearby, his voice laden with his own pain. The man was crouched in a mound of grey and only his eyes were visible through the part of his visor he'd wiped clean. "We should get away from here!"

As the falling dust gathered around him, and the sounds of distant explosions continued unabated, Lanson asked himself where this was all going to end.

TWENTY-FOUR

At the same speed with which it had come, the agony from the disintegration attack vanished, as Lanson's Galos-strengthened body recovered from the effects of the Ixtar weapon. The relief of it was immense, but alongside it was his realisation that since his kit hadn't disintegrated, he'd been outside the effect cone of the Ixtar weapon. He dreaded to imagine the pain of being caught in the centre of such an attack.

As his thoughts cleared, Lanson took in his altered surroundings. The smaller particles from the disintegrated building hung in the air, in apparent defiance of gravity, and in such quantities that he could see little other than grey. Before Lanson hauled his gaze away from the north, a series of overlapping detonations created a lighter patch, which told him that the Sagh'eld were continuing to bombard the wreckage of the *Ghiotor*.

"What the hell happened, Captain?" asked Gabriel.

"The *Ghiotor* disintegrated one of the Ex'Kaminars and then the Sagh'eld took out the *Ghiotor*," said Lanson.

"The *Ghiotor* was—"

"Don't ask me how it happened, Sergeant." Lanson exhaled, forcing himself to confront the truth. "The Sagh'eld deployed a weapon we haven't seen before."

"Some weapon."

"At the moment, it's the least of our worries," said Lanson. "The debris from the *Ghiotor* is going to crash down and we're way too close. I reckon that section of the nose had a mass of fifty billion tons."

"Shit," said Gabriel. "How long until it hits?"

"Not long enough," said Lanson. He made a snap guess based on an estimate of the Ixtar vessel's previous altitude, minus a few seconds. "Forty seconds from now. Maybe."

"We can't do a damn thing to avoid that," said Gabriel, giving his visor another wipe. "We'll have to ride it and hope we come through."

"The Sagh'eld are targeting the wreckage as it comes down," said Lanson. "A dozen Gorlan strikes should be enough to break it up."

"Let's hope so. I'd best tell the others."

The rest of the mission personnel were hardly more than ephemeral figures to the south, standing in the place where Lanson had recently been monitoring the Sagh'eld warships. Gabriel talked fast and then dropped himself face-down behind a knee-high pile of dust. It wasn't much cover, but it was some.

Lanson was already prone, and he watched the other soldiers throw themselves to the ground. Then, a shock rolled through the ground, gently like a ripple in a calm pond. Another shock followed immediately after, this time with enough strength to make the ground shake. Lanson gritted his teeth, waiting for the big one to come.

Away to the north, the largest piece of wreckage impacted unseen. Hardly any time later, the ground jumped beneath Lanson, throwing him more than a metre into the air, while the energy of the shockwave made him feel like he'd been smashed into a wall. The dust was thrown up too, and it engulfed him, reducing his vision to zero. Lanson had no sight of the ground, and he attempted to twist so that he would land on his side. Thudding shoulder-first into the ground, he grimaced at the renewed pain.

"Stay down!" he yelled on the comms.

A howling wind followed the shockwave, clawing eagerly at everything in its path. Particles of metal were whipped away in great sheets, and they swept past Lanson as he lay curled up, waiting for it all to end.

Eventually, it did end. The wind died off, rapidly, not gradually, and that dust which hadn't been carried south settled once more. Lanson was half-buried and part of him wanted to lay still for a time and gather his thoughts.

Instead, he climbed to his feet, wiping his visor clear as he did so. The aching he was expecting to feel from the shockwave didn't materialise and he felt in perfect health.

"Any injuries?" asked Gabriel on the squad comms.

"Only among the Sagh'eld, sir," said Corporal Hennessey. "All their ground troops are dead - the disintegration attack must have killed them."

Lanson's eyes went to his suit HUD and, sure enough, the Ravrol security systems were no longer tracking any targets. He supposed the disintegration attack had destroyed the monitors within its effect cone, but there'd be adjacent ones which would have survived. Perhaps a few Sagh'eld troopers had also escaped with their lives. Lanson hoped not.

"We should find some cover, Captain," said Gabriel.

"Yes," said Lanson. "Let's go west."

The idea which had been threatening to emerge from hiding was still somewhere in the back of his mind. He tried to pin it down, but it remained elusive.

"West it is, sir," said Gabriel.

Together, Lanson and Gabriel jogged towards the rest of the squad, their feet kicking up clouds as they forged through the now diminished piles of dust.

From what Lanson could tell when he looked south-east, the disintegration weapon had cut a swathe through the base and into the ground beneath it, forming a slope. How far the destruction extended he couldn't be sure, since the airborne particles cut down his visibility. However, the half-decayed walls of structures loomed like jagged, fog-shrouded mountains.

The particles continued to fall, though not with such density as before, and Lanson twisted around, in case any of the surviving Sagh'eld warships were visible.

That was the moment he heard a grumbling, stuttering sound coming from the north-west. It was a Sagh'eld Rodos drive, but it didn't sound right, as if its output was falling. Lanson turned further, but he couldn't see anything.

The Ravrol monitors were still tracking the enemy warships and a check on his HUD showed him that the three Tagha'ans were high up in the planet's atmosphere. However, the second Ex'Kaminar was only a few kilometres away, at a low altitude and heading slowly south-east across the landing field.

"We've got a battleship coming our way," said Lanson.

"Looking for us?" asked Gabriel.

"Its engines don't sound right, Sergeant. Maybe it's coming in to land."

"Which won't stop it firing a missile or two if its sensor team detects us."

"Exactly," said Lanson.

He increased the pace, following the other mission personnel who were already on their way, leaving trails of footprints in their wake.

"This structure ahead looks like it might have some of its roof left, Captain," said Corporal Hennessey.

The place indicated was fifty metres away. About half of its facing wall was standing, though the corrosion on its surface suggested it might come down at any time. What had once been a doorway was now little more than an opening of no describable shape.

"There ain't no roof on that, Corporal," said Castle.

"Let's have some positive thinking, Private."

The squad were still ahead of Lanson and Gabriel. Corporal Hennessey was first through the doorway. "Like I told you – no roof," she said. "Just walls."

In moments, everyone was inside. The building's interior had completely disintegrated, while the outer walls – which must have been constructed from a tougher or thicker alloy – had partially survived.

Other exits led from the structure, though Lanson was only interested in the one leading west, which was about forty metres distant. He looked briefly towards Gabriel and then set off that way. As he negotiated the dust piles – which dragged at his feet in the same way as dry sand – Lanson gave as much attention as he could to the HUD map inside his suit helmet. He was looking for something, without knowing exactly what.

The sound of the failing propulsion distracted him, because it suddenly appeared to be coming from much closer. Turning his gaze upwards, Lanson expected to see the grey undersides of a Sagh'eld Ex'Kaminar. Instead, he saw only the near darkness of the planet's dusk. A check of his HUD informed him that the battleship hadn't deviated from its previous course, but it was now only three kilometres away.

As Lanson hurried across the piled dust, the weakened alloys of the building began to break apart with the vibration. A sheet of metal dropped from the top of one wall, falling and striking the ground, where it exploded into particles.

Lanson increased his pace, before bringing himself to a halt at the western exit. He poked his head out, hunting for the incoming warship. It still wasn't in sight, and the Ravrol monitors informed him that the enemy vessel was almost scraping the ground, which meant the intervening structures were tall enough to keep it hidden.

The next building wasn't far – across what had once been a road. The walls of the structure were high and deeply pitted but showed no sign of imminent collapse, however the vibrations from the warship's propulsion were shaking free a continuous shower of particles. Several windows had fallen out, and they were lying in pieces on the ground. As Lanson was watching, the vibration shook free another window, which fell and broke apart when it impacted with the ground.

"There's an entrance about fifty metres south," said Lanson, pointing that way.

"Will the door even open?" asked Private Teague doubtfully.

"Not a chance in hell," said Lanson. "That's why Private Galvan is going to blow it open for us."

"Yes, sir!" said Galvan.

"We can't wait here for him, Captain," said Gabriel.

"We'll all go," said Lanson. "Ready?"

He didn't wait for a response, and darted from the doorway. The layer of particles was much thinner here, which made Lanson's feet slither as he accelerated. He didn't slow down and he didn't look back until he was up against the wall of the next building and a few metres from the closed door. From here, he could see that the access panel was completely disintegrated, which confirmed that force was the only way to gain entry.

"Private Galvan, open that door!" Gabriel ordered.

Galvan wasn't slow on his feet and he dashed past, holding his gauss rifle in one hand and a blue cylinder in the other. Skidding to a halt, he tucked the cylinder under his left arm and then gave the door a solid punch with his right hand. Flakes of alloy broke off the metal surface.

Having tested the strength of the door and found it wanting, Galvan planted the charge in the middle, about halfway up.

"Five seconds!" he yelled, accelerating south along the wall.

The rest of the soldiers had long ago learned Galvan's fondness for a short timer and none of them had come any closer than ten metres. Even so, they shuffled north along the wall and Lanson did likewise.

With a muffled thump, the charge detonated, blowing a ragged cone of metal particles into the street. The mission personnel were against the wall, and nobody was hurt as a result of the blast. Lanson didn't wait for the dust to settle, and he ran towards what he hoped would now be an opening.

Galvan's charge had done the business, creating a roughly circular hole in the wall, about twice the size of the original door. Already the dust from the explosion had thinned and Lanson hurried into the building beyond.

The opening led directly into a large room and Lanson looked about while the soldiers made their way inside. Almost everything had crumbled, though in some cases only partially. Lumps here and there had likely once been consoles, though Lanson couldn't be sure, nor was he interested to find out.

Once the soldiers were off the street, he dashed across to the room's western exit. His eyes found the access panel, which was only partly disintegrated but definitely not operational.

"Private Galvan, you'll have to blow this one open as well," said Lanson.

"Yes, Captain."

In the few seconds it took Galvan to prepare, Lanson listened carefully to the Ex'Kaminar's faltering propulsion, which sounded like it was on the brink of failure. Suddenly, the noise cut out entirely, leaving only an ominous silence.

Before Lanson could shout a warning, he felt the solid thump of impact. The floor jumped, but he kept his feet. The walls and ceiling shook, but they didn't come down.

"An Ex'Kaminar would normally maintain a hover," said Lanson. "It's hit the ground, which means its Rodos drive has failed completely."

"What might have caused that, sir?" asked Gabriel.

"I don't know, Sergeant," said Lanson. "But even if the battleship is completely out of action, the *Ragnar-3* will have a hard time against the three Tagha'an heavies which are still out there."

"I'm worried, Captain. The Ex'Kaminar may be down, but what if its shuttles are operational? Those warships carry plenty of troops, and its crew might order an exploration of this area of Ravrol. Maybe we should go south."

Lanson couldn't deny the logic, yet he felt reluctant to follow Gabriel's suggestion. "I want to take a look at the battleship," he said at last. "If its weapons are functioning, I'll need to make the crew of the *Ragnar-3* aware."

"Yes, sir," said Gabriel, though he didn't look entirely convinced.

Turning his attention to the HUD map, Lanson noted that the Ex'Kaminar's nose was almost directly north of his position, at a distance of about a thousand metres, and the battleship's hull was positioned east to west.

The situation remained dire, but Lanson was keen to find out what exactly had befallen the Ex'Kaminar. Perhaps he was overthinking it, and the obvious reason – that the battleship had suffered catastrophic damage during its engagement with the *Ghiotor* – was the real reason.

However, the *Ragnar-3* was incoming, and its crew would need as much intel as Lanson could gather. He was determined he wouldn't let them down.

TWENTY-FIVE

Private Galvan's explosive charge tore a hole in the weakened door, large enough for everyone to pass. The absorbed heat from the blast left the metal too hot to linger, so the soldiers hurled themselves one-by-one into the next room.

"That door was a lot tougher than the last one," Galvan remarked. "The effects of the disintegration weren't nearly so bad."

Since Lanson didn't want to be slowed by the necessity to blow open every single door, he hurried over to the western exit. He could see that the access panel was online, but it wasn't until he successfully tested it that he felt reassured.

"Anything to keep us here, Captain?" asked Gabriel.

"Not that I can see, Sergeant. This door works, but these consoles are either completely shut down or they've been damaged by the *Ghiotor*'s attack."

"What's got you heading west, sir? It's like you have a plan."

"I don't have a—" Lanson frowned, and then it came to him

– the idea which had been haunting him for so long. "Let me check something out, Sergeant."

"Yes, sir," said Gabriel, his eyes narrowed as he peered at Lanson. He kept his questions to himself.

Giving his full attention to the HUD map of the base, Lanson ran a query on its datafile.

> *Identify: Location: Armoury.*

The response came back at once.

> *Results [52]. View?*

A total of fifty-two armouries were located on Ravrol, which was far more than Lanson wanted to explore, so he increased the focus of the query.

> *List: Location: Armoury [Tier 0]*

Again, the response appeared immediately.

> *Results [3]. View?*

Lanson felt his heart beat a little faster and he sent a command to overlay the armoury locations onto his HUD. When he zoomed the map right out, he could see the three blue markers which had just appeared. One was far to the south-east and another was located in the exact centre of the southern landing strip. However, the third Tier 0 Armoury was much closer. In fact, it wasn't more than six hundred metres west of Lanson's current position.

"Sergeant Gabriel, I'll tell you why we're heading west," he said.

"Sir?"

"There's a Tier 0 armoury that way."

Gabriel didn't say anything for a moment and then he nodded in understanding. "A Tier 0 armoury might contain portable Galos launchers."

"That's what I'm hoping for," said Lanson. "Maybe we can make life a little easier for the *Ragnar-3* when it arrives."

"In a little under four hours," said Gabriel. He didn't often smile, but he did now. "It would feel good to punch back against a warship for a change."

"Maybe you'll get your opportunity, Sergeant," said Lanson. He sent over the coordinate details of the western armoury. "Overlay those details onto your HUD map."

"Done," said Gabriel. "Six hundred metres between us and the armoury."

"Then let's get moving."

Lanson was already at the western exit, the door to which had closed again automatically. He opened it and entered a short corridor leading to another door. Beyond that, another room, this one with four exits. A command console was located in the centre of the floor, but this time Lanson wasn't even vaguely tempted to log on. Now, his mind was firmly on the possibility of hauling a bunch of Galos launchers from out of the Tier o armoury and firing them at the Sagh'eld assholes over the base.

Taking the exit west, Lanson led the mission personnel into an open space with seating, screens, replicators and what might have been plant pots in each corner. The ceiling was decorated in another of the starscapes Lanson had first seen on Dalvaron. He remembered the beauty of the infinite and part of him yearned to look upwards, if only for a moment.

Lanson wasn't stupid enough to succumb to the urge and he kept his gaze averted as he headed once more west. He still wished to obtain a visual on the crashed Ex'Kaminar, but he'd feel a lot safer if he was holding a Galos launcher in his hands.

Or maybe I won't. What was the diameter of the blast at Dalvaron? Twenty thousand metres? More?

Certainly, the Galos launchers were too potent a weapon to be fired at point blank range, and Lanson wasn't eager to sacrifice himself – since he was the only one with Tier o access to the Aral systems – or anyone else for that matter.

How to effectively use the Galos launchers was an obstacle to overcome later, should the nearby armoury indeed contain any such weapons, and Lanson didn't waste time dwelling on it.

Pausing at the western access panel, he glanced at his HUD to reassure himself that the Ex'Kaminar hadn't launched shuttles. Nothing new flew in the Ravrol airspace.

As far as Lanson knew – from his time on the Vachal destroyer *New Beginning* – the Sagh'eld built their warships with redundancy so that the failure of a warship's main power source wouldn't prevent the personnel onboard from operating the exit ramps or the shuttle bay doors. It was therefore puzzling why the enemy hadn't launched any transports, unless the engines on those vessels had also failed, or the battleship's crew saw no strategic value in a deployment.

Or everyone on board is dead.

The thought came from out of nowhere and Lanson wondered if it could possibly be true. He'd seen the *Ghiotor* destroyed by a sphere of dark energy. A sphere which Lanson hated to admit resembled that created by a Galos detonation, albeit on a much, much smaller scale. Since the Ravrol ground defences were out of action, the attack could have only been generated by a Sagh'eld warship. If the enemy had developed a new super-weapon, an Ex'Kaminar would be the first place they'd install it. Perhaps, Lanson thought, something had gone badly wrong for the Sagh'eld.

Realising he was drifting once more into distraction, Lanson cleared his thoughts. He continued heading west until he arrived at the outermost room within the structure. A single door led to the outside.

"I should take a look, Captain," said Gabriel.

"A missile will kill us all either way," said Lanson.

"I know sir, but—" Gabriel didn't finish his sentence, and

probably didn't know how to anyway. "Time for night vision enhancement," he said. He didn't wait more than a second or two before he reached out and switched off the lights.

Lanson turned on his suit helmet's night enhancement just in time to see Gabriel operate the door panel. It was almost full dark outside, but the sensor in his suit turned everything into shades of green, which allowed him to see well enough, though not perfectly.

Straightaway, a scent came to him, sharp and dangerous, like technology mixed with the cold, heartless, emptiness of the void. He recognized the odour at once, from his time in the Cornerstone underground bay. Lanson wasn't the only one to understand.

"Galos tech," said Corporal Hennessey, her head tilted and her nostrils flared.

"Not just Galos tech," said Lanson. "This is what it was like when the first Galos cube was about to detonate."

Sergeant Gabriel was busy looking through the doorway, without poking his head outside. "The entrance to the next building is about thirty metres away," he said. "And directly opposite."

"What about the Ex'Kaminar, Sergeant?" asked Damico.

In a darting movement, Gabriel leaned outside and then withdrew. "There's no cover between us and the battleship." He grimaced. "You might want to take a look, Captain."

Lanson took Gabriel's place at the door and then leaned into the street. His view north was unimpeded, and the night vision enhancement from his helmet sensor allowed him a partial view of the Ex'Kaminar. The enemy vessel was a little more than a thousand metres from the doorway and its hull loomed high, like a wave of darkness ready to come crashing down upon Ravrol.

Something was amiss. The Ex'Kaminar was faintly blurred,

as though it were slightly out of focus, and, at intervals of less than a second, jags of black energy flashed soundlessly along its flanks.

"We're in the shit, folks," said Lanson, withdrawing his head and turning to face the others.

"The usual kind of shit, or the real deep kind?" asked Corporal Hennessey.

"The real deep kind," said Lanson. "Judging by the looks of that Ex'Kaminar, the Sagh'eld have been experimenting with a Galos-type weapon, and they've suffered a technical problem. There's an ongoing reaction on the battleship."

"Does that mean the Ex'Kaminar is about to detonate, sir?" asked Corporal Ziegler. "Or are we going to find ourselves in combat with a bunch of turbocharged Sagh'eld soldiers?"

That was the trouble with the Galos tech – it seemed to produce a *roll the dice* kind of outcome, where the most common results would be destructive in the extreme, but every once in a while, something different would happen. On this occasion, Lanson suspected he and the others were facing a plain old explosion of incredible magnitude, though he had no evidence to back up this conclusion, beyond a feeling he had.

"The enemy would have launched shuttles by now, if they were able," he said. "So, I don't think we have to worry about Sagh'eld troops." Lanson took a breath. "If I had to put money on the table, I'd say that everyone on the battleship is dead, and that the runaway reaction was caused by a failure in whatever hardware generated the blast that took out the *Ghiotor*."

"Our ride out of here is a long time off," said Damico. "And with those three Tagha'an heavies still waiting up there, we can't even steal a shuttle and head into space with it."

"Maybe we should go looking for a transportation node that will take us to a different planet, Captain," said Gabriel. "You said Commander Matlock would have set the *Ragnar*-3 to exit lightspeed far enough away from here that it wouldn't get caught in a surprise attack. We could leave this planet to the Sagh'eld, and if you're right about the Galos reaction on the Ex'Kaminar, there won't be much left for them when the battleship explodes."

Gabriel was putting forward a good argument and Lanson pursed his lips in thought. "I don't want to lose the *Ragnar-2*, Sergeant."

"In which case you'll have to take the gamble, sir," said Gabriel, his expression not giving anything away of his own feelings. "Stay or go."

To check if Gabriel's suggestion of escaping the planet was even feasible, Lanson queried his HUD map for the nearest transportation nodes. The closest was about nine hundred metres south-east. It wasn't far, though the route was more exposed than the journey to the armoury, and therefore contained a greater element of risk.

However, Lanson was keen to get hold of some handheld Galos launchers, because weapons like that could change the course of almost any conflict. He was torn over what to do and cursed his indecision.

A change of circumstances was enough to help Lanson make up his mind. A faraway rumbling of propulsion climbed rapidly in volume.

"There's a warship incoming," said Lanson. "It's something big."

He stepped closer to the door, but before he leaned outside, he checked his HUD map. The Ravrol sensors were no longer tracking three Sagh'eld heavy cruisers and the Ex'Kaminar. Now, they were tracking an additional vessel, and this new one was huge.

Lanson closed his eyes for a moment and asked himself if he should have ever left the *Ragnar-3*.

TWENTY-SIX

Whatever was incoming, Lanson had to see it, in hope that it would provide a better understanding of the Sagh'eld plans. Movement on the HUD map confirmed that one of the heavy cruisers had accelerated to join the newly arrived spaceship, and the sound pressure created by the two propulsions was immense.

Lanson put his head into the street outside and he swore at the sights. A Sagh'eld superheavy lifter – all eight thousand metres of it, with high flanks, and underside bay doors running much of the length of its hull – was descending through the darkness. The vessel was outrunning the sound of its own engines and therefore it was at a lower altitude than Lanson had expected. He couldn't see the accompanying Tagha'an, which meant it was hidden by the vast hull of the lifter.

"What is it, Captain?" asked Gabriel anxiously.

"A superheavy lifter," said Lanson, remembering his prediction from earlier about how the Sagh'eld might intend to carry away the *Ragnar-2*.

He watched for another few seconds. The lifter decelerated steadily. Soon, it would come to a halt directly over the *Ragnar-2*. Then, those huge bay doors would open and gravity chains would haul the Aral warship into the lifter's interior. Allowing the Sagh'eld to escape with this technology was unthinkable.

Withdrawing once more into the room, Lanson thought quickly. One possibility was to look for a terminal from which he could remote-activate the *Ragnar-2*'s external weaponry. Up to now, he hadn't considered it an option, in case it triggered a response from the Sagh'eld which would end up with the Aral warship destroyed. However, with the enemy about to steal the prize, Lanson could deny them by forcing an attack on the *Ragnar-2*.

Despite the satisfaction he'd gain by making the Sagh'eld destroy that which they were hoping to claim, Lanson knew it would be an empty victory that would leave his own mission a failure. He could think of only one path that might lead to success, though of course it was the riskiest to travel.

Lanson made up his mind. "We're heading for the armoury," he said.

"Then let's get going," said Gabriel, as if he hadn't expected the decision to go any other way.

The first obstacle was the street, which was exposed to the enemy sensors. As he sprinted from the doorway, Lanson hoped fervently that the Sagh'eld were entirely focused on the lifter, rather than running sensor sweeps of the base.

His feet skidded once or twice on the thin layer of grit and dust, but Lanson made it to the opposite door without being incinerated. The scent of charged Galos tech was stronger now and, as he breathed in the odours, he sensed a craving in his body. He was suddenly gripped by a desire to run north towards the crashed battleship and place his hands upon its hull.

Lanson didn't succumb to the temptation, and he activated the access panel for the door nearby. The first of the soldiers entered the building and soon, everyone was inside the room beyond, where Lanson noticed the expressions of longing on several faces. It seemed he wasn't the only one feeling the draw of the Galos.

"The armoury is less than three hundred metres from here," said Corporal Hennessey. She used her arm to indicate the far exit. "Straight west all the way."

This entrance room contained nothing of interest and Lanson hardly paid any heed to the furniture. He jogged the twenty metres to the opposite door and planted his hand on the access panel, revealing a short passage.

The mission personnel followed the passage into another room. Then followed more passages and more rooms, in which the tech became increasingly sophisticated. Lanson spotted a type of console he hadn't seen before – a cylindrical, ten-operator model that went almost up to the ceiling – that he would have stopped to examine had time not been so pressing.

At what the HUD map indicated was the final door, Lanson took a deep breath and then activated the panel. The room beyond was a huge, open plan space, in which consoles of all shapes and sizes had been installed. Advancing inside, Lanson looked around, while the rumble of Rodos propulsions were an ever-present reminder that the Sagh'eld lifter hadn't gone anywhere.

It turned out the armoury wasn't on this level, and it was accessed by a security-locked airlift in the centre of the southern wall. Lanson summoned the car, while the soldiers kept a wary eye on the exits.

The car arrived and it only had room enough for three personnel to travel at once. "I'll come," said Gabriel. "You too, Private Chan."

The three of them squeezed into the lift, which only had
two stops – Level 1 and Level 0. Lanson selected Level 0 from
the operation panel and the lift car accelerated towards its
destination. The journey lasted almost thirty seconds, which
suggested the armoury was far underground. This came as no
surprise, given what Lanson hoped to find there, and he began
wondering if he'd find any other interesting toys that might give
the Sagh'eld a hard time.

"Slowing down," muttered Chan.

Having come to a halt, the lift door opened. Gabriel and
Chan were first out. They dashed along a short passage, before
stopping at the entrance to a room and looking carefully inside.

"Clear," said Gabriel.

Lanson exited the lift and the three of them entered the
room at the end of the corridor. The space was rectangular and
measured about twenty metres left-to-right and ten metres
across. Directly opposite where Lanson was standing, a sign
hung above a deep set two-metre-wide door.

Armoury.

"Reckon this is the place?" asked Chan innocently.

Lanson smiled thinly and advanced towards the access
panel set to one side of the armoury door. This panel was larger
than the others found on Ravrol, and it glowed a faint green.

This was no time for hesitation – not with the Sagh'eld
preparing to lift the *Ragnar-2* - and Lanson placed the palm of
his left hand firmly on the panel. For a time, nothing happened,
and he became acutely aware of the silence, which made him
feel as though he was being watched from a place unseen.

Just when Lanson was beginning to think something was
wrong, the five-metre-thick armoury door slid into a recess.
Beyond the door, a passage led to a room, dimly lit in blue.

A warning appeared on the access panel.

Permitted: 1

"I guess that means me," said Lanson.

He stepped into the passage and walked rapidly towards the room at the end, wondering what kind of defence mechanisms the Aral had installed to keep this place safe from intruders, and what would happen if Gabriel or Chan tried to follow him. Something deeply unpleasant, no doubt.

Emerging from the passage, Lanson entered the armoury. The air was cold and stale, and the walls were close, putting him mind of an ancient vault built to protect the greatest treasures of eternity.

Against the right-hand wall, an alloy rack supported four long-barrelled handheld rifles with large bores. Lanson stooped low to inspect them. The weapons exuded a faint coldness, but in appearance they were nothing out of the ordinary. However, their presence in the Tier o armoury spoke a different story.

Lanson rose and headed along the wall towards a half-metre crate with a closed lid. "There's plenty of hardware in here," he said on the comms. "I'm checking it out as quickly as I can, but I haven't located any Galos launchers yet."

Unexpectedly, Gabriel didn't respond.

"Sergeant?" said Lanson.

The comms remained dead. With growing alarm, Lanson headed back along the entrance passage. He could see Gabriel and Chan from here, but neither were moving. Lanson slowed to a halt.

"Sergeant?" he repeated.

The two soldiers still didn't move, as though they were frozen in place.

This must be one of the armoury security measures, thought Lanson suddenly. *Whoever is in the room outside is placed into zero-time until the armoury door is closed again. Or whoever is inside is speeded up a hundred thousand times.*

Had he not witnessed the accelerative effects of the Galos

cube on Cornerstone, Lanson would not have come up with this explanation so quickly – perhaps not at all. As it was, he felt sure he'd guessed correctly and, rather than exiting the armoury and possibly finding himself time-locked out for a second visit, Lanson headed back into the room.

The crate he'd seen earlier wasn't locked, and Lanson lifted the hinged lid. Inside, he found dozens of three-inch silver-coloured spheres, gleaming like Christmas tree baubles. Pulling one out, Lanson discovered it was much heavier than it appeared, and, like the rifles, it was also colder than the ambient air. When he brought the sphere close to his face, he could see it was etched with the finest and most intricate of patterns that could only be seen from a short distance.

Lanson was tempted to put a couple of the spheres into the leg pocket of his combat suit, but he decided against it on the basis that he had absolutely no idea what the devices were designed to do, though *create an enormous explosion* was high on the list of possibilities. Setting one off by accidently knocking it against a wall while it was in his pocket was not a desired outcome.

Next to the crate, a couple of ten-inch, black-clad cubes had been left on the armoury floor. Lanson didn't pay them any heed and moved on past to another wall-mounted rack, this one holding a single, long-barrelled hand cannon that looked as if it weighed sixty pounds. He was very keen to see what would happen when the gun was fired, but again, like everything else in the armoury, the risks of field testing were too great for him to bring the weapon with him.

Moving on with his search, Lanson found a variety of devices, all of which were certainly dangerous in the extreme, but which nonetheless created a child-like desire within him to find a remote mountain somewhere and start firing these weapons at it.

The Galos launchers – four in total - were within a one-metre-by-two metal crate. Lanson picked out one of the launchers and inspected it briefly, to make sure these were definitely what he was looking for. Having reassured himself, he gathered up all four. The weapons were heavy for their size, but they were fitted with carry straps that allowed him to loop two of the launchers over each shoulder.

"Four Sagh'eld warships, four launchers," he said, if only to hear his own voice.

Despite the undoubted stopping power of the weapons, the margins were too tight for Lanson's liking, so he looked around for something else to take with him.

Screw the risks. We might need the extra firepower.

Drawn like moths to a flame, his eyes landed on the massive hand cannon. Picking it up, he discovered it was as heavy as his first estimate. Letters etched on the short stock spelled out the words *Ezin-Tor*. Lanson doubted he was strong enough to wield the gun properly, but Gabriel, Ziegler or Damico wouldn't have much trouble. With a grunt of effort, Lanson slung the cannon over his shoulder to join the Galos launchers.

Reckoning he could carry a little more, Lanson gathered up two of the long-barrelled rifles from the rack near the door.

It was time to leave. Reluctantly, Lanson headed for the exit passage. To his surprise, the door at the end was closed, though he wasn't concerned, since he could open it again using the inner access panel.

Not so. When Lanson stopped in front of the panel, words glowed upon its surface.

Maximum permitted units: 5

"I'm on Tier 0, damnit," said Lanson in irritation. "I should be able to carry out as many weapons as I want." He touched the access panel and the door stayed closed.

The choice as to which items from his haul should stay

behind was easy. He lowered the two rifles to the ground. The words on the screen didn't vanish.

Maximum permitted units: 5

Cursing again, Lanson returned to the armoury and placed the two rifles back on the rack where he'd found them. As soon as he stepped into the exit passage again, the door at the end opened without him interacting with its access panel.

As soon as Lanson had completely exited the armoury tunnel, the door closed behind him and words appeared on the outer access panel.

Armoury lockout: C92

Lanson didn't bother trying to discover the meaning of the lockout code. Gabriel and Chan were no longer in zero-time, and they both stared at Lanson in puzzlement.

"Where did those weapons come from, sir?" asked Gabriel. "I—"

"You and Private Chan were locked in zero-time while I was in the armoury, Sergeant," said Lanson. "I've got us some of the good stuff." He shrugged the two Galos launchers off his shoulder and handed them to Private Chan. "Yours to carry, soldier."

"What about that cannon, sir?" asked Gabriel with unmistakeable interest.

"It's the Ezin-Tor, Sergeant, and I can only guess what will happen when it's fired. Think you can carry it along with your AR-50?"

"Yes, sir."

Lanson handed over the Ezin-Tor, and was immediately relieved at the lessening of his burden. Gabriel hefted the weapon easily enough and turned it over to inspect it fully.

"You'd best not fire it in enclosed spaces, Sergeant."

"Probably best I don't fire it at all, sir," said Gabriel, slinging the cannon over his shoulder.

The visit to the armoury was over. Heading back to the airlift, Lanson was more than pleased with the vastly increased firepower now available to the mission personnel, though he didn't think for a moment it was going to be an easy job to destroy three Sagh'eld heavy cruisers and a superheavy lifter from ground level.

Still, there was now a chance, where previously there had been none.

As the lift doors closed and the car began its ascent, Lanson smiled grimly to himself at the carnage he felt sure was on his near horizon.

TWENTY-SEVEN

Soon, Lanson, Gabriel, and Chan were once more in the large room at the top of the lift shaft. The soldiers gathered with expressions of great interest, mostly directed towards the Ezin-Tor.

"Been getting yourself something new, Sergeant?" asked Corporal Hennessey.

Knowing that the soldiers wouldn't listen closely while they were distracted by the Aral cannon, Gabriel shrugged out of its strap and offered everyone a closer look.

"It's a gun, and no I don't know what happens when it's fired," he warned.

Gabriel allowed the soldiers only a few seconds to gawp and then slung the weapon again.

Meanwhile, Lanson had hurried across to one of the monitoring stations nearby and powered it up. He was aware the mission personnel would be waiting for his guidance, but he wanted a view of outside before giving orders. Gabriel joined him at the console.

"We have one shot at each enemy warship, Captain," he

said. "There're range finders on the Galos launchers and I asked Private Castle if he was able to determine the maximum firing range when he was targeting the *Ghiotor*."

"And?"

"He wasn't, sir. It's possible one or more of those Sagh'eld heavies is out of range."

"Is anyone else trained to fire a launcher, or will Private Castle need to take all four shots?"

"Corporal Ziegler is the squad backup if something happens to Private Castle, sir, and Private Davison has a knack for weapons, whatever the type."

"That makes three," said Lanson, calling up the external feeds.

"The rest of us know how to operate a launcher," said Gabriel. "I wouldn't like to pick anyone else in the squad and tell you that soldier is guaranteed to score a hit."

"It might be that Private Castle is required to fire twice," said Lanson. "If that's the only option."

"Yes, sir, I'll go and speak to my squad."

While Gabriel returned to the soldiers, Lanson adjusted the sensor feeds he was receiving from the external monitors. The superheavy hadn't changed position. It was directly over the landing field at a three-thousand-metre altitude, with its main bay doors wide open like the maw of an alloy god.

The lift hadn't begun yet and Lanson was glad the Sagh'eld had taken this time to prepare, since it had allowed him to visit the armoury and return. However, he wasn't surprised at this display of caution by the enemy, since the superheavy would likely be at its mass capacity limit once the *Ragnar-2* was within its bay.

Aside from the lifter, two of the Tagha'an heavies were higher and at a similar altitude of about a hundred kilometres. Clear space of about fifty kilometres separated the two vessels.

The third cruiser was directly behind the superheavy at a distance of about three thousand metres. Lanson didn't think this vessel would be directly visible from the southern edge of the landing strip, though in theory it would be vulnerable to destruction from the Galos launcher shot aimed at the superheavy.

Beckoning Gabriel, Castle, Davison and Ziegler over, Lanson pointed out the locations of the enemy targets and asked for opinions on how best to tackle them.

"Those higher-altitude Tagha'ans might be out of range, Captain," said Castle. "The only way to be sure is by targeting them to find out if the Galos launchers will obtain a lock. And they're too far apart to be caught in the same blast."

"We'll take separate shots at each," said Lanson before turning to the next problem. "The lifter and its escort heavy are too close to our position. Perhaps of equal importance, they're near both the Ex'Kaminar on the landing field and the *Ragnar-2*. A single detonation from one of those launchers might encompass all four vessels."

As Lanson spoke, he caught a hint of the cold, dispassionate odour of Galos tech, the same as he'd noted when he'd crossed the street south of the battleship. Turning his gaze to the far corner of the room, Lanson thought he detected blurred edges on the consoles over that way, but when he concentrated, the blurring disappeared as if it had been only a creation of his imagination.

"Would a Galos explosion destroy the Ex'Kaminar or create...you know...a chain reaction or something?" asked Davison.

"We're in the realm of guesswork here, Private," said Lanson.

"How long before the Sagh'eld commence the lift, Captain?" asked Gabriel.

"Soon," said Lanson. "Minutes."

"Not enough time for us to reach a safe distance on foot," said Ziegler. "And not enough time to find a shuttle either."

"The Sagh'eld would shoot down a transport in seconds," said Lanson. He grimaced and resisted the urge to crash his fist onto the top panel of the console. "There has to be a way!"

Suddenly, the propulsion sounds of the enemy vessels became overlaid by an immense bass, which Lanson sensed rather than heard.

"Shit," he said. "That's the lifter's gravity chain generators."

"They don't sound like any gravity chains I ever heard," said Davison, turning his head, as if he was trying to pinpoint the source.

"That's the strain of an eighty-billion-ton lift, Private," said Lanson. "The Sagh'eld are about to haul up the *Ragnar-2*."

Having come this far, he was furious at the thought of the enemy taking the *Ragnar-2* out from under his nose. A red mist threatened to descend, but Lanson forced himself to hold onto his rational thoughts.

"We're going to destroy those high-altitude Tagha'ans," he said. "If we're lucky, it'll make the superheavy and the final cruiser run for the hills."

"And once they're at the right distance, we can blow the crap out of them too," said Castle with satisfaction.

"Or at least buy enough time for the *Ragnar-3* to get here," said Lanson. "It has the firepower to deal with the Tagha'an and the lifter."

"Less than three hours until our warship exits lightspeed," said Gabriel. "We'll have to keep the remaining enemy forces away for that long."

"Let's do this," said Lanson. Adrenaline was coursing through his body, leaving him fidgety and keen to act. "It's 280 metres back to the eastern exit."

"There's another exit north-west of here, Captain," said Gabriel. "It's less than a hundred metres away."

"We're leaving most of the squad here, Sergeant," said Lanson. "If the enemy have time to launch their weapons, I'd rather they detonated 280 metres east rather than a hundred metres north-west."

Saying the figures out loud made the distance seem like insufficient protection against a Sagh'eld missile strike, so Lanson ordered those members of the squad who wouldn't be carrying Galos launchers to head directly west, under Corporal Hennessey's command.

As Hennessey and her five soldiers ran for the western exit, Lanson dashed for the eastern door, with Gabriel, Castle, Ziegler and Davison close behind. He entered the next room and continued without slowing. The bass of the lifter's gravity chains began to increase steadily and the blurred edges which Lanson thought he'd seen earlier returned, only this time he wasn't sure if the effect was caused by the superheavy's gravity generators, or by the Ex'Kaminar battleship.

Faced by the might of technology, all Lanson could do was keep running east, and hope he and the others would be fast enough, skilful enough and, damnit, lucky enough, to knock out a couple of twenty-billion-ton Sagh'eld warships and cause the remaining vessels to accelerate for the horizon under maximum thrust.

It wasn't long before Lanson arrived at the entrance door to the street. Drawing to a halt at the access panel, he belatedly realised he didn't need to be here. He could have – probably should have – gone west with Corporal Hennessey. However, Lanson was here now, and he wasn't about to order a hold on the attack while he sprinted to safety.

"Private Castle, you're taking a shot at the easternmost

Tagha'an," said Lanson. "Who wants to take a shot at the western heavy?"

"I'll do it," said Davison.

"Good," said Lanson. "You're going to exit this building, annihilate a couple of enemy warships and then get back under cover. If the superheavy and the final Tagha'an head for the skies, you'll take the Galos launchers from Sergeant Gabriel and Corporal Ziegler and attempt to wipe out the last two vessels."

"Unless we're both chewed up by Kraal fire," said Castle.

"That's right," Lanson agreed. He thumbed towards Gabriel and Ziegler. "In which case your backups will finish the job."

"I'm ready whenever you give the order, Captain," said Castle.

"What about you, Private Davison?"

Davison turned the Galos launcher over in his hand and studied the weapon's tiny display panel for a moment. He shrugged. "Ready as I'll ever be, sir."

"This is the time," said Lanson. He touched the access panel and the door opened onto darkness. Straightaway the heady, yet terrifying scent of Galos tech on the verge of detonation filled his nostrils, while the heavy beat of the lifter's gravity chain generators made conscious thought a challenge.

Castle was first out, and Davison was right behind. From his position by the doorway, Lanson watched as Castle – no more than two or three metres away - raised the Galos launcher, wielding it like a sawn-off shotgun.

"Take this, you assholes," said Castle.

The Galos launcher produced a soft *whump* as its projectile was ejected from the tube. Then, Castle sprinted back towards the doorway, his feet kicking up grit from the disintegrated Ex'Kaminar which still covered the ground.

Private Davison fired without comment or drama. His Galos launcher spat out its own projectile and then he stood there, watching.

The travel time of the Galos projectiles was short, and Davison announced the outcome almost at once.

"Two detonations!" the soldier exclaimed. "Damn, those are big explosions!"

"What's the lifter doing?" asked Lanson anxiously. He knew it was about to do something, since the bass from the gravity chain generators abruptly vanished and the thunder of two Rodos drives became overwhelming.

"The lifter is..." Davison began. "Shit, it's heading east! I think the Tagha'an is going with it."

Lanson cursed too, though the sound pressure of the Rodos drives completely drowned him out. He checked his HUD for confirmation. Sure enough, the high-altitude Tagha'ans were gone, while the final two Sagh'eld warships were on their way east at a low altitude and under maximum thrust. Such was their acceleration they'd soon be outside the visibility arcs of the Ravrol sensor arrays.

"We should get away from here," said Lanson urgently. He indicated west and headed that way.

"What if the lifter returns, Captain?" asked Ziegler. "We might have a shot at it."

"The lifter isn't coming back until its crew are one hundred percent confident their vessel won't be taken out in a Galos detonation," said Lanson.

"The only way they can be sure is—"

"That's right, Corporal. Once the Sagh'eld figure out the launch point of our Galos attacks, they're going to incinerate this area of Ravrol and everything around it."

"I don't recall you mentioning that earlier, Captain," said Davison.

"You should listen more closely, Private," said Lanson.

Exiting the room adjacent to the wall, he continued west at a full run. Two of the four Sagh'eld warships had been obliterated and, considering their destruction had been enacted by ground forces, it was a tremendous result.

However, the job wasn't yet done. The superheavy and the third Tagha'an would soon be out of sensor sight. At some point after, Lanson was sure the heavy cruiser would execute a high velocity flyover of the Ravrol base, while deploying weapons onto the area where the Sagh'eld believed the Galos attacks had originated.

Somehow, Lanson had to think of a way to escape death until the *Ragnar-3* exited lightspeed. After that, maybe there'd be a chance to bring the mission to a successful conclusion.

TWENTY-EIGHT

Lanson's party joined up with Corporal Hennessey and the other members of the squad six hundred metres from the eastern entrance. The place where Hennessey had called a halt was an underground room on the western edge of this huge security complex. As well as containing useful hardware – including two command consoles - the room also offered four exits, each protected by a solid blast door. The western door led to steps which exited directly onto a south-to-north road that joined the landing field. Should escape become a necessity, this place had several options.

"Good choice, Corporal Hennessey," said Lanson. "I'm expecting the Sagh'eld to launch a significant assault on the northern edge of Ravrol. In fact, I'm surprised it hasn't happened yet."

"Are we planning to sit tight, Captain?" asked Gabriel.

"Yes - and this is as good a place as any," said Lanson, dropping himself into one of the command console seats and bringing the device out of sleep. "If the Sagh'eld want to breach this underground room, they'd need to direct a hell of bombardment onto the ground level above us. I don't think they have the means to pinpoint our location in order to do that."

Lanson hadn't got so far as accessing the Ravrol external monitors when he heard the distant rumbling of an explosion.

"Missile strike," said Hennessey.

"The first of many," said Lanson.

Feeds from the base monitors appeared on the console's viewscreens and Lanson worked quickly to select the ones he wanted and to adjust their focus. He caught sight of multiple detonations somewhere to the east, which ripped apart buildings and hurled debris into the air. Seconds later, another salvo of Sagh'eld missiles exploded, this time further to the east.

"The enemy vessels aren't detected by the base monitors," said Lanson. "They're launching from across the horizon."

"What if they hit the Ex'Kaminar?" asked Private Chan.

"Let's hope they don't, Private," said Lanson.

He had one of the feeds aimed at the stricken battleship. The vessel seemed completely out of focus, though not so much that Lanson couldn't see the nonstop bursts of dark energy which crackled about the Ex'Kaminar's hull like a spiderweb. A Galos event was going to take place sometime soon, he just didn't know when.

"Did the Aral create a satellite ring around this planet, Captain?" asked Gabriel.

The question drew Lanson away from his inner questions on the battleship.

"I checked earlier, Sergeant," he said. "The Aral established satellite monitors, but they're all offline. Either the hardware failed – which is unlikely - or the Sagh'eld destroyed the satellite ring when they arrived."

"So, we're relying on the ground arrays," said Gabriel.

"That's right, Sergeant. Ground arrays that can't see a damn thing on the far side of the planet."

A third salvo of missiles struck Ravrol, creating a wall of plasma flame hundreds of metres long, and ripping apart several buildings. The Sagh'eld were still targeting an area east of where Lanson and the others had taken cover, but he was sure they'd soon expand the scope of their attacks. Given the colossal destructive power of the Galos launchers, the Sagh'eld couldn't afford to get this wrong. Lanson expected that eventually, the Tagha'an would execute a high-velocity flyover of Ravrol, in order to deploy incendiaries and wipe out anything which had survived the missiles. He didn't want to guess his survival chances when that happened.

For many long minutes, the bombardment continued. The Sagh'eld had evidently miscalculated the launch position of the Galos attacks, and the missile strikes were predominantly directed east and south.

"There isn't much left that way which isn't wrecked," said Hennessey, watching the feeds from a short distance back.

"Nope," said Lanson, staring hard at the screens. "It won't be long until—"

A half dozen missiles crashed into the base somewhere near the underground room. The sound of the blasts carried loudly and Lanson felt the shockwave through the soles of his combat boots. Still, the ceiling didn't come down and the power supply to the hardware wasn't interrupted. However, one of the feeds went offline and Lanson hunted rapidly for another sensor array he could aim at the building overhead.

The next salvo detonated a little to the south, once more creating a shockwave which swept through the room. A second feed went blank, prompting Lanson to once more search for an alternative, though the operational feeds gave him enough information to form an unfortunate conclusion – the first of the missile strikes was a short distance east, the second a short distance south. The logical next target was directly overhead.

"Shit," Lanson muttered, waiting for the impact. His concern wasn't so much that the missiles would penetrate the underground room, more that the explosions would make it difficult or impossible to escape.

A minute passed and the impacts didn't come. In fact, the Ravrol monitors detected no further detonations. Lanson wasn't reassured – rather he believed the lull was only temporary and that soon, the Tagha'an would race across the horizon and deploy incendiary cannisters across this area of the base. Glancing over his shoulder, Lanson noticed how much the soldiers were on edge. Their instincts were telling them that something bad was on its way.

One minute became five and then fifteen. No missiles struck the base and the enemy spaceships remained out of sensor sight. Lanson was certain the Sagh'eld hadn't given up, but he was at a loss to explain their behaviour.

Then, a series of readouts on the console added to his puzzlement.

"The sensors have detected seismic activity nine hundred klicks east of Ravrol," said Lanson. "*Significant* seismic activity."

The readings climbed until everything was shuddering. A rumbling came to prominence and Lanson heard creaking and groaning sounds coming from the hardware in the room. And still the seismic activity didn't stop. Lanson slid from his chair, thinking he could better retain his balance when he was on his feet. For the next fifteen seconds, the quake violently shook the ground and it was everything he could do to stay upright.

After what seemed like an age, the seismic activity dropped off abruptly and everything became steady once more. Fortunately, nobody had suffered serious injury, though a few of the soldiers had been thrown to the floor or had collided with the hardware in the room.

"Good job the Aral built this place solid," said Corporal Ziegler. "What the hell caused that quake?"

Lanson had been busy fighting to stay upright and had not given thought to the reason for the earthquake. Now, the answer slotted itself right into his head.

"An impact," he said.

"Only a warship has the mass to shake an entire planet," said Hennessey. "Assuming we can rule out an asteroid."

"That was no asteroid," said Lanson.

He had a rising sense of dread about the events taking place beyond the sight of the Ravrol base, and he watched the feeds for confirmation of his fears.

"What is it, Captain?" asked Gabriel intently.

"I think it's the—"

Lanson cut himself short. One of the eastern monitors had detected a shape approaching over a distant mountain range. The moment he saw it, Lanson's heart fell.

A warship approached – a vessel he well remembered from his time on Scalos. Bristling with weapons and with a hull measuring eighteen thousand metres from nose to stern, this warship was every bit as much a threat as the *Ghiotor*.

"The *Tyrantor*," said Lanson.

"What brought it here?" asked Corporal Ziegler.

"A comm from the *Ghiotor*," said Lanson. "Or a lucky guess based on data from the Infinity Lens."

"Has it come for the *Ragnar-2*, Captain?" asked Hennessey. "Or—?"

"Or is it here to kill me?" Lanson finished. "I don't know."

He stared at the feeds for a time, feeling something akin to hatred. Every success on this mission was followed by a new obstacle, and each obstacle was higher, and harder to surmount than the one before it. And here was the *Tyrantor*, come to royally screw things up.

"At least the Ixtar destroyed the Tagha'an and the super-heavy for us, huh?" said Hennessey.

"On this occasion, I'd rather be dealing with the Sagh'eld," said Lanson. He took a breath and did his best to suppress the negativity. "But like you say, Corporal, we've only got one enemy warship to handle now, rather than two."

"Maybe the crew on the *Tyrantor* will take a look at the Ex'Kaminar and decide it's best if they get the hell out of here before it blows," said Ziegler hopefully.

Lanson had seen the energy shield on the *Ghiotor* absorb the blast from Private Castle's Galos launcher, and he wondered how much more the warship's defences could have taken before they collapsed. It seemed likely that the Ex'Kaminar was going to produce an explosion with a far larger radius, but Lanson found himself wondering if the intensity of the blast would be any greater. Perhaps the *Tyrantor*'s shield would be strong enough to keep the warship intact.

Cursing the degree of guesswork involved, Lanson continued watching the approaching enemy vessel. Certainly, the crew of the *Tyrantor* were in no hurry and the warship's velocity remained low.

"It's heading straight for the landing field," said Gabriel.

Lanson nodded without speaking. The *Tyrantor* was close enough now that he could see it in greater detail than in his previous encounters. Like the *Ghiotor*, the vessel was high-flanked and bulky, and fitted with immense armour plates designed to soak incoming missiles, with or without the protection of its energy shield.

On and on came the *Tyrantor*, until it filled much of the northern horizon, its propulsion creating a sound like thunder. The vessel drew to a halt directly over the southern edge of the landing field, several thousand metres east of Lanson's position, and oriented east-to-west.

"What's it doing?" asked Ziegler.

"I don't know," said Lanson, unable to take his eyes away from the feeds. He stared, noting the low-profile repeater turrets, along with the hatches covering the warship's missile clusters. Try as he might, Lanson couldn't figure out the intentions of the *Tyrantor*'s crew.

An answer wasn't long in coming. Without warning, the Ex'Kaminar on the landing field exploded into dust, the density of which turned several of the nearby feeds into impenetrable grey.

"Looks like the Ixtar disintegration weapons don't set off the Galos cubes after all," said Hennessey.

"Or they don't trigger an event when a Galos reaction has already begun," said Gabriel. He cursed. "I'm pretty sure the universe would be a better place if the Aral had never invented those damn things."

"Me too, Sergeant," said Lanson. Inwardly, he was surprised that the disintegration weapon had neutralised the Galos reaction, but he reminded himself that nothing about this Aral tech was predictable.

Over the course of the next few minutes, the dust from the Ex'Kaminar began to settle. Meanwhile, Lanson had switched feeds away from those affected by the dust and he watched the *Tyrantor* as it repositioned once more.

When the Ixtar warship came to a standstill, it was directly over the *Ragnar-2* at a five thousand metre altitude, with its nose to the west and its stern to the east.

"What now?" asked Ziegler.

"Watch," said Lanson.

Just like he'd expected, shuttles began launching from the *Tyrantor*. Lanson counted six in total, and they were a mixture of mid-sized transports, along with two much larger vessels, each of which was three hundred metres in length and armed with both missile launchers and repeater cannons.

"The Ixtar are going to capture the *Ragnar-2*," said Gabriel.

"I reckon," said Lanson. He checked the time on his HUD. "The *Ragnar-3* is more than an hour and a half from exiting lightspeed. Maybe if we can make it onboard, we'll have a chance against the *Tyrantor* once the Singularity functions are unlocked."

Lanson didn't know who he was trying to convince. The *Ragnar-3* was no match for this opponent, he felt sure of it. Besides, the Ixtar might well have cracked the security on the *Ragnar-2* and escaped before his own warship arrived.

Having come so far, Lanson couldn't help but feel he'd reached the end of the road.

TWENTY-NINE

Despair threatened and it took every ounce of Lanson's resolve to keep himself from conceding the mission was a failure. The trouble was, he couldn't think of a way to turn the current situation into a victory. He spent several minutes in thought without coming up with a solution. While he was pondering, Sergeant Gabriel and Private Damico exited the room to ensure the route back to the surface hadn't been blocked by the Sagh'eld missile attacks.

"The way's clear," said Gabriel upon his return. He watched Lanson for a time. "We have the two Galos launchers, Captain. If we score simultaneous hits on the *Tyrantor*'s energy shield, it might be enough to destroy the vessel, or drive it away. We forced the *Ghiotor* into lightspeed with just a single Galos strike."

"The downside to your suggestion is that the *Ragnar-2* will be destroyed, whatever happens to the *Tyrantor*," said Lanson.

He checked the numbers again. The previous Galos attacks on the Sagh'eld heavy cruisers had confirmed that the detonation spheres were twenty-six thousand metres in diameter. That meant an attack aimed exactly at the farthest visible point of the *Tyrantor*'s stern – measured from the nearest edge of the landing field when accessed from this room - would create an explosion large enough to encompass more than half of the enemy vessel, while, in theory, allowing the soldier firing the weapon to remain just beyond the extremes of the blast. The margins were tight, but that was nothing out of the ordinary.

"Isn't the destruction of the *Ragnar-2* the next best thing to capturing it, sir?" asked Gabriel quietly.

"It might come to that, Sergeant," Lanson admitted. "However, that vessel – and the others like it – could be the key to humanity's survival."

"Even if we don't know how," said Gabriel.

Lanson nodded. "These Ragnar warships are tied in to the Infinity Lens. If the Human Confederation is to survive, we either need to have complete control of the Lens, or we need to put it out of action. Right now, the *Ragnar-2* is a piece of a larger puzzle, and I'm reluctant to see it destroyed." He smiled thinly. "Besides, I don't like to lose."

"Me either, sir."

Turning his attention once more to the feeds, Lanson watched the Ixtar shuttles. The four smaller transports had set down next to the *Ragnar-2*'s facing flank a few minutes ago, but so far, no soldiers had disembarked. Meanwhile, the two larger attack shuttles hovered at a five-hundred-metre altitude.

"Here they come," said Corporal Hennessey, who was never more than a pace or two away from the command console.

Sure enough, the ramp doors on each of the transports were opening, and the Ravrol sensors detected movement beyond. After a few seconds, squads of Ixtar soldiers descended the ramps to the landing field. Lanson tried to keep his anger in check as more and more of the aliens emerged from the transports.

Eventually, the flow of troops ended, and those who had disembarked – hundreds upon hundreds of them – turned in good order towards the *Ragnar-2*.

"There's something else coming out," said Hennessey, peering at the feeds. "From the westernmost shuttle."

A two-metre cube, escorted by another squad of Ixtar, floated down the transport's exit ramp. Shortly after, a second cube was brought from the bay of the adjacent shuttle.

"Security breakers," said Lanson.

"Wasn't the *Ghiotor* able to crack open the Dalvaron security systems remotely?" asked Corporal Ziegler.

"It was," said Lanson. "But the *Ragnar-2*'s comms are programmed to reject inbound transmissions from unauthorised sources."

The Ixtar brought out no more security cubes, and the two which were now on the landing field began floating towards the *Ragnar-2*.

"Will the enemy be able to break the *Ragnar-2*'s security before the *Ragnar-3* exits lightspeed?" asked Hennessey.

"I haven't got the faintest idea, Corporal," said Lanson. "Our only experience of this is when the Ixtar attempted to steal the *Ragnar-3* on Ilvaron. I remember it wasn't a good time for observation and note-taking."

Having assumed he'd be able to remotely activate the *Ragnar-2*'s onboard weapons from a suitable console, Lanson was now experiencing doubt, despite his Tier 0 security status. Out of curiosity, he attempted to create a data link with the warship. His previous attempt to communicate had failed completely. This time, Lanson's link request produced a response, though one which left him scratching his head.

> *Component Missing. Link unavailable.*

"What the hell?" he said.

"Maybe the Aral never got round to finishing the construction," said Corporal Ziegler.

"The build is complete, I'm sure of it," said Lanson.

He didn't know why he was so certain, and yet if the *Ragnar-2* really was completed, then it should be able to accept a datalink. Something was bothering Lanson and he couldn't put his finger on what it was.

"Let's check out the construction documents," he muttered.

It didn't take him long to find the build plans for the *Ragnar-2*. The documents numbered in the hundreds of thousands, but they were well enough organized and he soon found what he was looking for.

"Well, shit," said Lanson in complete surprise. He looked at the feed of the *Ragnar-2* and suddenly it all made sense.

"What is it, Captain?" asked Gabriel.

"I thought the Aral had built six different Singularity class warships," said Lanson. "They didn't – they built only one."

"Then the *Ragnar-2* is—" Gabriel stopped short as if he couldn't quite believe it either.

"It's one component of a greater whole," said Lanson. He pointed at the document on his screen. "The *Ragnar-2* is upside down at the moment, so that its outer armaments aren't damaged by contact with the landing field, but there are no weapons on the rest of its hull because those are the surfaces which are meant to link to the other components of the warship. The *Ragnar-3* is designed to sit right on top of the *Ragnar-2*, while the other four components connect to its flanks and its forward section."

"Making one big *screw you* warship," said Hennessey.

"That's right," said Lanson, hardly able to contain his excitement.

As if this discovery had opened the flood gates, new ideas

came rushing into his brain. Searching rapidly through the *Ragnar-2*'s design documents, Lanson found the confirmation he was after.

"The *Ragnar-2* was built with automated defences," he said. "Just like the *Ragnar-3*."

"Are you saying we can fire our Galos launchers at the *Tyrantor* and the *Ragnar-2*'s defences will neutralise the blasts?" asked Gabriel.

"That's exactly what I'm saying, Sergeant."

Lanson sat back in his seat and chewed his lip in thought. A plan was now fully formed in his head, though it contained a few uncertainties. "If we could guarantee the destruction of the *Tyrantor*, this would be so much easier," he said. "Since we can't be sure, we'll have to wait."

"What do you mean, sir?" asked Gabriel.

"Success relies on the *Ragnar-3*'s arrival, Sergeant. If we drive away the *Tyrantor* early, the enemy crew might just wait for their energy shield to recharge and then return. Except then we won't have any Galos launchers left."

"So, we attack once the *Ragnar-3* is here," said Gabriel. "And then hope we can figure out how to make it couple with the *Ragnar-2* before we all escape into the sunset."

"Do I detect a note of cynicism, Sergeant?"

"Hell no, sir. We had no plan before, and now we have something." Gabriel smiled. "Even if it's going to take a miracle to pull it off."

"I think we're owed a miracle or two," said Lanson. He looked at the timer he had running on his HUD. "Seventy minutes until the *Ragnar-3* breaks lightspeed," he said. "Plus the extra minutes it'll take to explain the plan to Commander Matlock, and for the warship to lightspeed to Ravrol from wherever in this solar system it arrives."

"What if the Ixtar security breakers give them access to the warship before the *Ragnar-3* is here?" asked Hennessey.

"If that happens, we'll have to act at once," said Lanson. "Our only hope will be to destroy the *Tyrantor*. If the Galos launchers don't have enough punch, then it's game over for us."

With the plan outlined, Lanson spent a few minutes discussing the details with Gabriel, Hennessey and Ziegler. When the talking was done, Lanson set himself for the mental stress of watching the Ixtar and hoping their security breaking tech wasn't as good as the Aral warship's defences.

Seventy minutes became sixty and then fifty. The Ixtar on the landing field weren't doing much, though of course they were only waiting until they could board the *Ragnar-2* and secure it.

Although Lanson maintained an outward calm, inside the pressure was building. Each new minute seemed to last twice as long as the previous, until even the seconds went by at a crawl.

Nearby, the soldiers talked quietly among themselves. They knew the stakes, though they didn't appear too much on edge.

"Forty minutes, Captain," said Gabriel.

"They're going to be the longest of my life, Sergeant," said Lanson.

"The worst that happens is we all die," said Gabriel. "Then we won't be here to care that we failed."

"I disagree," said Lanson. "The worst that happens is we fail this mission and we live."

"Then we'll be around to fight another day, sir."

Lanson reflected on Gabriel's words. On the surface of it, the soldier's philosophy appeared shallow. Live or die. Do your best. However, the more Lanson thought about it, the more he came to appreciate the simplicity. He could only give his all and if it wasn't enough, then he'd still be able to look at himself in the mirror knowing that he carried no blame.

Drawing himself back into the present, Lanson was pleased to note that another seven minutes had gone by. The Ixtar on the landing field hadn't yet forced an opening into the *Ragnar-2* and they were running out of time. Soon, a couple of massive Galos blasts would strike their warship.

"Twenty-five minutes," Hennessey announced a short while later.

Now that Lanson was calmer, he no long felt the need to stare unblinking at the sensor feeds. Instead, he idly dug through the Ravrol files, hunting for information on the Infinity Lens. The data containers were buried deep, beneath multiple layers of security that his Tier 0 access allowed him to bypass. However, the Infinity Lens files were missing.

What the—?

Lanson executed an audit on one of the data containers and when he scanned the list, he found an entry he didn't understand.

> *Access 91#Z*

The access code wasn't a valid one, so Lanson was unable to determine what action had been taken on the files, besides them being removed. Further checks revealed that the Aral security systems hadn't assigned a user id to whoever had accessed the data containers, though the time stamp indicated the events had taken place five thousand years ago. Lanson recalled his earlier discovery that the last commands issued to the Ravrol systems all had the same time stamp. The time stamp here was the same.

Lanson hated mysteries, especially the ones he was unable to solve. Exiting the Infinity Lens data containers, he instead accessed the data array holding information on the construction of the Galos cubes. Once again, the files were gone and a query on the audit trail turned up the same access code as before, along with the same time stamp and same lack of recorded user id.

Realising that too much of his attention was being occupied by this search for answers from the past, Lanson hauled himself away. The hunt had, at least, produced one positive outcome – the *Ragnar*-3 was now only ten minutes from exiting lightspeed.

Fighting against his agitation which threatened to rise once more, Lanson stared at the feeds.

THIRTY

Another five minutes passed, and just when Lanson's hopes began creeping upwards, he spotted one of the doors midway up the *Ragnar-2*'s facing flank open for about two seconds, before it closed again.

"Damnit," he said. "The Sagh'eld have either broken the warship's security, or they're on the brink of it."

"They'll have to take a shuttle up to that entrance," said Corporal Ziegler.

"I doubt that's going to delay them for longer than a few seconds," said Lanson, rising from his seat.

"Is it time to act, Captain?" asked Gabriel.

Lanson cursed. Had the Ixtar security breakers taken only another fifteen minutes, the plan's chance of success would have been so much higher.

"Let's get this done," said Lanson.

The soldiers required no preparation, and they gathered up, eager to begin. Gabriel led the way to the western exit, with Private Castle and Private Davison right behind. Private Chan was carrying Castle's usual rocket tube, so that the other man would be less encumbered for the coming shot.

Lanson was fourth in line, and he climbed the stairs beyond the western exit rapidly. The stairwell was tight and claustrophobic, such that Lanson could touch both side walls at the same time. At the top, Gabriel opened the exit door, but stayed inside. The planet's night was evidently short, and the soft light of morning spilled through the opening. Here, the sound of the *Tyrantor*'s propulsion was a terrifying weight that threatened to crush anyone living.

"The moment we step out of this door, we'll be visible to the enemy sensors," said Lanson.

"It's a fifty-metre run to the edge of the landing strip," said Gabriel. "I scouted here earlier, and there's some debris that will help keep us covered."

Lanson nodded and glanced behind. Corporal Hennessey was next in line, her eyes narrowed and her face set. "Once the enemy is neutralised, we'll wait at the edge of the landing field for the *Ragnar-3*."

"Two minutes and it'll be here," said Hennessey.

"We're all connected to the Ravrol comms, so contact with the warship will be straightforward, but we're leaving the talking to Private Wolf," Lanson warned.

"It's time to go, Captain," said Gabriel. He was holding the Ezin-Tor in both hands now. "Maybe I'll have a chance to test this out after all."

Without further hesitation, Gabriel dashed from the exit, with Castle and Davison coming right after. Lanson followed onto a grit-strewn road that was piled high with wreckage from buildings destroyed in the Sagh'eld bombardment. Slabs of alloy balanced precariously against half-standing walls adjacent to the road, and Lanson spotted broken pieces of console and other shattered tech from within the base.

It wasn't the debris which had him worried. The *Tyrantor* was low in the sky to the north, an unstoppable construction designed to bring death, and destroy worlds.

Lanson felt anger more keenly than he did fear, and he sprinted north. Gabriel was already ten metres ahead, and the soldier ducked beneath a sheet of twisted metal.

Trusting that the rest of the squad was still with him, Lanson lowered his head and entered the space beneath the alloy sheet. Light and shadows played tricks with his vision, but the three soldiers ahead were all the guidance he needed.

Having emerged once more into the wan light of dawn, Lanson ran towards the wall to his left. Scattered lumps of misshapen tech lay there, which would offer some cover, albeit scant. Darting between two mangled consoles, he headed for a thick slab of metal which was resting against the same wall, creating a space that was shielded from the *Tyrantor*'s sensors.

Lanson was several metres from the slab when he was afflicted by a racking pain, which he felt in every nerve of his body.

"Death ray," he said, his voice sounding detached and remote.

Having been attacked by this weapon before, Lanson's Galos strength allowed him to shrug off the effects quickly. He stumbled once, but then righted himself and made it beneath the slab. Gabriel was standing at the entrance, facing south towards the rest of the squad and making urgent hand gestures.

"The rest of you hit the dirt!" he yelled. "Act like you're dead!"

As one, the soldiers dropped where they were standing. Private Galvan thrashed and groaned unconvincingly before he lay still.

It was quick thinking from Gabriel – a plan that would hopefully make the crew on the *Tyrantor* believe their death weapon attack had been successful and thereby reduce the chance they'd launch a plasma missile just to be on the safe side.

Turning north again, Gabriel crept forward while not venturing so far that he'd be visible to the *Tyrantor*.

"The edge of the landing field is ten metres from the edge of this slab," he said. "There's a corner from which we should have visibility on the *Tyrantor*'s stern."

"Where's the *Ragnar-3*?" Lanson muttered.

The warship was thirty seconds overdue, though it wasn't unheard of for some variation to creep into a lightspeed journey. In addition, he didn't know precisely when the *Ragnar-3* had begun its transit. The uncertainty was something Lanson and the others would have to deal with.

"Are we commencing the attack immediately, Captain?" asked Gabriel.

Lanson desperately wanted to hold, even if it was only for a short time longer, but he couldn't risk letting the Ixtar capture the *Ragnar-2*.

"Yes, Sergeant. It happens now."

Neither Castle nor Davison waited for a direct order. They broke from cover and sprinted for the corner. A moment later, Gabriel went after them and Lanson found himself doing likewise.

If the Tyrantor launches a missile, I'm dead anyway.

Private Castle came to a slithering stop about two metres onto the landing field. He already had the barrel of the Galos launcher pointing in approximately the right direction and the fine tuning took him only a moment. The stubby launcher thumped with discharge.

Meanwhile, Davison had also come to a halt at the corner. He took a fraction longer to aim and fire, but the lack of tension in the soldier's stance told Lanson that the shot was a good one.

By now, Lanson was also at the corner, and he was in time to witness the twin Galos detonations. The two spheres of utter darkness were so tightly overlapped it was impossible to distinguish between them, and they came so close to where he was standing it seemed to Lanson as if this was the nearest he'd ever been to death.

An ovoid of red appeared around the visible section of the *Tyrantor*. Within the blinking of an eye the warship's energy shield faded and then vanished. The Galos detonation spheres disappeared too and Lanson caught a glimpse of corroded armour and falling dust.

Then, the *Tyrantor* vanished into lightspeed.

A sharp cracking sound followed as the air rushed in to fill the space vacated by the Ixtar warship and a strong wind rushed by, bringing dust and particles of metal with it. Lanson braced himself until the air was once more still.

Although the *Tyrantor* was gone – for how long was anybody's guess – it had left behind a scene of devastation. The Galos detonations had carved a deep bowl in the landing field, as well as obliterating a huge section of the Ravrol facility's northern end. The matter which had existed only seconds before was simply gone, with nothing to indicate what had once been here.

Turning his attention north, Lanson spotted the *Ragnar-2*, which had been caught in the extremes of the explosions. The vessel's forward two thousand metres were over the edge of the crater, though it had no chance of falling in while its engines were running. So much had happened and so quickly, that Lanson had failed to watch for an activation of the *Ragnar-2*'s defences. The warship had survived, and that was all that mattered.

It wasn't only the *Ragnar-2* that had emerged unscathed from the Galos explosions. All six of the Ixtar shuttles had also escaped, along with the soldiers on the ground. Lanson used his helmet sensor to zoom in. The enemy were clearly agitated, but it didn't look as if they were preparing to evacuate.

"Those Ixtar must have been protected by the *Ragnar-2*'s defences," said Lanson.

"Lucky assholes," said Castle sourly. "Now we've got six shuttles and a few hundred ground troops to deal with."

"The *Ragnar-3* will take care of them," said Lanson. "When it gets here."

As he was speaking, he saw one of the smaller transports rotating slowly, bringing its nose around to the south.

"Move!" yelled Lanson, grabbing Private Castle and pulling him back towards the corner.

The soldiers reacted at once and they dashed south. Lanson had scarcely covered a half-dozen metres when a fusillade of gauss slugs struck the wall on the opposite side of the street. Glancing back, he was reassured that the Ixtar shuttle no longer had line of sight on him or the soldiers, though he was sure the transport's pilot would be acting to correct that.

"We have to get off the street," said Gabriel, finding cover beneath the slab of metal.

The rest of the squad – those who'd acted dead after the *Tyrantor*'s earlier attack – were already on their feet and a good distance closer to the door leading to the underground room. Corporal Hennessey paused to look back, but Gabriel waved her on.

When he emerged from the southern end of the slab, Lanson heard the faint sound of a shuttle's propulsion coming from somewhere north. Looking quickly over his shoulder, he saw the enemy vessel in his periphery, two thousand metres away and not much larger than a dot.

Gauss fire tore into the road a few metres from where

Lanson was standing. Shattered pieces of tech were pulverised and shards of it were hurled south towards the fleeing soldiers.

Gabriel was two paces ahead of Lanson and he performed an about-face, before scrambling back towards the slab. "Get under cover!" he roared.

The four soldiers crouched low, waiting for the gauss fire to end. After a time, the bullets stopped coming, but, when Gabriel crept north, he reported that the shuttle hadn't gone anywhere.

"I can hear another engine," said Lanson, listening carefully. "I think it's one of those attack shuttles."

"Damnit," cursed Gabriel. "The transport to the north has us pinned down, while the others come to flush us out."

"A damn shame I don't have my shoulder launcher with me," said Castle.

"Captain?" said Gabriel, the Ezin-Tor still in his hands. "Maybe it's time."

"I think it's definitely the time, Sergeant."

Maintaining his crouch, Gabriel tucked the butt of the cannon into his shoulder and shuffled a short distance forward. The gunner on the Ixtar shuttle started firing again and gauss slugs punched into the metal slab, creating a tremendous racket.

"Let's see what happens—" said Gabriel.

He fired the Ezin-Tor. The gun produced a low whumping sound and, a half-second later, the repeater fire stopped.

"I wouldn't normally say this but...holy crap," said Gabriel.

As soon as the shuttle stopped firing, Lanson crawled rapidly north and was just in time to see the vestiges of a fading explosion that looked like a missile blast, except that it was black like a Galos detonation, rather than the scalding white of plasma. Debris was falling towards the ground.

"We made it back into the building, Captain," said Corporal Hennessey on the comms. "We had to close the door - one of those attack shuttles headed over the street to the south."

From where he was hiding beneath the slab, Lanson couldn't see the enemy vessel, though he could hear its propulsion reflecting off what remained of the walls. Fortunately, his suit comms was linked to the Ravrol monitors, and the attack shuttle's position showed on his HUD.

"Is that cannon ready for another shot, Sergeant?" he asked.

"I reckon so," said Gabriel, turning awkwardly so that he was facing south, while staying close to the slab.

The soldier crouch-walked a few paces along. Gabriel was fully aware that, once he was exposed, he didn't have much time to aim and fire before the gunner on the shuttle spotted him and launched missiles at the slab. In Lanson's mind, it was a stroke of enormous good fortune that the crew on the Ixtar vessel didn't know where he and the others had taken cover.

"Ready," muttered Gabriel.

With a burst of movement, he pushed to his feet and launched himself towards the southern opening between the slab and the wall. Hauling the Ezin-Tor barrel onto target, Gabriel fired once and then twice, each discharge producing a deep thumping sound. Then, he spun and dashed deeper into cover, with the power source of the Aral cannon whining loudly in his hands and the sounds of twin explosions rumbling in the street to the south.

"It's coming down," Gabriel said with grim satisfaction.

Lanson was eager to see, and he advanced towards the southern end of the slab, just in time to watch the remains of the three-hundred-metre shuttle impact with the street and the wrecked buildings to the west.

The vessel's hull was a mess and it appeared to have suffered a combination of explosive and corrosion damage –

two vast holes had been torn into its flank, while the armour plating across its entire visible hull was crumbling rapidly. Particles of dust had been thrown into the air as a result of the impact.

The mass of the attack shuttle was significant, and it produced a noticeable shockwave beneath Lanson's feet. He looked instinctively upwards and saw that the slab had shifted. It made a groaning and a scraping sound and then the upper edge slid down another few inches.

"We have to get out of here," said Lanson. His eyes went to the HUD map. The other four Ixtar shuttles were only now beginning to react to the destruction of the vessel over the street and they were accelerating this way. "North!" he said. "Quickly! Private Castle, go get your launcher!"

"Yes, sir."

While Castle went south, Lanson, Gabriel and Davison headed in the opposite direction, emerging from beneath the slab at a run. The corner wasn't far and, from there, Lanson hoped Gabriel would be able to take out the remaining four shuttles.

The Ezin-Tor was a great weight, but Gabriel didn't fall behind. He slowed to a halt at the corner and positioned himself so he could fire across the landing field, yet without being too exposed.

"Take this, you assholes," he said.

Lanson didn't want to miss the fireworks and he was positioned so that he could look over the other man's shoulder. The four Ixtar shuttles were accelerating directly this way, leaving the troops behind at the *Ragnar-2*.

The first Ezin-Tor shot struck the second attack shuttle, producing a huge explosion which engulfed its nose and the forward half of its hull. A second shot plunged into the same place and the shuttle burst like an overripe fruit, the force of the blasts sending pieces of debris flying in every direction.

"One down," snarled Gabriel.

He fired for a third time, striking one of the passenger shuttles on its nose. Dark flame blossomed and the transport began to spin out of control, its trajectory now downwards.

Too late, the last two shuttles banked, hoping to escape the Ezin-Tor. This wasn't a time for mercy and Gabriel's next shot tore one of the transports into three separate pieces. The final shuttle was stubborn, and it required two shots before it was sent hurtling to the ground.

By now, the whining sound from the Ezin-Tor had an unmistakeable edge of strain. In addition, Sergeant Gabriel's outline had become blurred and the rest of his body was possessed of the faintest shimmering, as if he were shifting in and out of reality.

Private Davison was affected too and, when he looked down at himself, Lanson found that he was also shimmering. He didn't feel any different, but that didn't mean everything was fine.

"What's going on, Captain?" asked Davison. The soldier's voice sounded different. It was as loud as normal, but with a faraway quality, like his words had been amplified across an unfathomable distance.

"The Ezin-Tor," said Lanson, detecting the same remoteness in his own voice. "It contains Galos tech, or something like it."

"There're hundreds of enemy soldiers on the landing field, sir," said Gabriel. "Should I keep shooting, or hold?"

"Hold for the moment," said Lanson. "Without shuttles, the Ixtar can't board the *Ragnar-2*."

"Damn," said Gabriel, sounding almost like he was in a state of shock. He patted the barrel of the Ezin-Tor. "Give me a squad with a dozen of these and I could take down a battleship."

"It's the *Tyrantor* I'm worried about," said Lanson.

His eyes went to the gradually brightening horizon.

Where's the Ragnar-3?

THIRTY-ONE

Lanson soon had his answer. A dot appeared high in the atmosphere, approaching at high velocity. He didn't even have time to zoom with his helmet sensor before the dot resolved itself into the unmistakeable shape of the *Ragnar-3*. The warship began decelerating with the kind of savagery which could only be accomplished with advanced propulsion tech.

"It's here!" said Private Davison.

"Why no comms link?" asked Gabriel.

"I don't know," said Lanson.

Even though he'd given Private Wolf the task of making comms contact with the *Ragnar-3*, he attempted a link of his own. The warship's receptors were open, but they weren't accepting inbound requests.

"What the hell?" said Lanson. His eyes traced the warship's trajectory. The vessel was heading directly for the *Ragnar-2*.

"Captain, look!" said Davison, pointing across the landing field.

The *Ragnar-2* was climbing upwards, though not with any

great urgency. Lanson heard the warship's propulsion rumbling, and that in turn was overwhelmed by the sonic booms and the thunder of the *Ragnar-3*.

Once it had achieved an altitude of two thousand metres, the *Ragnar-2* rotated around its longitudinal axis, so that its external armaments were pointing towards the landing field and its upper section was facing the sky. The Ixtar soldiers on the ground nearby could do little other than watch.

"The warships are going to combine," said Lanson.

He was right. The *Ragnar-3*'s descent continued, albeit at a much-reduced velocity. Now that its rotation was finished, the *Ragnar-2* climbed on a heading that would see the two warships meet in mid-air.

Lanson stared. The manoeuvre was clearly happening under the control of a computerized guidance system, so precisely was it happening. At the last possible moment, the two spaceships decelerated, and the *Ragnar-3* landed neatly on top of the *Ragnar-2*. A series of loud clunking sounds echoed across the landing field as the linking posts from the latter vessel slotted into concealed housings on the *Ragnar-3*.

It was done. The *Ragnar-2* and the *Ragnar-3* had combined into a single vessel, which looked disproportionately tall and certainly incomplete. Atop the new warship, the huge twin-barrelled cannon looked as menacing as ever, but aside from that, the vessel's appearance was nothing less than peculiar.

"I've got a comms channel to the *Ragnar-3*, Captain!" said Private Wolf. "Commander Matlock says she was locked out of the hardware as soon as she entered this solar system. She's back in control."

"Tell Commander Matlock about the *Tyrantor!*" said Lanson. "It could return at any moment!"

"Commander Matlock acknowledges, sir. She's going to

execute a pickup from the landing field. The rest of us are heading up to join you."

Lanson was in two minds about ordering Commander Matlock to pilot the *Ragnar-2-3* – or whatever the hell it was called now - away from the planet at maximum velocity. He held his tongue. Just this once, he was going to ride his luck.

Only a few kilometres across the landing field, the Aral warship began accelerating directly south. The sharp sound of Gradar turrets ejecting projectiles rolled across the landing field and Lanson shifted his gaze to see the Ixtar soldiers being pulverised by the onslaught. He felt no emotion at the unfairness of their deaths.

The Gradar repeaters stopped firing after a short time, and the *Ragnar-2-3* came to a halt with its portside flank overhead and its undersides no more than twenty metres from the ground. A dozen or so buildings west had been crushed by the warship, but Ravrol had suffered enough that a few more breakages didn't matter.

A long flight of metal steps unfolded from the hull of the warship that had recently been the *Ragnar-2*.

"You'd best go first, Captain," said Gabriel, as the steps touched the ground.

Lanson nodded once, noticing as he did so that the other man was no longer shimmering. Whatever the Ezin-Tor had done to him, the effects had worn off. This time, at least.

Climbing as rapidly as his legs would allow, Lanson looked back only once, to make sure the rest of the squad had caught up. He needn't have worried. The soldiers were as motivated as ever and they sprinted up the steps towards the airlock above. Lanson hurried on, wondering if the *Tyrantor* would reappear just when he was on the brink of an escape which, not so long ago, had seemed impossible.

Lanson didn't stop when he entered the airlock, and he

hurried through into the warship's semi-dark interior. This was his first time on the *Ragnar-2*, but nevertheless he instinctively knew which way to turn. Lanson made for the bridge.

"We're all on board," said Gabriel on the comms. "Closing the airlock."

Commander Matlock didn't wait for the steps to retract. Instead, she put the warship into a state of maximum acceleration. The sound of the engines was electrifying and, even though the life support system kept the interior stable, Lanson could tell at once that the spaceship's thrust had increased significantly. Doubtless he'd soon learn about any other changes resulting from the combination of the *Ragnar-2* and the *Ragnar-3*.

A few minutes later, and with Lanson still on his way to the bridge, Commander Matlock announced that she was about to send the warship into lightspeed. Not long after, and with no interference from the *Tyrantor*, the Aral warship exited this unnamed solar system.

At last, Lanson felt he had a moment to relax. After all that had happened – from Dalvaron to Ravrol, he and everyone else had turned the mission into a success.

However, this, he knew, was just the beginning. With both the Sagh'eld and the Ixtar hunting for the Infinity Lens, the Human Confederation remained in the gravest of danger.

Somehow, Lanson had to take control of this ancient tech before his enemies achieved their own goals. Then, perhaps, humanity might survive the dangers to come.

Sign up to my mailing list here to be the first to find out about new releases.

ALSO BY ANTHONY JAMES

Survival Wars (Seven Books) – Available in eBook, Paperback and Audio.

1. Crimson Tempest
2. Bane of Worlds
3. Chains of Duty
4. Fires of Oblivion
5. Terminus Gate
6. Guns of the Valpian
7. Mission: Nemesis

Obsidiar Fleet (Six Books – set after the events in Survival Wars) – Available in eBook and Paperback.

1. Negation Force
2. Inferno Sphere
3. God Ship
4. Earth's Fury
5. Suns of the Aranol
6. Mission: Eradicate

The Transcended (Seven Books – set after the events in Obsidiar Fleet) – Available in eBook, Paperback and Audio

1. Augmented
2. Fleet Vanguard
3. Far Strike
4. Galaxy Bomb

5. Void Blade
6. Monolith
7. Mission: Destructor

Fire and Rust (Seven Books) – Available in eBook, Paperback and Audio.

1. Iron Dogs
2. Alien Firestorm
3. Havoc Squad
4. Death Skies
5. Refuge 9
6. Nullifier
7. Scum of the Universe

Anomalies (Two Books) – Available in eBook and Paperback.

1. Planet Wreckers
2. Assault Amplified

Savage Stars (Seven Books) – Available in eBook and Paperback

1. War from a Distant Sun
2. Fractured Horizons
3. Galactar
4. Fulcrum Gun
5. Laws of Ancidium
6. Empires in Ruin
7. Recker's Chance

Forged Alliance (Eight Books – set after the events in Savage Stars) – Available in eBook and Paperback

1. Dark of the Void
2. The God's Titan
3. Vilekron
4. Ascendant of Berongar
5. The God's Reckoning
6. Shadows of Kilvus
7. Endurus
8. Flint's Justice

Guns of the Federation (Seven Books) – Available in eBook and Paperback.

1. Xaros – Jungle Planet
2. War Vessel of the Ax'Kol
3. Voltran Unchained
4. Darkness on Sagitol
5. The Andos Vector
6. Repulsor
7. Death Never Wins

Printed in Great Britain
by Amazon

22873467R00158